MATRIMONY IN MURDER

LESSONS IN MURDER, BOOK 10

EDALE LANE

Matrimony in Murder, Lessons in Murder Book 10

By Edale Lane

Published by Past and Prologue Press

Edited by Melodie Romeo

Cover art by Melodie Romeo

First Edition September, 2024

CONTENTS

ACKNOWLEDGMENTS

I want to thank my beta readers Karen Fitz, Mark Gaylor, Maryann Kafka, Debbie Fahlman, and Dawn McIntyre for providing valuable insights and catching grievous mistakes before they could get out into the world. I must also recognize my esteemed proofreader/copy editor Dione Benson for another professional job well done. A special shout-out to my Facebook group members who voted in several rounds to help me choose the right cover.

I was especially inspired while writing this book by the commitment blessing my partner Johanna and I celebrated on August 10, 2024. My research applied to the book and our service, also held in an affirming church.

For Johanna

I

Morningside Park, Roanoke, Virginia, Saturday, May 11th

"Ow!" Jenna slapped her arm and scowled. "Why don't mosquitoes ever bite you?"

"Because I slathered on the Skin So Soft like I told you to do," Randi quipped and shot her a smug glance. At least the shade of the wooded park trail served as a welcome relief from the blazing afternoon sun as Jenna and Randi strolled beside their intimidating, wouldn't-hurt-a-fly German Shepherd. Tucking away his lolling tongue, Byron cocked his ears and swung his head around to inspect Jenna at the sound of the slapping noise. He must have determined all was well, as he took the interruption in stride and wagged his tail.

It's so hard living with a know-it-all, Jenna thought in irritation. Then, easing her gaze over Professor Miranda McLeod from head to toe, with her silky, tawny tresses tied back in a bouncing tail, her intuitive brown eyes smiling from behind her glasses, the long, lean frame of her body draped in a tight rainbow heart T-shirt and leg-showcasing shorts, Jenna's heart thumped. Randi had suggested she rub on the lotion, swearing to its effectiveness, and it had been Jenna's idea to bring Byron to this park. After all, it was conveniently located, and the trail was the right length for a brisk walk. And it smelled good—or was that Randi's Skin So Soft?

"I know," she muttered, her frown deepening as she swatted at another one hovering in front of her face like a tiny version of a horror movie monster.

"It isn't a sign of weakness, you know," Randi responded, with empathy in her tone. "You don't have to always be tough, taking on bears with just a fingernail file, or dispatching a gang of criminals with your bare hands."

Jenna laughed. "You assume I own a fingernail file." They exchanged a humorous look. But her soon-to-be wife had a point. Jenna would go to extraordinary lengths to prove her toughness. She was about to take Randi's hand when she had to ward off another attack from the vicious insects.

"My point is, you'll use science to your benefit to solve a case," Randi posed, "and yet you brush it aside in other instances."

"Science?" Jenna planted her feet and spun to Randi with skepticism dominating her expression. With one hand resting on a cocked hip and the other extended in animation, she proclaimed, "There's no scientific evidence that a beauty product—not created as a bug repellant—can dissuade the inclination of mosquitoes to bite people."

Randi's eyes twinkled, her brows quirked, and her lips curved. "And yet, it works." She brushed a quick kiss to Jenna's lips before pivoting to face the trail, pulled along by the end of Byron's leash.

I love her! It wasn't the first time Jenna had confessed this to herself, or everyone else she met, and it wouldn't be the last. Sometimes, when she was in one of those moods, Jenna wondered who she'd even be now if not for having Randi in her life. She definitely wouldn't be this happy because she never had been in the thirty-two years before meeting her. *And now we're getting married.* Her joyous mood couldn't be dampened for long—not even by mosquitoes.

In a few strides, she caught up to Randi's long-legged gait. "I suppose I could try it next time we go to the woods for something."

"Here." Randi stopped again, and her obedient dog waited in a sit. She scrubbed her arms along Jenna's and then brushed them across her face. "Maybe some of it will rub off on you and do some good."

Oh, the implications of that statement! Every bit of Randi that had rubbed off on Jenna had done marvelous good and then some. "We can't have you scratching throughout our wedding."

A couple of joggers passed, paying them no mind, while a chirping bird in the branch overhead did the same. In the relative solitude of the park trail, Jenna kissed her. "Thanks. I can't wait to marry you."

Randi's gaze melted to a lipid pool of bliss, stealing a glance at her engagement ring. "Me too. It's so close, and everything is ready. We just have the shower tomorrow and the rehearsal Friday, then bells ring and we're off to your surprise honeymoon!"

Jenna rolled her eyes and groaned. "You *still* won't tell me where we're going?"

They started back down the path, Jenna smelling like a weak application of skincare product. At least she didn't feel another bite. Sunlight filtered through the green canopy, reminding her of the beautiful spring day.

"I'll help you pack," Randi replied with an adorable smile.

"And this shower thing." Suspicion and unease worked their way into Jenna's voice. "I don't get that. I mean, why is it even called a shower anyway?"

"Because," Randi giggled, "family and friends shower you with gifts and blessings and well-wishes. Now, Angie sends her regrets, but she can only take off the weekend of the wedding, not for both. But Trisha has taken over planning everything."

"That's what I'm afraid of." Jenna knew Detective Trisha Jamison better than she did the sister she'd recently reconnected with after sixteen years. "She'll do up some fancy shindig that I won't even fit in at. Besides, aren't showers just for the bride? I know we're both brides, but can't I have a bachelor party? They seem more fun."

Since Jenna wasn't swatting or scratching, Randi took her hand in the cool shade of the wooded trail as a cyclist, hunched over the handlebars of a dirt bike, pedaled by. "She promises it will be fun, and the guys will be there too. Don't think of it as some frilly, doily-laced Victorian tea party; it'll be fine, and you'll have fun."

"Where is it again?"

"At Wasena City Tap Room & Grill, your favorite cop hangout, tomorrow evening from six to ten—because, you know, work Monday morning. Trisha and the gang rented it out, so only our group will be there. And don't say four hours is too long; it includes eating dinner. Some people won't stay the whole time, but four hours gives flexibility for friends and cops to come and go."

"What about your college folks?"

"They're invited too," Randi said, "and Ellen and Jo will be there, plus Eric and his new wife. My sensei is going to try to make it, and a few of my adult karate students. Pastor Luna said she'll swing by after evening jazz vespers for some cake. So, a mix of your cops and my cadre of friends—our people."

Jenna squeezed Randi's hand and bumped hips with her. Their afternoon exercise had waned into a lazy saunter. At least Byron enjoyed a medley of unfamiliar scents, if not the invigorating rush of a jog.

The closer to the ceremony time crawled, the more jitters Jenna experienced. *What if something goes wrong?* Randi had easily expressed her belief that something always went wrong; it's what made life interesting, and Jenna should chill. It wasn't like Jenna merely conjured up things to worry about; she had seen every way things could go wrong on her job.

At least neither of them had jealous exes who would show up and cause trouble. Jenna had talked to her old heartthrob, Tori, several times since her engagement to Randi, just to be certain. Tori claimed to be happy for them and had even sent a gift after politely turning down an invitation to the wedding. "I've seen the prize and the woman who's getting it," Tori had said over the phone. "I won't be there to screw things up for either of you. Congratulations, Jenna. She's a better fit for you than I could ever be, even if she is a total Mary Sue." Nobody would call U.S. Navy Lt. Commander Tori Varon a Mary Sue.

"OK," Jenna admitted. "It might be fun. I guess it's a rite of passage I have to go through before I can be officially married to the greatest gal on the planet. I'll manage, although I'm more concerned about these secret honeymoon plans of yours. And how come you got to plan everything? Where was I when you and Jamison cooked up this shower event?"

"Where you always are, dear," Randi answered with far more patience than Jenna deserved. "At work, solving a case, putting criminals behind bars, and keeping the world safe. You know I'll never complain about your career; just don't get your nose out of joint if I move ahead and plan things in your absence. Oh, and by the way." Randi stopped and turned to Jenna once more. They were near the end of the trail, with the sounds of people talking and cars pulling in and out of the parking lot fifty yards away.

Jenna gazed at Randi warily, with a tickling feeling there was something important she had forgotten to do. Randi released her hand to jab a finger into the bone between her breasts. "May eighteenth, one o'clock, to get dressed and ready for the ceremony at two—be there." The command was followed by a hard kiss, warning Jenna, *Or else.*

A flood of desire rushed through Jenna at Randi's rare display of dominance, and she suddenly wished they weren't in a public park. Then her phone buzzed.

"Wild horses—no, a herd of T-Rexes—couldn't keep me away." She pulled the cell phone from her shorts pocket.

"I don't think T-Rexes had herds," Randi mentioned in a speculative tone as if giving the matter weighty consideration.

"Ferrari," Jenna answered with her official sharpness.

"There's a fatal accident that needs your attention."

Jenna straightened and duty swept away frivolity at the sound of Captain Jerome Myers' voice on the line. *A Saturday and the captain's calling about a fatal accident?*

"Yes, sir."

"I'm shooting you the address. Murphy and Stone responded, and dispatch looped me in, but I'm out of town, so you're in charge. Dr. Valentine and the crime scene techs will meet you at the site. I know you're getting married in a week, but it shouldn't take that long to wrap this up. Then I'll put your name on the do-not-call list until you're back from Never Never Land, or wherever your wife's hauling you off to. Mine was Niagara Falls. I have to admit, it was romantic. I'll be back in on Monday, so, if your findings can wait till then, I'll be happy."

"Thanks, Captain, for your confidence. I'll discover what happened."

"I know you will, Ferrari." His voice was warm, fatherly, proud.

For an instant, her own father's face and voice flashed through her mind. She had spent a lifetime knowing he wasn't proud of her, didn't care a flip about her, only to discover it had been a misconception, a mistake, and a miscommunication he had been too proud—and too ashamed—to admit. They weren't all the way right yet, but Jenna and her dad had come a long way since the day a year ago he'd called to ask for her help. *He still hasn't committed one way or the other if he and Mama are coming to our wedding.* It was too dismal a thought, so she shook it away.

"Dispatch?" Randi asked when Jenna opened the text on her phone to check the address.

"Captain Myers; a fatal accident. Too bad we didn't bring both vehicles."

Randi picked up her stride down the path, letting Byron stretch his legs, and Jenna jogged to keep pace. "Shall I take you home for your car or drop you off at the station? Or I could just take you straight to the scene."

"That would be an imposition. You have finals to get ready for next week, and when are you going to grade those tests?"

Randi's grin stretched from ear to ear. "The kids are getting off lucky—all multiple choice for the first time in forever!"

She's a really good teacher, Jenna thought in admiration. "The house is closer. I'll take my car and text you when I know how long I'll be."

"Wonderful! Maybe you'll be home in time for a late dinner."

At the side of the big blue pickup, Randi opened the back door for Byron, who jumped in with practiced ease. Jenna needed the running board to climb up while Randi slid in like the truck had been tailormade for her.

"I hope so." Just imagining what culinary delight Randi would whip up aroused Jenna's senses. No fire in the hearth tonight, or at all until the weather got cold again. No, the ceiling fan would be on, and some of Randi's soothing music playing. Bandit, the cat king of the domain, would rub against her leg, and maybe an action movie or even a predictable romantic comedy would do—as long as she had Randi wrapped in her firm embrace. Best of all, Randi made her feel inexplicably loved—something she looked forward to feeling for the rest of her life.

2

From the curve in the road, Lieutenant Detective Jenna Ferrari surveyed the scene, taking in the steep twenty-foot embankment and the mangled vehicle lodged against a sturdy pine tree. Lights still whirred without the annoying screech of sirens as two patrol cars, the official CSI car, and the medical examiner's wagon parked in the lane because the shoulder here wasn't wide enough for them. A uniform with a stop/slow sign directed traffic safely around the scene.

It was easy to see this was a dangerous curve, but the weather had been perfect, the traffic was always light, and it was generally too early for drunk drivers. *Was he going too fast?*

Jenna kneeled to examine the tire grooves pressing into the soft earth where the vehicle careened over the steep drop-off and into the line of trees in the forest downhill. Newer neighborhoods and some old farms had been terraced into the base of this mountain, and the main access road curved with switchbacks to create a gentle incline, which was indeed preferable to a straighter, steeper path to navigate in snowy weather. If a person didn't live up here or come to visit someone, there was no reason to use this road.

Young Officer Matt Murphy stepped up to Jenna in his sharply-pressed uniform with his close shave and neatly trimmed blond hair just showing from under his black hat. To his credit, he smelled more like Irish Spring than the sweat she noticed rolling down his face. "Sorry to bother your Saturday, Lieutenant, but some things about this crash don't add up."

"I find the only times you've ever bothered me off duty have led to the arrest of murderers, so don't sweat it," Jenna replied. Confidence in the sharp boy scout informed her this would likely be another such instance. "Fill me in, and then I want to inspect the wreck myself."

"Right," he replied and pulled out his notes. "The car—a gray 2021 Toyota RAV4 Hybrid, a crossover SUV, registered to Mr. Nolan Todd Baxter—left the road about where we're standing and crashed into the trees below. So far, we have found no witnesses to the accident. A resident of the neighborhood," he motioned to the row of houses above and to their left, with stunning views of the valley, "called it in when she noticed the accident. Brenda Zellner. She's over there with Officer Stone. Pretty shaken up, as she knows the victims, or at least their car. I didn't let her go down there." Murphy gave Jenna a look as if to affirm he'd never contaminate a crime scene.

Jenna nodded. "How was she sure it was the Baxters' SUV?"

"Oh, because of the elementary school bumper sticker," Murphy replied. "She said Alexia Baxter is—was—a kindergarten teacher, and she had that bumper sticker on both their vehicles." He shook his head in grief.

Knowing the victims' identities saved time, but Jenna was certain Murphy had more relevant information to impart. "And you think this was more than a simple crash because?"

Murphy rested a hand on his hip, glanced down at the car surrounded by crime scene investigators and a tall, inky-haired medical examiner with big black glasses, and sighed. "That's the part I need to show you."

Despite her egocentric impulse to scramble down the slope on her own to prove her toughness, as Randi had recently noted, Jenna took Murphy's offered hand, and they traversed the rugged terrain together. Besides, it would be rude to deny him the chance to exhibit his innate chivalry. Jenna hadn't taken time to change clothes and still sported the blue jean shorts and T-shirt she'd worn to the park. Only then did she realize how uncoplike she must appear in the top Randi had made for her with a photo image of Bandit the cat and Byron the dog in a cute pose emblazoned across her ample breasts. *Oh, well, too late now.*

Jenna stopped to pull on a pair of black rubber gloves—which she always had at the ready—before steadying herself on the bumper of the upended vehicle.

"Oh, it's you!" called out the familiar voice of CSI Destiny Wilcox as she poked her head around the other side of the SUV. "I want the whole car towed back to the lab," she stated, "but we're collecting samples from the tires and bumpers before they haul it back up the hill and possibly dislodge a crucial bit of evidence."

Jenna caught her gaze and nodded, internally praising Wilcox as pride in her associate swelled. It was reassuring to know the best people in the department were working the case with her.

"Wilcox, what about this?" Beanpole novice CSI Davenport popped his head out of the treeline holding up a piece of mangled metal.

"We'll talk later," Jenna said to Destiny, dismissing her to perform her job. Then she turned to Murphy.

"I strongly suspect that Mr. Baxter wasn't driving his Toyota when the crash occurred," he reported.

Balancing herself with a hand against the car, Jenna followed him a few steps to where Dr. Rudolph Valentine hunched through the passenger side door, the back door open between them. At once, Jenna spotted the odd arrangement. A young, Black female's body rested strapped into the back seat while a White male of a similar age lay unbuckled in the front passenger seat, hemmed in by the inflated airbag. No one occupied the driver's side, and its airbag had not deployed.

"Good call, Murphy," she said. Although even a rookie should have realized this wasn't a simple case of a fatal car accident, her astute colleague had probably noticed more. "What else?"

"No skid marks on the pavement," he reported. "Nothing to indicate the driver tried to break or swerve—like he or she intentionally drove over the side."

"Were any of the doors open when you arrived on scene?" Jenna inched forward to examine the young woman who the 911 caller identified as a kindergarten teacher. She wore casual clothes, sneakers without socks, and her shoulder-length black hair was matted in the back with what looked like dried blood.

She slumped to the side, only held up by her shoulder harness. Peering closer, Jenna didn't see a handbag or cell phone on the back seat or the floorboard.

I don't typically carry a purse, she thought. *But, if her phone, keys, or wallet aren't in her pockets ...*

"These doors were closed," Murphy answered. "Officer Stone and I had to pry them open to check on the passengers." He shook his head. "No pulse when we found them, and their skin was cool to the touch. Now, the driver's door was shut, but not all the way—you know, like how when you give it a push and it doesn't completely latch."

"Yeah." Jenna wondered how long the car had been here before someone noticed. Glancing up the hill, she spied the woman leaning against Officer Stone's squad car with her head lowered, propped in a hand. She had questions for her, but first, "Dr. Valentine."

The medical examiner straightened, and, though he was downhill from her position, Jenna had to look up to meet his eyes.

"Oh, Lieutenant Ferrari," he answered in his non-southern, New England accent as if he'd been too deep in thought to notice her arrival. "Captain Myers said he was sending you out. This is no simple accident, and while I can't tell you anything officially until after the autopsy, I can share some professional observations."

"Please." Jenna stepped around the open back door to stand closer. He, too, was in his Saturday garb—jeans and a New England crab shack T-shirt.

He gave his glasses a nudge and motioned toward the man, presumably Mr. Baxter. "Liver temperature suggests both victims' TOD was approximately four hours ago, but this is where it gets odd." He pointed to an insult to the back of the man's head. "This depressed skull fracture appears to be the cause of death, yet there's nothing in the vehicle near the back of his head to have caused it. And this contusion and scraping on his forehead," he added, carefully pivoting the man's head for Jenna to see, "is incidental. Plus, the lack of bleeding indicates it was received postmortem. The same for the female victim. I need to perform thorough autopsies, but my experience tells me both deaths were the result of blunt-force trauma to the back of their heads. Now, maybe Wilcox and Davenport will find something inside the car that could have caused these injuries when they get it back to the lab, but—"

"They could have been dead before the crash occurred," Jenna completed. "We need to find the missing driver. Either he or she killed them, or they know who did."

"That's my supposition." Dr. Valentine raised his chin and waved to two assistants manning a gurney at the top of the hill.

"Send me a copy of your report as soon as you're finished," Jenna said. "Is it all right for me to touch the bodies now? I'd like to confirm identification."

He nodded and stepped aside. "You could say death is in my job description, as I work on and for the dead every day. Still, when a young couple like this comes across my table, it's always a tad sadder."

Jenna felt the same way as she fished the man's wallet out of his back pocket. Opening it, she spied the Virginia driver's license with the photo of a White man with a sculptured jaw, a crooked nose, and a cultured brow arched over caramel eyes beneath muddy brown hair. "Nolan Todd Baxter, age twenty-six, organ donor." She rattled off the address, hoping Murphy was writing it down. When she maneuvered around to the back, she smiled to see that he was.

A search of the woman's pockets, on and under the seats, and in the cargo compartment turned up no purse, wallet, or cellphone. She observed the glass in the back passenger window was intact. "Hey, Murphy, you're about her age. Know any woman who'd leave the house on purpose without her phone?"

"Can't say that I do, Lieutenant. It's even the rare guy who'll drive off without his phone."

"Search the area around the crash site and under the SUV when the tow truck gets it out of the way," Jenna instructed. She and Murphy had to move to make room for the dieners to do their job.

"We'll do," he avowed. "Looking for a purse, phone, any personal items, and anything clue-worthy."

"I want to talk to the woman who called it in."

"Alrighty."

Murphy didn't ask if Jenna needed help; he was smart and tactful enough to know not to. But he took her elbow all the same as they scrambled up the embankment that smelled like fresh dirt, crushed grass, and death. She couldn't allow his gallantry to offend her, especially since it was a trait she admired in the young officer. He had no qualms about taking orders from a woman; that was all that mattered.

With her dignity undamaged, Jenna finger-combed her short crop of black hair and brushed off her clothes before approaching Officer Stone and the closest person she had to a witness.

"Lieutenant Ferrari," the more seasoned, sturdy Officer Vicki Stone acknowledged as Jenna approached. She wore her long blonde hair twisted up under her uniform cap, a smart choice considering the heat of the afternoon. "I've been talking with Brenda Zellner, who called in the accident. She's a neighbor and has been very anxious." Her tone blended official with compassionate in just the right combination to meet Jenna's standards, and she nodded to her in approval. "Tell the lieutenant what you told me."

Red-rimmed, moist eyes revealed the young brunette woman's distress. Leaning against the squad car, hugging herself, Brenda matched Jenna's diminutive height. She appeared to be in the victims' age group, the one Murphy would fit into, around ten years younger than Jenna and Randi's. While Stone wasn't quite old enough to be Brenda's mother, she satisfied the role for the time being, lending her mature support in a crisis.

"Is it them?" Brenda's lips quivered along with her voice while her woeful gaze locked onto Jenna's. "Is it my friends? Are they dead?"

There was no point in giving her false hope. "I am very sorry, Ms. Zellner. We've positively identified Nolan Baxter. Could you describe his wife to me?"

Brenda covered her sob in her hands and sniffed before answering. Officer Stone extended an arm around her shoulders in silent comfort while the young woman sucked in a jagged breath. "They just got back from their honeymoon," she lamented. "Alexia's my friend. She's twenty-four, African American, with high cheekbones, about your height, slender, and so sweet. She's always wearing a smile and the children love her."

Jenna nodded and said, "That describes the second victim. I'm so sorry, but both of your friends are deceased. I realize this is difficult; it would be for a trained police officer too. But I need you to answer a few questions that will hopefully help make sense of this tragedy. Can you do that for me, Ms. Zellner?"

"Brenda," she uttered in a weak voice. "Ms. Zellner is my mother."

"OK, Brenda. We need to pin down the time of the accident more closely. You placed your 911 call at three-o-eight, correct?"

"I guess so. I mean, my hair appointment was at two-fifteen, and it took a little over half an hour. Then I picked up a couple of things at the dollar store next door and headed back up the hill to home."

"You live in the same neighborhood, the one up there?" Jenna pointed to the terraced rows of houses overlooking the valley.

"Yeah. I mean, I have an apartment over my parents' garage. It's better than paying ridiculous prices for something in town, and I still have some privacy. My boyfriend invited me to move in with him, but I'm old-fashioned, and Mama and Daddy said we should wait until we're married to live together."

She turned a forlorn expression to the right, where Dr. Valentine's assistants loaded gurneys laden with body bags into the van. Another tear rolled down her cheek. "Alexia moved in with Nolan because they got a good deal on the house, and it took both their incomes to qualify. They were engaged already, and I told Mama it was fine—that's what people do nowadays."

"How long ago was this?" Jenna inquired.

"Last August. I remember because it was the week before school started back, and Tommy and I came over to help them unpack and get the house in order."

All the information Brenda had was relevant, but Jenna needed to fix the timeline. "That was kind of you. You're a good friend, and I'm sure Nolan and Alexia appreciated it. Brenda, you said you went to your two-fifteen hair appointment. What time did you drive by here on the way?"

"It must have been around two," she speculated. "It doesn't take long to get there, and I know what you're going to ask next. No, their car wasn't down there in the ditch when I left. I always look at that curve because there've been a few wrecks there. One time—oh, three or four years ago—somebody else died in that same spot. They put up a white wooden cross and people brought flowers for months."

If Brenda's statements were accurate, Dr. Valentine was indeed correct. The couple was already dead when the crash occurred and probably had been for several hours.

"Brenda, I'm going to ask Officer Stone to follow you home in her patrol car to see that you make it safely, and, later, after you've had a little time to process everything, I'll set up an appointment to talk with you again. You've been very helpful, and I believe you can be even more helpful and do right by your friends. Would that be OK?"

"Yes, Lieutenant—what's your name again?" Brenda mopped her face and straightened, now two inches taller than Jenna.

"Ferrari." She handed her a card. "Go spend the evening with your parents, now. Dr. Valentine will take good care of your friends."

3

Neither Jenna, Captain Myers, nor dispatch had called in any of the other detectives; typically, it only took one person to oversee a fatal accident scene, but the evidence Jenna observed pointed to murder. She called Jamison.

"Hey, boss!" the perky younger detective exuded upon answering. "Don't worry about the party. I'm not making everything fancy dancy or anything of the sort."

"I'm sure it'll be great," Jenna replied in her no-nonsense cop voice.

"What's the matter?" Jamison's frivolity flew, replaced by a serious tone.

"We caught a case. No one called in the team because they thought it was a traffic accident fatality. How fast can you get to Mill Mountain Estates?"

"Bennet and I are at Vic Thomas Park, so about fifteen minutes if he drives me there."

"You have your camera and a kit?"

"Always," Jamison avowed. "I keep a spare in Bennet's trunk. He says to tell you we're on the way."

"Tell him I owe him one." Jenna slid her phone back into her pocket and strode over to the tow truck driver. "We need to hold off pulling the wreck up the hill until my other detective gets here," she ordered. "Fifteen more minutes. She's going to document everything on camera for the record."

"Awright," he drawled, and spit a dab of juicy chewing tobacco on the ground away from where Jenna stood. "That there's a dangerous curve. They oughta put up a guardrail or somethin'. This is the second fatality I know of here. Idn't that a rule or somethin', like puttin' up stop signs? If someone gets killed there, the city has to do somethin'."

"Believe me, I'll be looking into it on Monday," Jenna assured him. While not part of downtown, the location still lay within the Roanoke city limits, and the driver was right; the dangerous curve should have a guardrail. Even if there had been one, it wouldn't have helped the Baxters.

Stone returned from Brenda's house to help Murphy, Wilcox, and Davenport search for anything thrown from the vehicle or something to point to the missing driver. With Jamison's digital camera rolling, the tobacco-spitting operator moved his tow truck, lining it up on the lifeless Toyota SUV. He pulled a lever, and hydraulic feet clamped onto the asphalt, raising the truck's back tires off the road. Another lever lowered a crane, and a third started spitting out a length of chain with a big-ass hook at the end. *Huh,* Jenna thought. *He's making sure his truck doesn't budge while hauling the wreck up.*

"Lieutenant?" Wilcox rousted Jenna from her thoughts. "Come look at this."

Jenna crossed the few yards to where Wilcox crouched by the side of the road and joined her. "The tow truck was parked here." She motioned to the deep tire marks from the heavy work vehicle. "So, we didn't see this earlier." Wilcox pointed, and Jenna responded with satisfaction.

"That footprint could be from the driver," she stated. "Maybe he bailed up here by the road before it went over the side. That would make sense as he wouldn't want to risk being injured himself."

"I'll snap a few photos and make a cast of the impression, since Detective Jamison is busy documenting the vehicle retrieval," Wilcox said. "Rest assured, I'll go over the car with a fine-toothed comb. We should pull something from the unknown driver—a fingerprint, DNA, hair, or fiber. Sherman and Deng are on next shift, and they'll follow through. They're no slouches. I'm looking forward to the festivities at the Tap." She flashed Jenna a gleaming grin, and Jenna felt heat rise in her cheeks.

"I appreciate you working late," she said, then huffed out a breath. "And making time to come to the party."

While Wilcox took pictures and mixed casting batter for the footprint, Jenna turned her attention to the SUV being hoisted up the incline with a noisy winch. Dr. Valentine's van had left, and a scattering of uniformed cops still combed the area. By the time the tow truck pulled away with the wreck loaded onto its flatbed, the sun hung low behind the trees and twilight closed in.

"We didn't find hide nor hair of a purse, phone, or wallet," Murphy reported.

"She didn't have it with her," Jenna concluded, "because she was already dead when somebody put her in that back seat." Having time to mull over the evidence so far, she was certain of it. "You and Officer Stone head on back. You're probably due to be off shift."

"We're excited about the bash tomorrow night," he said brightly, changing the subject. "I hope you'll like my gift."

"Oh, you don't have to—"

"Of course I do!" he exclaimed. "The invitation said I could bring a date, and I want you to meet Missy. But, don't worry—we won't monopolize your time or anything."

This social event was going to happen, and Jenna realized she was OK with it—maybe even looking forward to it. She didn't get big birthday parties as a kid or bother with sorority or frat parties in college. She figured this wouldn't be like either, and she'd know most of the people there. Randi would be with her. Would there be music? Could they dance?

A smile curved Jenna's lips despite the dismal circumstances. "I look forward to meeting her. That Missy is one lucky girl, and I intend to tell her so. Now, go home."

Murphy beamed like he'd reeled in the winning bass at a tournament. "Thanks! Have a good night—or as good as possible."

As Murphy strode off, Jamison glided up. Jenna noticed her appearance for the first time since she had arrived; it was the most casual she'd ever seen the glamorous younger detective—a cheery, strawberry-splattered button-up top and white shorts. A snug ball cap hugged her flowing ginger strands, and a hint of sun reddened her model's nose and cheeks.

She spoke wearily, her words coated in regret. "I didn't get to take pictures of the victim's positions in the car."

"Murphy and Stone were first on scene," Jenna informed her. "They took care of it." She stole a glance at Assistant DA Bennet Altman, who leaned against his luxury car in what looked like tennis attire, arms crossed, and head lowered. When he caught her gaze with bold, brown eyes, the athletic man with neat chestnut hair pushed off and strolled toward them.

"We had a picnic and then were playing frisbee golf with some friends in the park," Jamison supplied. "I told him to go on and leave me, but you know Bennet. He's such a sweetie."

"We still have to check out the Baxters house and inform their next of kin."

"I figured as much," Bennet said. "Evening, Lieutenant."

"Sorry to interrupt your Saturday."

He tried to smile, but it just wasn't there. "It happens in our lines of work. So, I took the liberty of looking up the Baxters' details, you two being busy and all." He pushed a button on his phone. "Alexia has no living relatives, according to what I could find. Her bio says her parents and brother died in an accident five years ago while she was attending the University of Virginia. No aunts, uncles, or grandparents mentioned anywhere. However, Nolan has family in town—parents and a younger sister. I just texted you their names and address."

"Thanks, Bennet. I appreciate you bringing Jamison out." Jenna gave Trisha a questioning look and rubbed her mouth. The faintest whiff of Skin So Soft tickled her nose, reminding her how her own plans had been jolted off track.

Jamison turned into Bennet, laying her manicured hands on his broad shoulders. "Sweetie, notifications are hard, and I think you should go home, shower, and get caught up on any casework you brought home for the weekend. We have the prenuptial party tomorrow night. Jenna will take me home and I'll call. You should probably eat because it could get late."

"Are you sure, babe?" He cupped her cheek with a smooth hand and gazed at her with concern. It felt strange to Jenna to witness this softer side of the hard-hitting lawyer. "I don't mind—"

Jamison pressed a finger to his lips before moving in to touch them with hers. She batted enchanting green eyes at her beau and said, "I'm sure. Aaron and Cindy got lucky this afternoon. We would have trounced them for sure. Go home; I'll call you."

Everyone else had left, and the crickets and cicadas sang loudly into the darkening night. Bennet responded with a quick kiss, bade them farewell, and headed back to his sedan. Jenna opened the passenger door for Trisha. "He's got a dreamy side I'd have never pictured," Jenna said. "I can't imagine what he's like when y'all are alone."

Jamison giggled. "He's a sweet teddy bear. I'm sure you've got a dreamy side too. Randi said—"

Jenna conveniently closed the door on that topic, both literally and figuratively. Rounding the front, she took her seat and cranked the silver Honda Accord. "I hope we find an unlocked door," she said and sped up the long hill. Thankfully, Jamison didn't finish whatever cockeyed story of Randi's she had been about to repeat.

She parked on the curb in front of the Baxters' house. The garage door was open, and an old Ford Focus occupied the side opposite the empty spot. A dim light shone through the front window, likely coming from an interior room, but neither the garage nor front porch lights were on. Jenna and Jamison approached the house with caution and stopped to secure fresh pairs of disposable gloves.

Jenna pushed the doorbell and knocked. "Is anyone home?" she called out. "This is the police." With no answer, she tested the knob. Locked. "Let's check the garage."

Scanning her surroundings, Jenna detected no sign of a struggle here, although some soil lay in a haphazard ring around a dirty shovel propped in a corner.

"That's odd," Jamison mentioned. "All the other tools are hung neatly on that rack over there."

"I'll have to get Wilcox over here," Jenna said. "And before we go, I want some uniforms out here to tape everything off." Laying her grip on the doorknob into the house from the garage, it turned.

Jenna exchanged a glance with Jamison and drew her sidearm. Her partner grimaced and whispered, "We came straight here from the park. I had a kit in his trunk but didn't bring my gun."

Jenna nodded, eased open the door, and called out, "Police! Is anybody home?" Silence.

Once inside, they cleared the premises and inspected every detail. It appeared the couple lived alone. Photographs featured big smiles and love-sick expressions. There was already one with Alexia in her wedding dress, safe in the loving embrace of Nolan wearing a tux. Jenna sniffed the air. "Bleach."

"It's stronger over here," Jamison said from the living room.

Passing a discerning gaze over each aspect of the space, Jenna searched for anything out of place. She perused the floor, furniture, and décor until her eyes were drawn to a cheerful painting. She stepped closer, studying the canvas. "There's a spot that doesn't belong. It isn't part of the picture."

Jamison was at her shoulder in an instant. "Is it a blood drop?" She snapped a closeup with her digital camera.

"We'll let the lab decide. It doesn't look like a struggle occurred, except ..."

Jenna took two strides to her left, crouched, and pointed. "This looks like ceramic dust, and up here ..." She stretched to her feet in front of a bookshelf. "Is an empty spot. See the dust around the clean ring?"

"And some books are upside down," Jamison added. "If someone bumped into the bookshelf—"

"Or was hit in the head and fell against it," Jenna speculated.

"A vase or nicknack could have broken. The attacker cleaned up in a hurry, only collected the pieces, not the dust, and shoved the books back in any which way."

Jenna headed for the kitchen and pressed the foot bar to open the trashcan lid. "A Precious Moments teacher figurine," she concluded upon seeing the broken-off hands holding books and the decapitated figurine head wearing glasses. "They were attacked here, in their home, or one of them was, at least."

"Hey." Jamison marched in from the dining room. "Where's the dog? Several of the photos show a little dog in the picture."

Jenna glanced down to spy the food and water dishes on a pad at the end of the breakfast bar. "That's an excellent question."

Seeing the spinning blue lights reflecting off a window, Jenna headed to the front door with Jamison behind her. Opening it to the patrol car, Jenna issued orders. "I'm declaring this house a crime scene. I want it taped off and a thorough search made of the premises. Of particular interest would be any object that could be used as a murder weapon. Then canvass the area; find out if anyone saw or heard something."

"On it, Lieutenant," replied Officer Campbell.

Stepping out to the front yard, Jenna phoned the station. "Have CSIs Sherman and Deng arrived on duty?"

"They just got in," the desk clerk answered.

"Send them out here to my location in Mill Mountain Estates. I've uncovered the primary crime scene for the nonaccident fatalities from this afternoon."

"You've got it, Lieutenant. They should be there in twenty."

Blue lights and police cars must be rare sightings in this neighborhood because curious folks poured out onto their porches to gawk. An old man—had to be in his eighties—with stooped shoulders, a granite-etched scowl, and bald but for a thin, white ring, stepped off his porch and marched toward them.

"What's all this?" he demanded, slapping his lips around toothless gums. A scattering of white stubble erupted from his chin. Despite his apparent age and unkempt condition, he struck a powerful pose. Void of a beer belly or flappy arms, he looked like a fellow who kept himself in reasonably solid shape. As he squinted at Jenna, his disgruntled glower deepened. Hoping he might shed some light on his neighbors, she met him at the property line, Jamison right beside her.

"I'm Lieutenant Detective Ferrari and this is Detective Jamison from the RPD. And you are?"

The man worked his mouth and jaw and narrowed his bristly brows. "Ralph Halbach, Sergeant with the 25th Infantry Division back in 'Nam. That was a lifetime ago, I reckon. After the Army, I had thirty years with the U.S. Postal Service. Two lady cops." He raked a hand over the smooth top of his head and chuckled. "I'd've put my teeth in if I'd've known."

"Thank you for your service," Jamison said with a relaxed, welcoming expression. His annoyed visage remained unchanged.

"Mr. Halbach, do you know your neighbors, Nolan and Alexia Baxter?" Jenna asked.

"That young couple with the yappy dog? What'd they do?"

"I regret to inform you they were killed earlier this afternoon," Jenna related. "We're trying to put together a timeline and discover exactly what happened to them, and you can help."

Mr. Halbach scraped a gnarled hand down his scratchy face as his frown lines intensified even more. "Dead, you say?"

"Yes, sir," Jamison replied compassionately. "Did you know them well?"

"Naw," he let out in a growling drawl. "Different social circles, but I'd talk to 'em ever once in a while. Seemed nice enough though."

"Were you aware they recently got married?" Jenna probed.

"Heard sumpin' to that effect." Mr. Halbach huffed out a breath and shook his head. "What happened to 'em—an accident? They didn't strike me as the drug usin' kind."

"Their SUV crashed, but we're still investigating the incident. Could you tell me if you noticed them drive away this afternoon, maybe with a friend or someone else in the car?" Jenna studied the old man closely as he formed his response.

"I don't rightly recall. They were out of town for a week and just got back. I think. Nolan came out and mowed the grass yesterday," he mused in thoughtful reflection. "Might wanna ask some of these other neighbors. I fell asleep watchin' the ball game and can't say when they left."

"OK, thank you, Mr. Halbach," Jamison said in an appreciative tone.

"We may have some more questions for you later," Jenna stipulated, "but thank you. Would you consider this a safe neighborhood?" Jenna couldn't recall ever needing to come up here. Gauging by the newer houses with spacious yards, she expected it to be an affluent area. As ironic as ice cream in January, the poorest parts of town always experienced the most crime. What were they going to steal from folks who had nothing?

"Yeah, I'd say so," he mused. "No crook ever bothered me. Then again, I've got guns, so they'd be fools to try."

"Thank you for your time and stay safe." Jenna and Jamison walked back to meet the nighttime crime scene crew who had just arrived. "It's all yours," she said. "I think there's blood on the living room painting and someone cleaned with bleach."

"We'll get everything we can, Lieutenant," Deng assured her.

"Now for the hard part," Jenna admitted to Jamison and strode to the car.

4

———◆◇◆———

J enna took a deep breath, exchanged a grave look with Jamison, and
rang the doorbell. They had briefly discussed changing clothes first and
decided notifying Nolan's parents before they found out another way took
priority.

A dog barked, the front porch light clicked on, and a laughing young
woman with a sassy blonde ponytail and a cell phone held to her ear opened
the door. Upon perceiving no threat, the golden retriever stopped barking
and wagged its tail, its entire body gyrating with the motion.

"Just a minute," she said to whoever was on the other end of her call and
lowered the phone. "May I help you?"

Jenna and Jamison held up their badges. "I'm Lieutenant Detective
Ferrari and this is Detective Jamison. Are Mr. and Mrs. Baxter at home?"

Her cheery disposition fled, replaced by anxious concern. "Mom, Dad!"
she called over her shoulder. To the phone, she said, "I'll have to call you
back." To the detectives, she offered, "Come in," and pulled the door wide.

"What is it, hun?" sounded a male voice from deeper in the house.

"Are you Susan?" Jamison asked.

"Yes." This time, dread bloomed in her expression, as if she feared she was
in trouble. Susan laid her phone on a little table near the door and stole two
nervous steps down the hallway to take up a position behind her parents.
Having Jamison's approximate height and build, she resembled a stairstep
between her shorter mother and taller father. "They're police detectives."

"Police?" The older woman knit her hands together in front of her and shot her husband a nervous glance. Kathleen Baxter—Jenna recalled from the records ADA Altman had sent her—was a fifty-year-old elementary school teacher whose height and curves mirrored her own, although her shoulder-length, acorn brown hair sporting a classy wave was much more glamorous.

"I'm Joel Baxter." Nolan's father wrapped an arm around his daughter's waist, pulling her close. While the balding man with glasses was tall, his physique screamed that his sport of choice was armchair coaching. Jenna didn't need to remind herself she could easily take him down; however, she wasn't certain she could help him off the floor if he were to fall.

"What can we do for you, detectives?" he asked with guarded curiosity.

"Mr. and Mrs. Baxter, Susan," Jenna specified, using their names in a compassionate tone. "Is there somewhere we could sit down?"

"Is it Mama?" Kathleen slapped her hands to her cheeks as fear flashed in her eyes.

"No, ma'am," Jamison answered. "Let's sit in here, why don't we?" She motioned to a quaint sitting area on the side of the front entrance.

Jenna noticed the house was older than their victims' with furnishings and décor dating back twenty years or more. The room was clean except for the dog hair, no doubt ground into the out-of-style plush carpeting.

The family filled the couch, and Jenna took an ottoman, leaving Jamison the stuffed, wingback chair. Father, mother, and daughter all peered at her in apprehension and held their breaths. There was no easy way to say this.

"We regret to inform you that earlier today, your son, Nolan, and his wife, Alexia, were killed. We are so sorry for your loss."

Joel teared up, swallowed, and struggled to remain strong for his family. Susan burst into wailing tears and buried her head in his shoulder. Kathleen stared and blinked.

"I'm sorry, but I thought you said ..." She shook her head. "That can't be right. They just got back from their honeymoon a few days ago. I talked to Alexia on the phone before lunch. There must be some mistake."

Susan continued to sob while Joel inquired, "Were they in an accident?"

"No, sir," Jenna stated. "Someone killed them on purpose."

"That's crazy!" Kathleen's voice shot up an octave as her eyes widened.

"We understand this is the worst news a parent can receive," Jamison responded in a soothing, empathetic quality as she leaned closer from the edge of her seat, her elbows on her knees and palms up. "At this time, we have no reason to suspect you, your husband, or your daughter are in danger, but, until we know more, we've asked a patrol car to sit outside your house overnight."

"Joel, there's been a mistake!" She swiveled toward him and shook in obvious distress. "This can't be happening—it just can't!" The dog whined, sensing her distress, and laid his head on her knee.

"There now, dear," Joel attempted some comfort. Turning his gaze to Jenna, he asked, "What happened? Who did this, and why? Nolan and Alexia had friends—not enemies. They aren't involved with criminals or drugs, and they aren't so well off for people to rob them. Was it a drunk driver, a crazy person?"

A fleeting image of the poor, crime-ridden parts of town flashed through Jenna's brain, followed by the crime-scene house in the nice neighborhood.

"Dad." Susan sat up, touched his arm, and mopped at her face with her other hand. The comprehension that Jenna couldn't answer if he kept asking questions lit in his expression. He nodded and lowered his chin, and Jenna spied his lower lip tremble.

"I'm sorry, Mr. and Mrs. Baxter, but there's no mistake," she replied gently.

"This investigation is our top priority," Jamison assured the family.

"There was a car crash," Jenna confirmed. "However, we're treating this as a homicide. It seems someone tried to make it appear like an accident, but the evidence points to Nolan and Alexia being killed in their home early this afternoon."

"Our information doesn't list any relatives for Alexia," Jamison mentioned. "Do you know of someone—"

"No," Kathleen interrupted. She still seemed shocky, her face pale and the gripped knuckles in her lap white in contrast to her blue capris. "We're her family. I was friends with Alexia before she and Nolan started dating. She arrived, fresh and bright, at our school as a first-year kindergarten teacher, and, while you might think there's nothing to it, setting that initial foundation is crucial and quite demanding. It takes a special sort—a sweetheart like Alexia—and I was drawn to her right away. I introduced her to the staff, helped her learn the ropes, all the first-year teacher things. Then I was caught completely off guard when Nolan brought her to dinner one night as his new girlfriend. It's like they were meant to be."

Recognizing the family's need to share and remember their lost loved one, Jenna gave Kathleen the space to continue talking.

"And Nolan."

Jamison handed the grieving mother a tissue, which she took and dabbed her eyes and nose.

"He was the best son anyone ever had," Joel picked up the thread. "He made good grades in school, never got in trouble—well, he was a boy, but you know what I mean," he added and lowered his head into his hand.

"You don't think some asshole who had to wait in line or failed their driver's test came after him at home on a Saturday, do you?" Susan's expression had upgraded from morose to fierce, her eyes flashing with fury. "That's where he worked—at the DMV. It's not his fault the state doesn't hire enough employees or people are stupid and get their licenses suspended or revoked. I can't tell you how many times assholes had cussed him out or made threats to him at work."

"We will look into any threats," Jenna said, shifting her attention to Susan. "Did he mention a specific person?" *I'll have to check with the DMV, see what his supervisor says, if they have video camera evidence of any such threats.*

"No," she bit out in frustration. "I don't know of anyone specific. He didn't talk about work much, as you'd imagine. He talked about cycling and going to movies and ..." She stopped to sniff and wipe a hand under her nose. "Getting married." On that, Susan's voice cracked, she crumpled back into her father's embrace, and she was done.

"Is there anyone we can call for you?" Jamison offered.

Kathleen shook her head. "Can we see them? When can we see them?"

"I'll call and let you know," Jenna answered. "Probably tomorrow or Monday. Dr. Valentine is the best medical examiner I've ever met. He's taking good care of them. We'll talk more later." She stood and Jamison followed her lead. "We're going to leave you to your privacy now."

Joel peered up at Jenna with a haunted expression, as if he wanted to say something yet had no words. Then his wife let out in a frantic squawk, "Where's Picasso?"

"Picasso?" Jenna questioned.

"Their little dog," she answered in a distressed manner.

"We're looking for him," Jamison soothed with assurance.

"Her," Susan corrected. "She'll be scared and confused. You must find her."

"We'll make it a priority," Jenna promised, and she and Jamison showed themselves out.

"It's always so brutal," Trisha whispered as they trudged back to Jenna's car. "Such a nice family, broken like that."

"Yeah. The only thing we can do is catch the lowlife bastard who did it."

***

Randi used the rest of her Saturday to update her students' grades in the community college system, score the handful of late papers frantic slackers had turned in on Friday, and make the last selections for questions to go on her multiple-choice final exam. It was OK, she told herself, since she had assigned plenty of essays and reports across the semester. They had timed their wedding to be after school was finished, even if they had cut it close. She was giving the exams for her Monday-Wednesday-Friday classes on Wednesday and had declared Friday to be a discussion day to reflect on everything they'd read in English Literature. She suspected few students would attend.

There was a nifty machine in the teachers' workroom to score the exam grid sheets in seconds, so all she'd need to do was upload the scores into her program and let it average the grades. If anyone barely failed and deserved a boost, she'd add a few bonus points. Then, wedding rehearsal, wedding, and honeymoon! It caused a giddy feeling to effervesce throughout her body whenever she thought about it.

Knowing Jenna would be late, tired, and depressed after performing a death notification, Randi whipped up comfort food—spaghetti and meat sauce—with a side of salad. It simmered in her big, iron kettle, the lid locking in the flavor, while buttered garlic bread lay on a tray at the ready to pop into her new air fryer/toaster oven combo. Her sister, Ellen, had raved about hers until one day Jenna came home with the best brand to enhance their kitchen. Everything came out so much better in it that Randi had almost quit using the microwave and traditional oven.

In her recliner, the wine glass half-finished, she relaxed to the sounds of Aaron Copland's *Appalachian Spring* while playing a castle-building game on her phone. She quickly hit save when her notification sounded and switched to her text messages.

'On my way.'

'One of my favorite three-word phrases.'

"OK, Byron, last run," she called to the furry German Shepherd who lay on his favorite rug in front of the dormant hearth. With a perked, gleeful expression, he scrambled up, performed a frantic search for his ball, and trotted to the back door, ball in mouth. Although he would have chased it all night, Randi only had time for a few throws. "Now you do your business," she commanded.

Leaving the door to the fenced yard ajar, she headed into the kitchen and turned on the air fryer to heat. It wouldn't take long. By the time Jenna arrived, everything would be on the table, ready for her to eat.

A sneaky black cat, with white paws and a spot on his chest, wound between her legs, rubbing them luxuriously. "Meow." He looked up at her expectantly as she served the plates.

"Don't give me that," Randi chided. "I already fed you and Byron. What? Do you want to make yourself so fat you can't jump onto the furniture anymore?"

He blinked innocent cat eyes at her. Upon getting nowhere with his ploy, Bandit snubbed her, spinning on his toes and flicking his tail at her as he slunk away. Byron raced back in and dropped the ball at her feet. Randi smirked. "No more ball tonight. Jenna's almost here and *we* haven't been fed yet."

She locked the back door and moved her wine glass opposite Jenna's at the dinette just as the lieutenant strode in. "Sorry it's so late. I hope you—"

Rounding the corner came the sharpest, sexiest, most wonderfully complicated woman who had added the zest and sparkle to Randi's life she'd always dreamed of. Instantly, Randi recognized the fatigue in Jenna's keen, blue eyes, and the burden of an unsolved case weighing on her slumped shoulders. Stepping around the table, she pulled her into a hug.

"You didn't," Jenna grumbled.

"I wasn't going to eat without you."

"And spaghetti," Jenna added gratefully. She kissed Randi's cheeks and brushed her lips. "Thank you."

"Always," Randi replied with promise. "Come sit and eat and tell me about it."

Jenna sighed and plopped into her chair, still in the shorts and T-shirt she'd worn to walk in the park so many hours ago. "I'll need to shower after, and this looks and smells so delicious—exactly what I need." Randi wasn't surprised when she reached for the wine first.

Bandit approached, trying his routine on Jenna. "I already fed them," Randi reported.

"As I supposed." Jenna took her knife and fork and started cutting her spaghetti. "So, 'On my way' is *one* of your favorite three-word-phrases? Pray tell, what are the others?"

Randi's cheeks warmed, and her eyes gleamed. "Indeed." She wiggled her brows and stuck her fork into salad. "However, I suppose it falls after 'I love you' and 'Randi, oh God!'"

It delighted her to watch Jenna almost spew a mouthful of wine onto her plate as she snatched a napkin. "Don't do that to me!"

"But it's so much fun!" Randi countered, glad she could tease a smile out of Jenna after a hard day. "All right. Once you catch your breath, tell me about it so you won't brood all night. I suspect you'll be off to the office first thing to get as much progress on the case as possible before our shower-slash-bachelor-party."

Jenna took a sip of water this time and narrowed her eyes at Randi. "You know me so well. And yet, somehow, you still want me around."

"You know it! I've been busy, and it's late—let's call a shower-for-two dessert after this and get a good night's sleep."

With a mixture of good humor and honest affection, Jenna responded, "I love you. And ... Randi, oh God!" She let out an exaggerated, sensual moan, sending them both into laughter.

5

Sunday, May 12th

R andi had sent Jenna on her way that morning with a to-go coffee thermos, a full belly of fluffy, loaded omelet, and strict instructions to call her mom for Mother's Day. They had discussed the possibility of driving to Kentucky to see her before scheduling the day of their prenuptial party. Jenna's sour mood over her mother's wishy-washy attitude and failure to commit to coming to their wedding prevailed. "If she isn't coming to my special day, why should I go to hers?" she had told Randi during a rant a few weeks back.

To be fair, her mom hadn't dug in and declared, "No way, no how," but neither would she give Jenna a yes. She merely hem-hawed around the invitation, changed the subject, and arrived at, "We'll see."

Still, Randi was right. If she didn't call to wish her a happy Mother's Day, it would be like they hadn't spent a year working to establish a relationship—any relationship—even an uneasy one. She would call at lunchtime, be cheery, and not mention the wedding at all. She knew Randi would phone her too, considering she had no other mother to call. It seemed hardly fair to Jenna for Randi's loving, supportive mother to have died while hers, with a ramrod stuck up her ass, was still alive and kicking. Randi had said her parents accomplished what they'd been born to and left this earth with no regrets. *While Mama's burdened with tons of regrets, fear, doubt, and pain.*

Once at her desk, Jenna wrote *Call Mama* on a sticky note and pressed it to the bottom edge of her monitor so she wouldn't forget. "OK," she told herself. "Run background checks."

It felt odd to be in the criminal investigations office alone, as usually the whole team surrounded her. Thinking of them, Jenna glanced at the banner-sized painting Tech Specialist Ethan Bauman's significant other, Mario, had painted. The striking poses he'd chosen made her, Jamison, Bauman, and Owens look like the newest additions to Marvel's Avengers. It always gave her a dual sense of humility and pride to gaze at it.

"Background checks," Jenna reminded herself. She looked up everything she could find on Nolan Baxter, his parents and sister, and Alexia Smith Baxter. Where there were reams on Nolan and his family, who had lived in Roanoke forever, she turned up sparse background on Alexia.

Leaning back to sip her coffee, Jenna stopped when she read Susan Baxter was a senior at Roanoke Community College where Randi taught. Without Bauman's magic touch, it took her a while to find a back door into the college files to find her schedule. "Damn," she let out with a sigh when she saw the Shakespeare class listed. "I'll have to tell Randi. She's going to want to do something for the girl."

In another instant, her thoughts reverted to the case of the murdered college student whose body a certain Dr. Miranda McLeod had discovered in the snow and the instant liking she'd taken to the astute professor. That fateful day had led to this one and the flood of happiness that had redefined Jenna's life. So much had changed in a year and a half. She'd gotten help with her emotional issues, turned colleagues into friends, reconnected with her estranged family, and, most of all, found the love of her life.

Jenna shook her head and tried to focus. It was both frustrating and curious that Alexia Smith's records, social media, and everything else existed at a bare-bones level. A birth certificate from New Jersey, an article about her family's sedan being hit by a train, and a bachelor's degree in elementary education from the University of Virginia two years ago. Upon arriving in Roanoke, she opened social media accounts, got a job as a kindergarten teacher at Mrs.

Baxter's school, and suddenly a life sprang up, complete with photos, charity work, clubs, and friends. From her old posts, she'd met Brenda Zellner of this neighborhood around the same time she met Nolan. There were lots of pictures of her with Brenda and other young women, her and an orange, fluffy dog, her and Nolan, and her, Nolan, Brenda, and another young man in the same age group—presumably the boyfriend Brenda's mother didn't want her to move in with.

Alexia's circle of friends seemed to include some persons of color, but most were White. Jenna didn't find that particularly unusual, as her own college classes consisted predominately of white students. She had made several friends from different ethnic backgrounds, and her primary hang-out group included two Black girls. They said they would rather associate with Jenna and her academic circle than an all-Black crowd because of shared interests and aspirations. She merely assumed all people chose their friends that way and race didn't play a part anymore.

Nolan had worked for the Department of Motor Vehicles for the past five years, achieved a promotion, and taught a driving safety course. The courts often required drivers with multiple moving violations to take the course before resorting to revoking their licenses. None of the Baxters or their close friends had caused an ounce of trouble in the community, and Kathleen Baxter had been selected Teacher of the Year three times so far during her career.

Jenna brought up the officer canvasses of the neighborhood from the night before. She and Jamison had talked to toothless Ralph Halbach and the uniform officers had questioned the folks on the Baxters' other side and the three corresponding houses across the street. None admitted to hearing or seeing anything. "Nice young couple," the Johnsons said. "Adorable dog," the Lees professed.

The Kirbys—who were both African American—mentioned a concern over them being a mixed-race couple. "It's certainly not the negative attention-getter it was twenty or thirty or fifty years ago," Officer Campbell recorded Mr. Kirby's words. "Still, some of those white supremacist types don't approve. I sure hope they don't go on a rampage."

The idea of something like that disturbed Jenna on a guttural level. *Any quack "hater" who violently opposed a White man marrying a Black woman would be twice as malicious toward a woman marrying another woman.* It had been Jenna's experience that most of those anti-everything losers paid far more attention to men than women in general. Who cares about two women, when they could bash gay men instead? After all, they were the ones who threatened these creeps' fragile masculinities. But wouldn't they be more enraged by a Black man daring to wed a White woman? Such racial violence had become a rarity in their community, and Jenna prayed—which she didn't do often—it would vanish altogether.

Although Jenna marked the motive at the bottom of her list, it troubled her. *I don't want to put Randi at risk. What if a bunch of right-wing nutballs go after her, try to get her fired, or worse? Sure, the law and school policies are on our side now, but we're only an election away from losing all our rights.*

Jenna tucked it away. There was nothing she could do about politicians; however, she could uncover who killed Nolan and Alexia Baxter and arrest him or her.

She focused on her screen. Ralph Halbach was the original owner of his house, built eight years ago. Everything about him checked out—he was a Vietnam War veteran, retired postal worker, father of four, grandfather of eight. Only one child, a son named Carlin, lived in southwest Virginia, and he was a security manager at a warehouse in Salem. It was time to check in with the lab and Dr. Valentine.

Since she had to pass the lab before reaching the elevator to the morgue, Jenna peeked in to see if anyone was there. "Good morning," she greeted upon spotting CSI Deng in the lab. "Do you have anything for me?"

"Oh, Lieutenant Ferrari." The black-haired tech jerked his head up as if surprised to see her. "I just came in to start some runs. The spot you mentioned on the painting was human blood and I put it in the DNA machine along with some sweat Wilcox swabbed from the driver's side seat. I've organized the fingerprints for Marcus to handle tomorrow, measured the shoe impression cast CSI Wilcox made, and it belongs to a man's size nine. It appears too wide to be a woman's shoe, and the tread is what you'd find on a hiking or work shoe or boot. We'll compare it to all the brands in our data system and try to find a match. We retrieved plenty of hair samples from the victims' house, but, so far, all of them are dog hair or match the victims. Did you remove a dog from the scene—probably a Pomeranian?"

"No." Jenna brooded over that. *What happened to the dog? Did it get scared and run away? Was it stolen? Could dognapping have been the motive?* She didn't recall any mention of it winning contests or being of particular value other than as a pet. "Thanks for coming in today. Please keep analyzing and let me know if you come across anything else relevant."

"Will do," Deng assured her. He was capable; she'd just be happy when Wilcox and Dr. Gupta came in tomorrow to provide their input.

On the elevator to the basement level and home of the morgue, Jenna wondered if Dr. Valentine would be here on a Sunday morning. How late had he stayed last night?

Upon arriving, she found the glass and steel doors locked and a report folder jutting from a hanging wall rack. She plucked it out and smiled. "Thank you, Dr. Valentine—always the consummate professional." He had performed both autopsies before going home, probably staying until the wee hours.

Jenna took the files and headed back upstairs. The building was practically empty other than the front desk clerk, CSI Deng, and a uniformed officer she passed on his way to the restroom. About to enter her quiet office, she stopped and glanced over her shoulder at the noise coming from the back door. Officer Curtis Campbell—who she first got to know when they shared a trauma therapy group run by Dr. Grayson—and the older, heftier Officer Louis Girard, who must have drawn the short straw, banged their way in.

"Hey, Lieutenant!" called Girard with a wave. Campbell carried a black trash bag and a dismal disposition.

"What've you got there?" Something tightened in Jenna's gut at the expression Campbell bore.

"We were out there at the Baxters' house, where that young couple got murdered," Girard began as he lumbered down the hall, stopping a few feet in front of her. "There was this spot of fresh dirt in the backyard, like someone had been digging, only no flowers around or logical reason for it. So, being senior officer on the scene, I told Curtis to see what was buried there, figuring it might be the murder weapon."

"I had to dig near clear to China through loose soil until I finally found something, at least four, maybe five, feet down." Campbell shot Girard an annoyed expression before returning a miserable look to Jenna. "It ain't the murder weapon."

Jenna braced herself, expecting the worst.

"It was their little dog," Girard declared. "Bashed in the head, same as them, and pretty fresh. I want to put it in a drawer in the morgue for Dr. Valentine so he can determine if the same weapon was used and if her TOD was before, after, or concurrent with her owners'."

"Yes, certainly," Jenna answered, pleased Girard had anticipated her orders. "Officer Duff on the front desk can get you a key."

While she had hoped they would find the pet alive and well, Jenna had speculated they might not. She let sympathy for the cute, poofy Pomeranian from the pictures coat her in sorrow. She could imagine the toy dog attempting to protect her family from danger, getting in the killer's way, and being thumped for her troubles. It wouldn't take a powerful blow to kill such a small creature. It just seemed abnormally cruel to her and lit a fire of anger in her gut.

"I need to take a look." It was the last thing Jenna wanted to do, but it was important. First, she had to be sure it was the same pet as in the photos. Then she wanted to inspect the wounds.

Girard nodded to Campbell. His pallor faded to a sickly green as he opened the trash bag and extended it toward Jenna.

Stepping close, she studied the foxy face, now lifeless with dull eyes, and the once perk ears now wilted into the blood-matted fur on her head. The size and shape of the wound was similar to what she recalled from Nolan's and Alexia's. She would wait for Dr. Valentine's conclusion before writing it into her report, but she believed whoever struck killing blows to her victims had done the same to Picasso.

"There was a shovel in the garage," Jenna said, returning her attention to the officers. "We noticed it appeared out of place with fresh dirt around it."

"After we found the dog, we collected it and brought it in," Campbell said as he closed the trash bag. "Maybe the lab can get prints or DNA. We took pictures of everything too, to document it. The crime scene tape is still up."

"We searched every inch of the property, Lieutenant," Girard stated, "and no sign of a murder weapon. The killer must have taken it with him."

Jenna nodded. "Good work, y'all."

She pushed into her team's office, as quiet and vacant as she had left it. Trisha would be going to brunch with Bennet and his parents while Bauman had zipped down to Asheville, North Carolina for the weekend. She could picture Owens getting ready to take his wife out to a fancy dinner or heading out to watch one of his kids play baseball. Returning to her desk, the sticky note to call her mother caught her attention. *Ten-thirty; too early. She's probably at mass.*

Upon finding her coffee thermos empty, Jenna frowned. She would have to make a pot at the coffee station under the life-size painted busts of the criminal investigations team. With no one else to bounce questions off, she gazed up at the painting while the coffee brewed. "Why put the people in their car, run it off a cliff, and bury the dog? Why even kill the dog? It was too small to be a threat. Barking? Worried Picasso would attract the neighbors' attention? Mr. Halbach mentioned he could hear her bark sometimes. Still, why bother burying her—and so deep?"

She glowered and puzzled. "Did the killer think we wouldn't find her or, if we bought that lame attempt at passing this off as a car accident, suppose the Baxters had buried their poor, dead dog?"

Jenna was back at her desk researching like crimes, her coffee tepid and the cup half empty, when Sergeant Detective Ron Owens swaggered through the door. "Oh, you're here!" he exclaimed in surprise.

6

—◆◇◆—

"I was about to say the same thing to you," Jenna answered, genuinely surprised to see him. However, Owens wasn't in his everyday gray suit and white shirt, rather a sharp navy blue paired with a pinstriped button-down collar and dark blue silk tie swirling with gold paisleys. "Shouldn't you be taking your wife out to dinner?"

"Just did that," he answered and motioned to his fine attire with a playful smirk. Jenna imagined how sharp he would look in his tuxedo at her wedding. "But you should be resting up for the shindig tonight."

Jenna sighed. "Caught a double homicide. And you?"

"Ah," he exhaled and lowered his aging linebacker's body into the chair at this desk. "Still trying to crack that home invasion case from last week. I didn't want to get you roped into it because—you know—wedding and honeymoon coming up. Captain Myers made it clear you would be off for a week, minimum, starting this Friday. Now, I realize I haven't taken the lead on that many cases since my promotion, but if I can't take some of the heat off you, what good was it?"

"It was good to help pay for your oldest to start college in the fall," Jenna reminded him. "While I appreciate not having to lead every investigation sent to this office, why don't you tell me about these home invasions?" Curiosity pricked Jenna's attention, and she wondered if they could be looking for the same suspect.

Owens unbuttoned his summer-weight coat and loosened his tie. "The first break-in was Saturday night, April 27th. Nobody was home, a lot of valuables taken—high-end electronics, jewelry, cash, artwork—and robbery division was handling it until a week later. Someone broke into an older couple's home, bound them with duct tape, threatened them with a billy club, and ripped off their home for thousands of dollars' worth of valuables. That's when Captain Myers considered it could be the same perpetrators. With the added hostage-taking and intimidation, he handed it off to our office. Bauman's been working with me on it."

"Yeah, I'm aware you guys had a hot one while Jamison and I had to sort out a flophouse brawl that ended in a stabbing." Jenna recalled every disgusting and depressing detail.

"Well, we weren't about to trade cases with you," Owens declared. "I mean, yours would be closed sooner and, well, the obvious. And don't go saying chivalry is dead, Ferrari. I know you would be insulted if you thought a couple of men were riding to your rescue," he added with a hardy laugh.

Jenna grinned and shook her head. "I would've made an exception for that one."

"Well, anyway." Owens sucked in a breath and ran a broad hand over hair almost too long to be considered a crew cut. "In the third incident, four days ago, the home was equipped with a security system, and we got decent footage. There's three of them—two men and a woman—all pretty average-sized. They wear painter's coveralls, gloves, masks, and hairnets like the cafeteria ladies wear. Both couples who were home for the robberies said the intruders gained access without their knowledge, surprised them, duct taped and threatened them, and then carted off specific items of value without unnecessary breakage or mess—all very professional. However, in this latest occurrence, the man initially tried to stop them and got punched in the jaw. When they threatened his wife, the homeowner submitted and endured no more violence. The crime scene techs have recovered no prints or DNA, but a few fibers the lab identified as generic cotton work gloves. Our best lead is their body types, voices, and how they move preserved on the video cam footage. I was going to take another look at it, maybe feed some specs into the computer, and see how many like suspects it spits out at me."

"I'd like to watch it with you," Jenna said and walked over to stand behind him at his monitor.

"Bauman usually does this stuff," he grumbled as he plonked on his keyboard and clicked his mouse. "What are we going to do if he moves to Charlotte?"

"Moves?" A projectile of panic raced through Jenna. Bauman was the best computer expert in the department. His skills had helped solve scores of cases. "Has he said something to you about moving?"

"Naw," Owens let out in a low drawl. "It's just a matter of time. He can make more money in the private sector, and you know what finding the right one does to a person. Wouldn't you move if Randi did?"

"I think we'd discuss it together," Jenna considered, "and if it was in our best interest as a unit, sure. I mean, I wouldn't stay behind while she moved off to take a job at Harvard or Columbia or something."

"OK, here it is." Owens played back the living room camera view of the action. Three robbers, average builds, and the woman probably on the tall side as she blended in with the guys, only identifiable by two chest bumps and the curve of her hips. The middle-aged home owner exchanged heated words with the intruders, clenched his fists, and raised a defiant jaw, which the masked man punched. The other two secured his wrists with gray tape and pushed him onto the sofa beside his wife. One man waved a short bat at them—the kind truck drivers use to test the air in their tires. It wasn't a police-issue billy club, just the type that could be purchased at any truck stop.

The crew was efficient, quick, and selective. They didn't bash things or create a mess. Neither did they rough up the couple more than necessary to ensure their cooperation. None said much, although there were a few exchanges that could render an acceptable voice analysis. The intruders left the couple sitting on the couch with their wrists taped, and, after they were gone, the husband and wife picked at each other's bindings until they loosed themselves."

"Did Bauman already isolate the man's voice?" Jenna asked.

"Yeah—good job of it too. Nothing in our database, but when we bring in a suspect, we can check for a match. I don't think they knew the camera was there."

"I'm sure they would have disabled or destroyed it if they had," Jenna speculated. "These aren't kids, and they aren't high on drugs. They are careful, methodical, and professional. I'd bet they've done this kind of thing plenty in the past. What do you think would happen if they met heavy resistance? Or if a barking dog threatened to alert the neighborhood that they were committing a crime?"

Owens offered her a curious gaze. "So far, they haven't acted violently; however, we only have three break-ins we are aware of to use for comparison. Anyone might resort to violence for self-preservation. Silence the dog, subdue the homeowner ..." He shrugged. "Why?"

"My case," Jenna answered and filled him in on the details thus far.

"But nothing was stolen from your victims' house," Owens pointed out when she had finished.

"True, although if it was these guys, their routine was interrupted," Jenna countered.

"I suppose if they discovered they had accidentally killed the husband, let's say, since he would probably be the one standing up to them, they might go ahead and kill the witness. And, since none of the other robberies involved serious assault or manslaughter, they wouldn't want the police to connect this crime with the series of other thefts. If they walked away with computers, TVs, watches, and those kinds of items and were ever caught, it would be too easy to pin them for the murders as well. Better not to enact their regular M.O."

"But whoever put the Baxters into their car and drove it into a tree did an amateur job. It took us no time at all to determine they hadn't died in an accident. This crew seems too sophisticated for that—unless they wanted us to think an amateur committed the murders." Jenna scrunched her face in frustration. "Could be the same bunch. Things got out of hand. A young, confident cyclist, athletic type, being protective of his new bride—or her little dog, if they bashed it first—stands up to them when nobody else had. We could be working the same case."

A few things still bothered Jenna. None of the neighbors reported hearing anything. Wouldn't they have noticed a fight, the dog barking? Unless the home invaders whacked the dog first, distressing Alexia and sending Nolan into a protective, vengeful rage. He goes after the man who struck the dog and one of the other two beats him in the head with the short bat. Alexia was a witness, so she had to go too. They think, plan, and perhaps argue among themselves, thereby consuming the several hours after death before dumping the car over the incline at the dangerous curve. It could have happened that way.

"I won't object to having a second pair of eyes on this," Owens confessed. "But we're packing it in early before the party tonight. Speaking of, how long have you been in? Did you eat lunch?"

Rousted from her thoughts, Jenna glanced at the clock. *One-thirty. Time to call Mama.*

"I'll go grab something from vending and be right back," she told him and switched mental gears on the way to the lounge. She fed the machine change and punched the buttons for a protein bar, a bag of chips, and a Diet Coke. Randi would scold and lecture her on the importance of a proper diet. *Only because she loves me,* Jenna reminded herself.

Determining her conversation might require pacing, Jenna set down her snack lunch and pushed the call button on her phone. The pacing commenced before her mother even answered. "Hello?"

"Happy Mother's Day, Mama!" Jenna was pleased she could produce a cheery sound when every muscle from her toes to her jaw clenched.

"Oh, thank you, Jenna!" Renita Ferrari's voice came through as pleasantly surprised. "I'm so glad you called. Vince Jr., Angie, your dad, and I just got home from a lovely lunch at Cilantro in Paris after mass. We wished you could have joined us, but I know you have important work there."

"That sounds wonderful, Mama." Jenna was honestly glad the family had taken her out for Mother's Day. *Flowers!* She thought and slammed a fist into her thigh as she spun on her heel. *Why didn't I think of flowers?*

"And the lilies you and Randi had delivered to the house are so pretty. You picked one of my favorites. And since they're in a pot, I can put them out in the front yard to bloom every spring. Thank you, dear."

And thank you, God, for Randi! "You're welcome. See, we weren't forgetting about you just because we couldn't drive up this weekend. Speaking of traveling, you know you're invited to our wedding this Saturday. Vince and Angie are coming on Friday, and you and Dad could always ride with them and split the expenses." She had planned not to mention it; the words just spilled out.

"I know, honey." Mama had that tone in her voice—the one that told Jenna she wouldn't come if her life depended on it. "You know I love you. You're my daughter and I'm proud of you, your job, and your integrity. And I like Randi too. She's so kind-hearted and smart and I'm sure she's the best friend you've ever had. But Jennifer, why do you have to *marry* her?"

Her voice had evolved into a pleading whisper. Jenna's feet halted, and she took a deep breath, waiting—as Dr. Grayson had instructed—to choose her response carefully rather than blurt out the first angry words that bypassed her brain on the way to her mouth.

"Marriage is a sacrament of the church," she continued in her "mother-knows-best" manner. "And the Bible clearly states it's only to be observed between a man and a woman. Now, I know you love her, and she loves you; why can't that be enough? Please don't make a mockery of the sacrament this way. And you've roped your brother and sister into participatin' in this, this—"

"Abomination?" Jenna supplied wearily. She realized she had moved beyond being angry with her mother. There was no point in arguing or reasoning with her, no purpose in trying to persuade her to see things from any point of view but her own.

"I wasn't goin' to use that word," Mama professed in contrition. "I don't say things like that anymore."

No, you just think them. Jenna didn't say it aloud because it would only lead to an unwinnable argument. Instead, she took a different approach. "You see, the thing is, I'm not Catholic anymore, and we are getting married in a church. Randi's God doesn't find our relationship offensive at all, and I think I like her

God better than yours. So, if your loyalty and allegiance to the Catholic Church is stronger than your ties and professed love for your daughter—"

"Jenna, don't do that!" Distress tightened her mother's throat, causing the words to choke out in a half-cry. "What I did and said all those years ago was wrong, and I've apologized. You accepted my apology and said you forgave me."

"I do forgive you, Mama," Jenna reaffirmed. "But you just hurt me all over again when you use antiquated doctrine to try to make me feel guilt or shame. I say 'try' because it won't work—never again."

"I'm not tryin' to make you feel guilt or shame, Jenna. I'm just tellin' you how I feel, and what I believe. For my whole life, we were taught what was right and what was wrong, and I can't just switch that off. Honey, please don't be mad at me. I love you, and your Dad's tryin' to talk me into comin'. He says God'll forgive me and I'll regret it the rest of my life if I don't, but ... we'll see, OK? Give me a minute to breathe."

Jenna thought, *We told you about this months ago. You've had more than a minute.* On a discouraged sigh, she said, "All right. Whatever. Happy Mother's Day, Mama. I love you anyway."

7

Randi and Jenna arrived home from the Wasena City Tap Room & Grill by eleven o'clock—not too late to still have a good night's sleep. The bridal shower/bachelor party was a smash. The place was teeming with folks—many Randi had only met once or not at all—and she struggled to match names with the sea of unfamiliar faces. Still, it had been boisterous and delightful.

Ethan Bauman bustled home from his trip to play a video of department bloopers, many of which featured Jenna doing or saying something that came across as hilarious the way he manipulated it. Trisha Jamison led them all in several party games. Randi and Jenna ate delicious food, drank champagne, opened a tableful of gifts, and were hugged and kissed enough to pass on any germs that might have hitchhiked in with the guests. From the colorful lights and balloons to Captain Myers' toast, it was a celebration like no other Randi could recall.

"Dr. Grayson even came," Jenna commented as she and Randi undressed for bed.

It pleased Randi to see Jenna so light and chipper. Earlier, when she'd come home to change for the party, she had been pensive and closed off—not angry or depressed—more contemplatively resigned. Randi presumed it was from talking to her mother earlier. She'd called Renita too, only steered clear of asking if she and Jenna's dad were coming to the wedding. Randi had wanted to discuss how Jenna felt, but it wasn't the right time then and she didn't want to dampen her mood now.

"I knew she would come," Randi said. "You're one of her favorites."

"She doesn't have favorites," Jenna dismissed as she whipped off the nice pullover blouse she'd worn with navy slacks.

"Sure, she does—you!" Randi proclaimed, then rounded the bed. "Let me help you with that."

Jenna turned her back to Randi, who nimbly unbuckled her silky, black bra, allowing her touch to linger on Jenna's silky, olive skin. She brushed a kiss to her nape, followed by trailing more along her collarbone. She forgot about the bra, which seemed to have disappeared while she indulged herself. Randi's roaming fingers found the button on Jenna's pants and deftly undid it as she pressed tight to her bare back.

"I think I'm *your* favorite," Jenna crooned as she laid her head back to expose more of her neck and throat to Randi's kisses.

"You most certainly are." The words escaped in a husky tone that concluded with a sucking motion in the hollow of Jenna's suprasternal notch. Although the champagne, the festive vibes, and holding Jenna in her embrace aroused Randi to distraction, she couldn't resist getting in a little tease. "I'll have to bump all my other lovers to the back of the line." She got an elbow in the ribs for her trouble.

"Brat!" Jenna stepped out of her slacks and pivoted to face Randi with a seductive challenge in her bearing. "I know how to hide the bodies where they'll never be found."

"Sweetie, it's reassuring to know you'd go to all that trouble for me."

Jenna's playful smirk and dancing blue eyes set the stage as her hand gently guided Randi's head toward her waiting lips.

"Why not top off the night with the best dessert I know?" Jenna suggested as they stood beside a turned-down bed with the heat of their bare breasts pressed together. "And, no, I'm not waiting for you to run to the kitchen for whipped cream."

Randi laughed, tickled to the core with delirious joy, and threw Jenna onto the bed. "You asked for it—one triple-scoop orgasm coming up!"

***

Monday, May 13th

"Good morning, Officer Stewart," Jenna greeted as she strode past the front desk. A buoyant spirit had a spring in her step and a tune in her heart after last night's festivities—both with the gang at the Tap and in private afterward. She planned to knock this case out, get married to her one-and-only, and head off on a mystery adventure. It perturbed her that Randi refused to acknowledge if any of her guesses were correct, and, man, could that woman keep a secret when she wanted to! Jenna reminded herself to never play poker with her.

"Good morning!" the older officer chimed back. "Thanks for inviting me to your bash last night. I'm always looking for a reason to celebrate."

"Well, thank you for coming."

Jenna smiled and was about to head back to her office when Stewart's manner shifted. "I heard about that case you caught over the weekend." He grimaced, shook his head, and ran a bony hand over his fuzz of black hair. "I know the Baxters—the older ones—not personally, but I know who they are. Good folks. Hey, you don't think race had anything to do with it, do you? I mean, a young, local White man marries a Black woman from up north somewhere?"

While the thought had crossed her mind, coming from an African American police officer gave the possibility more weight. Twenty-first century or not, there were always a few pockets of racism that kept turning up. Stewart would know more about that than she would. Jenna frowned.

"Now, Lieutenant, I know things are a right better now than in the past, but some folks still believe miscegenation should be against the law." He covered his mouth with a fist and coughed out three indistinct sounds that could be interpreted as the letters, "K, K, K."

"Yeah," she growled. "I thought of that, and we're pursuing all leads—speaking of which, I hope to get some today with our lab friends returning from the weekend."

"Oh, you'll get them all right," Stewart avowed in an assured tone. "Let me know if I can help."

"Will do."

A glance down the hall revealed the door to the DNA lab was open. Gathering hope to her chest like a shield, Jenna pivoted and strode to the lab. "Glad to see you made it bright and early after last night," Jenna praised with a smile of greeting. "You and your hubby looked like you enjoyed yourselves."

"Oh, Lieutenant Ferrari, we surely did!" exclaimed the only professional in the station who stood shorter than Jenna. Dr. Asita Gupta's black hair flowed down her back in a tail, and a broad grin dominated her round face. "You and Dr. Randi make such an adorable couple. My husband knows her from back when she dated that young mathematics professor and would visit over at their building. She is very well respected at the college."

"I have no doubt," Jenna affirmed, "and she said it was a joy to finally meet you. Please tell me Deng set up the machine correctly and we have DNA results this morning."

"Yes," Dr. Gupta replied as she tamped down her enthusiasm, switching to business mode. "But I haven't had time to make any comparisons yet. I only just walked in and am surprised you didn't take another hour."

"All right, tell you what," Jenna suggested. "I'll make my rounds and be back in about twenty minutes. Will you have something then?"

Despite having donned her professional manner, a cascade of laughter fell from Dr. Gupta's lips. "Oh, Jenna. When will you learn that science takes time?"

"Don't hold your breath," Jenna answered, half joking. "By then, science will have discovered ways to speed up. I'll be back."

She checked in with Dr. Valentine, thanked him for the reports he left, and asked about Picasso.

"Yes. I was surprised to walk in this morning and find a new resident in my domain," he replied.

He strode to the wall of refrigerated drawers and pulled out one near the bottom. Gently lifting the tiny dog, he laid her on his shiny, stainless steel examining table and flicked on a spotlight. Powder puffed from the sterile, rubber gloves when he popped his hands into them.

"My wife had a wonderful time at your pre-wedding party last night," he commented as he prepared for the necropsy. "Well, I did too, but I'm not much one for social gatherings."

"We were glad you could come. I think the joke you told went over well too."

"If you thought that was funny, how about this one?" he asked brightly. "What do you call a car dealership owned by a former coroner? Rigor Motors."

"Hilarious," Jenna deadpanned and shook her head. "Coroners and medical examiners must be extremely popular," she suggested. "People are always dying to meet them."

"Ha, ha," Dr. Valentine mocked. "What did you say our victim's name was?"

"Picasso." Humor faded, and empathy for the family pet took its place.

"This head injury is consistent with the ones inflicted on Mr. and Mrs. Baxter," Dr. Valentine pronounced gravely. "The wound circumference is the same in all three victims. And, while I can't conclude that the same implement was used to cause each case of blunt force trauma, I can testify the same type of weapon was employed. Considering the wood fibers and the size and shape of the skull fractures, I stick with the determination of a baseball bat or its equivalent. I'm sure the lab will test like instruments to match a size or brand."

Peering down at the fragile, furry pet, lying still and cold on the table, Jenna swallowed a lump in her throat and nodded. The Pommy was no larger than her cat—probably smaller. Byron might have been able to hold his own, even bite and injure his attacker.

"Did you check her mouth and teeth?" she asked. "Maybe she got a piece of the perpetrator."

"Not yet," Dr. Valentine replied with consternation. "I'm just getting started. I don't suppose we need to know what the pooch had for dinner; however, in case this was premeditated, she could have been drugged." He pried open her diminutive jaws, shined in his headlamp, and poked about with a metal probe. Trading the probe for tweezers, he plucked out a tiny fiber. "Perhaps from a pants leg," he mused, "or shoelace. I'll send it to the lab and perform a full necropsy. Poor thing. If Mom and Dad were no match for their attackers, Picasso never stood a chance."

"You think more than one?" Jenna inquired. *The home invasion crew has three members. Much easier to subdue a young couple with three of them.*

He shook his head. "The evidence doesn't indicate the number of assailants; there was likely a single weapon employed. Saying 'attackers' was only a speculation."

"OK. One more thing."

Dr. Valentine, headlamp on, glanced up from his examination of the body with a questioning expression.

"The Baxters—Nolan's folks—would like to see Nolan, Alexia, and Picasso. They don't know the dog is dead yet," she stipulated. "But they want to come in as soon as possible."

"Let's set up a viewing for one this afternoon then," he replied. "That will give me plenty of time to finish here, write my report, and have their children presentable."

"Thank you. I'll let them know."

Back on the main floor, Jenna trod to her next stop—CSI Wilcox's lab. She and Davenport, the primary day-shift specialists, were already at work testing evidence when Jenna walked in.

"Good morning." Her greeting had lost some of its luster since she'd used it on Officer Stewart.

"Oh, Lieutenant Ferrari!" Destiny Wilcox rang out as a brilliant smile widened in contrast to her earthy face. "Your party last night was so much fun. And the bag of party favors to take home, so thoughtful."

"I especially appreciated the video reel," commented twiggy, wet-behind-the-ears Davenport. He may still sport pimples, but at least he had a brain.

"I'm glad you could both come," she confessed, getting that out of the way. Now, on to business. "What do you have on the Baxter case?"

"You were right about blood on the painting," Wilcox said. "Deng put a sample in the DNA machine. We also recovered fingerprints from inside the car and residence, and Marcus has them running comparisons. The splinters recovered from the victim's head wounds came back as maple, and the mass spectrometer also identified traces of a nitrocellulose lacquer and simple brushing varnish."

"A baseball bat," Jenna concluded. "While ash and birch are also traditional woods for bats, maple is far more popular these days. Add in the finish—"

"And the size of the skull impact area," Davenport interrupted. "We already determined it's consistent with the end cap and barrel of a traditional bat. Next, we'll need to measure various brands and styles."

"So, bigger than a tire bat or nightstick," Jenna concluded. *That's what the home invasion crew carried.*

"I'd think so," said Wilcox, who, judging by the expression she wore, knew less about sports than Jenna and Davenport. "We also swabbed the driver's seat and wheel, retrieved a DNA sample, and also put it in for testing."

"Girard brought in a shovel yesterday and Dr. Valentine is sending you up a fiber from the little dog's mouth—yes, another victim, same weapon used, Valentine thinks. I'll check by later."

"We'll find something you can use," Wilcox promised.

"You already have." She could push the home invaders down on her nonexistent list of suspects. "But I'll take more."

Jenna made a stop by Jose Marcus's fingerprint lab, leaving her discouraged by the apparent lack of evidence. Over a hundred samples were lifted from the car and residence, and they all matched exemplars from family members and close friends. So, unless Brenda managed to kill them while at her hair appointment, or little sister got the jump on them, Jenna concluded the killer had worn gloves.

It makes sense if it was a break-in or premeditated. Add that most people wear gloves when using a baseball bat to protect from blisters, and all the shoveling to bury the dog.

"Dr. Gupta, I said I'd be back," Jenna announced upon entering her lab.

"Yes, and I've had time to print out the test results." Dr. Gupta crossed the sterile room, gleaming with white, silver, and a touch of scrubs blue, with a file folder. Handing it to Jenna, she reported, "The blood on the painting matches Nolan Baxter and the sweat sample is an unknown. It doesn't match any database or the exemplars from family and friends. If you bring in a suspect, we can run a comparison."

Jenna sighed in disappointment as she glanced over the graphs and charts with their peaks and valleys, not completely understanding what each marker meant. "So, nobody who's been in the military, teaches school, drives for a trucking company, has any kind of security clearance, or was arrested on prior felony charges."

Dr. Gupta shrugged. "It depends on how old your unsub is. Nobody collected DNA or kept records before the nineties. Testing wasn't even developed until the nineteen-eighties. But you could safely assume your suspect has no former felony arrests and works in a career that doesn't require DNA testing."

Jenna leaned her elbows on the counter and stared blankly at the pages of scientific script. A spark of inspiration struck as she suddenly recalled a family tree project Randi's sister, Ellen, had been talking about at the party last night. In a search to discover her family's heritage, she had enlisted a genealogy company to unravel branches of her family-tree, leading back to Ireland. "What if we have long-lost cousins we never met or are related to someone famous?" she'd speculated. A major component of the project was having her DNA tested.

"Hey," Jenna said, straightening with renewed promise. "What about running an ancestry search? You know, find out generic things like sex, race, hair and eye color, and what part of the world the person came from? We can't use it as evidence in court because a lot of folks could match the selected markers, but it can help us build a profile. I mean, we could eliminate scores of potential suspects, say if we knew the perp, for example, was Chinese—or wasn't Chinese."

Dr. Gupta's face brightened to match Jenna's level of enthusiasm. "Of course! Forensic genetic genealogy. I read about a case recently where an unknown felon's aunt uploaded her DNA to a public genetic database in hopes of connecting with relatives. Using a familial match to their unidentified sample, police were able to arrest and convict a dangerous child molester. I'll get right on that and see what we can uncover."

Proud of herself for producing a bright idea, some of that former spring returned to her step as Jenna swaggered down the hall to her office.

8

Jenna's team members were all busy at their stations when she walked into the criminal investigations office after making her rounds. She headed straight for the coffee.

"Great party last night." Owens whirled his chair around to face her with his gray suitcoat flopped open, revealing his ample girth. "Now my wife wants to throw some kind of party for our twentieth anniversary that's coming up, and I blame Jamison."

"Me?" Trisha squeaked. Her green eyes widened in innocent disbelief as she, too, spun her chair to face Jenna.

"Can't blame Jamison for being superior at everything she puts her hand to," Jenna replied jovially. "I consider such proficiency an asset. If anyone deserves blame, it's Bauman for making us all look like a bunch of clowns around here." Though her voice rang with irritation, Jenna winked at her tech guy to assure him she wasn't angry about the blooper reel.

"No, lieutenant," he stammered. "It was just supposed to be funny."

"It was funny," Owens confirmed. "Now, Jamison." He leveled an accusatory stare at her. "There is such a thing as being too good at your job. I don't have your financial backing. My wife thinks I can spring to rent out a venue and host a dinner and an open bar. I tried explaining to her it would take at least a semester of college tuition away from Ronnie Junior. Why can't I just take her out to dinner like a normal husband? No. You," he pointed at Jamison, "had to show her the sunnier side of life. The least you could do is bring me a cup of coffee."

With a relaxed sigh, Jamison met Jenna at the coffeepot. "We took up a collection to pay for the shower and the Tap gave us a good deal because of all the business the police station brings them. Maybe I could share some cost-cutting ideas with your wife."

"Ah, forget it," Owens allowed with a wave of his hand. "We'll come up with something reasonable."

"Bauman, how was your weekend? You haven't started packing to move, have you?" Jenna asked.

His indoor-white face paled even more behind wide, black-rimmed glasses, and Bauman gulped. "Me, move?" he repeated in a shaky voice. "Uh ... not yet. I don't know, Lieutenant. I mean, people talk about stuff, but I haven't committed to anything. Why would you think—"

"We all know you could triple your salary going to the private sector," Owens acknowledged and took a full cup from Jamison. "Thanks, kid. And don't sweat the party thing. I'm just messing with you." A smile returned to her face.

"Randi says Asheville is a nice community," Jenna commented as she returned to her desk. "Artsy and progressive."

"Yeah, it is." Worry clung to Bauman's expression, informing Jenna he was thinking seriously about it but wasn't ready to say so.

"So, are you still working the home invasions with Owens today?" she asked, changing the subject.

"Unless you need me for something else," he answered.

"There's not much in the way of tech on our case," Jenna replied. "But if you could extrapolate from your video footage the exact measurements of the robbers' bat, I could really use that information."

"Sure. Not a problem." He turned to his computer and got to work.

"Still thinking we're on the same case?" Owens asked.

"Not really. I think your guys' bat is too small to have caused my victims' wounds. And Jamison?" She flicked her gaze to Trisha. "Girard and Campbell found Picasso buried four feet deep in the backyard."

"Ah, that's too bad." She drooped into her chair and took a sip of her coffee. "I called the city first thing this morning to report about the dangerous curve where the Baxters' SUV crashed. They said it's on their list to have a guardrail installed, and, with any luck, they'll get to it by October."

Jenna scowled. "City hall. They're even slower than the courts. All right. Let's dig into Nolan and Alexia's pasts and see if we can turn up an angry ex or any other motive for murder."

"You've got it, boss," Jamison pronounced, and they both started digging.

About an hour later, Jamison went to refill her coffee. "I might have run across something of interest."

Jenna rolled her neck and turned her attention to her partner. "Share, then."

"Before he started dating Alexia, Nolan had a bad breakup with a woman named Claire Avery." She added cream and two sugars. "Claire exhibited some angry, bitter behavior, posting her displeasure on social media for months, and she swore to get even. The rants cooled off for a while, then picked back up a couple of weeks ago when Nolan and Alexia's wedding photo appeared in the newspaper. She posted a short video—had to have been totally wasted—where she calls them every name in the book and says Nolan will be sorry."

"She's worth checking into," Jenna replied. "Send me her info and I'll give her a call. Let's see if she's willing to contribute her DNA for comparison with our unknown. Even if not, we can get her shoe size. And I'd like to know where she was on Saturday."

With a pert nod, Jamison sent Claire's contact information to Jenna's station. She used the office phone to call Ms. Avery at her place of employment—a local pet store and grooming center.

Once the store supervisor connected her, a pleasant voice introduced itself as Claire Avery.

"Ms. Avery, I'm Lieutenant Detective Ferrari with the Roanoke Police Department. Are you aware that an acquaintance of yours, Mr. Nolan Baxter, and his wife were killed over the weekend?"

"Shut up!" she snapped. "Who is this and why are you messin' with me?"

"I'm really with the police," Jenna repeated. "We're asking you to come in and answer a few questions that might help us discover who murdered them."

"Murder?" The young woman sounded incensed and still didn't seem to believe she was talking with the police. "Now, listen here. I'm not doin' any such thing. I'm at work, and Fifi is waiting for her shampoo and cut. Whoever this is, don't call here again." The line went dead, and Jenna returned the desk phone to its charger.

"That was a short call," Jamison observed.

"Yeah. Looks like I'll have to send a patrol car to collect the angry ex. Either she didn't believe me, or she's stalling."

"You said the Baxters are coming at one," Jamison reminded her. "It's after eleven now. Let's grab lunch and bring Claire in after the Baxters have left."

"Good call, Jamison. Delivery?" Owens and Bauman had left to interview a person of interest in the home invasion robberies, so Jenna and Trisha had the office to themselves. "I'm always up for pizza."

Jamison's lips twitched. "I was thinking of a salad from the deli down the street, but thin-crust pizza shouldn't throw off my diet."

"Diet? You're already model thin," Jenna observed.

Trisha giggled. "How do you think I stay that way?"

***

Randi scurried around between her morning classes to visit all of Susan Baxter's teachers, let them know her brother and sister-in-law had been murdered, and suggested excusing her from final exams. Only her grumpy physics professor required persuasion, as the others were fully on board. By the time she got to the dean's office, the request was purely academic.

"I saw something about the murders in the paper." Dr. Adam Stanley, Ph.D, scrunched up his square face studiously as a furrow formed between his eyebrows. He rubbed his chin and met Randi's gaze with sympathetic eyes. "I didn't know the victims were related to one of our students."

Randi was pleased this dean had turned out to be more professional and less lethal than her last supervisor. Besides not having murdered anyone—that she knew of—Dean Stanley possessed a deeper level of comprehension regarding most topics and had enacted positive changes at the community college.

"The police withheld the names to protect the privacy of the victims' families," Randi informed him. "Susan has been an exceptional student and is slated to graduate in a few days. She doesn't need to be worried about exams while swamped with grief."

"I completely agree," he stated, lifting his chin. "And if she can't make the ceremony, we'll mail her diploma."

"Thank you. I already talked to her other professors, and everyone agreed. Do you want to call her house, or go by?"

Randi watched the apprehension wash over him. He licked his lips and raked a shaky hand through his thinning, gray hair. "I think it would be better if someone she knows and respects goes out to tell her. I mean, she may respect my title, but I've never had any personal interaction with Miss Baxter." Randi understood how he felt—afraid and awkward to pay his regards to a grieving family he didn't know. She was going to volunteer anyway.

"I'll go and extend yours and the faculty's condolences," Randi said.

Dean Stanley let out a breath and nodded. "Thank you. I think that would be best. You had her for two classes, right?"

"Three, actually. Her freshman introduction to English Lit as well as last year's English Novel and this year's Shakespeare. Her major is in psychology, but she likes to read, so she plugged in a lot of literature as electives."

He nodded and stood to show Randi out. "Tell her ..." He paused to gather his thoughts. "Tell her we're all thinking about her, and not to worry about school, and let my office know if she needs anything pertaining to graduation, records, or anything else. She's one of ours. Let her know she's one of ours."

***

Jenna texted Randi after the Baxter family left the station, broken and in tears. Randi replied she'd be going to see them after class with a flower arrangement from the college.

'I think it was the last straw for Susan when they learned the dog had been killed too,' Jenna texted.

'Such a tragedy. You'll make their killer pay, though.'

While deriving some satisfaction from Randi's declaration, Jenna still felt the weight of responsibility for protecting the citizens of Roanoke. *Why can't I prevent murders before they happen?* Her brain realized that wasn't always possible and that arresting criminals and seeing them locked up likely did prevent more murders. She thought about the psychic woman, Rhiannon. She'd prevented her murder. *Too bad she can't see them all coming in her crystal ball and give me a heads up.* Even if Jenna had believed a little in Rhiannon's supposed abilities, she understood enough to know that wasn't how "the gift" worked.

She gave Jamison a crack at running the recording from the observation booth and left Claire Avery to stew for fifteen minutes in the interview room before she walked in. *Something else we'll need to train somebody for if Bauman leaves.*

"Finally!" Claire huffed out and slapped her palm on the table. She wore a white cotton smock with cheery cats and dogs splashed over it and an angry snarl. "You hauled me in here for no reason and then left me sittin'. Am I under arrest for somethin'?"

Temper, temper, Jenna thought, lifted a brow, and cooly took her seat. "Ms. Avery, I'm Lieutenant Detective Ferrari, the officer you hung up on earlier today."

Her tantrum stopped and her oval, ivory face went blank. "You mean that wasn't a prank call?"

"I told you I was with the police."

Claire's denim-blue eyes rounded. "You mean Nolan is really dead?"

She appeared shocked; too shocked? Jenna scrutinized every movement and facial tick to determine how truthful she was being. "Yes, ma'am. A man I have evidence you were associated with in the past and his new bride." She didn't want to mention the dog yet—see if the suspect slipped up and said something about Picasso.

"Well, I," Claire began, her expression falling into sorrow, "I didn't know."

"Ms. Avery, how well did you know Nolan Baxter?"

As if snapped out of a dream, Claire flashed darts from her eyes at Jenna. "You know full well he used to be my boyfriend, or you wouldn't have hauled me in here in a police car. But we broke up two years ago, and I've moved on." She folded her arms over her chest and set her foot swinging from where one leg crossed the other.

"So it would seem." Jenna opened the file in front of her on the table filled with pages Jamison had printed out. "Then again, there's this video you posted on social media just two weeks ago where you called him and Alexia, 'cock sucking—'"

"Stop it!" Claire slammed her hands on the table and her feet to the floor. "I was drunk and feeling sorry for myself. I forgot I'd posted it and I'll certainly take it down after this. You can't think I wished them harm."

"You said you wanted to cut off his—"

"Don't!" the young woman interrupted again. With frustration apparent on her face, Claire impatiently pushed aside the overgrown bangs of her brunette bob. "Just don't," she repeated in a soft, regretful manner. "I thought he was the one. We had so much in common—outdoor activities like cycling and canoeing, an interest in cars, comedy movies, and, of course, dogs. I just loved his golden retriever, and he was the only person besides me that my dachshund tolerated. I can't completely blame him for our breakup, although I did at the time. I didn't see how bossy I was being or demanding and just tried to fix it all with sex." She sighed. "That didn't work. So, I was angry, especially since he found someone new so soon after we split, while I ..."

Claire shook her head and exhaled a heavy breath. "I didn't mean what I said in the video—just jealous he was getting married before me, I guess."

Jenna nodded. She wasn't completely convinced, although she could imagine a young woman responding that way.

"Who didn't like Nolan?" she asked. "Who else was angry with him, especially for marrying Alexia?"

"I don't know," Claire offered weakly. "He worked at the DMV and revoked people's licenses—well, the state of Virginia revoked them, but he had to deliver the bad news. Three years ago, some dude clocked him one, but I don't know about any recent incidents."

"What about co-workers, neighbors, your friends who might have shared your wrath toward him?"

"Not that I can think of. When we dated, he didn't live out on the mountain but in his parents' basement apartment. And most of my friends urged me to go out and find someone new."

It was time for Jenna to ask the crucial question. "Where were you on Saturday between eleven a.m. and three o'clock?"

"Shopping." Claire's expression shifted to alarm when she realized the implications. "I didn't—I couldn't!"

"Shopping with whom?" Jenna recalled something about young women liking to shop in packs, or at least pairs.

"Nobody."

"Did you use a credit or debit card or write a check for any of your purchases?"

"I didn't make any purchases," she answered with a baffled expression, adding, "except for a snack and soda, but I paid cash for those."

If this lame story was true, it belonged in the twilight zone. "You mean to tell me you went shopping by yourself for at least *four* hours and didn't buy anything?"

"Well, yeah," she answered innocently. "It's called window shopping. Hello?" She stared at Jenna like she had two heads. "It's fun. You browse, try on a few things, make a list to give your parents before Christmas ..."

"Ms. Avery, what size shoe do you wear?"

"A nine." Claire blinked as if puzzled over the relevance. Jenna glanced at the suspect's feet, determining she was telling the truth. A woman's nine would be a couple of sizes smaller than the impression taken beside the road, but she could have worn a larger shoe.

"Would you mind if our lab tech comes in here to swab your cheek for a DNA sample?"

Claire's features hardened, and Jenna could imagine steam puffing from her ears. "I told you I didn't kill Nolan and whatshername! You have insulted me and hurt my feelings, and no—you may not have my DNA. I have rights! I did nothing wrong and I'm going to leave now."

Jenna escorted her to the door, but, before opening it, issued a warning. "This outburst will only make me look harder at you as a suspect. Prepare to have your life turned upside down, Ms. Avery. If you have so much as an unpaid parking ticket, I'll find it."

Claire clamped her jaw shut, thrust her nose in the air, and marched out.

9

"What do you think, Jamison?" Jenna asked when they were back in the office. Jenna had developed a habit of prompting her protégé to examine testimonies and find flaws or inconsistencies when she was helping her prep for the detective's test; no reason to stop now.

"On the one hand, she certainly has a hot temper and possibly a drinking problem, with the whole posting drunken rants on the internet thing," Jamison answered. "But you don't think—"

"Back to basics, detective—motive, means, and opportunity. Where does Claire Avery stand?"

Jamison slouched into her armed swivel chair with a sulk. "Jealousy is a powerful motive, as is revenge," she admitted. "Not to mention the woman-scorned deal. And, OK, opportunity because her alibi is as shaky as a stack of Jell-O. Although I have to admit, I've done that plenty of times—stay out all day shopping alone and not buying anything."

Jenna pinned her with an annoyed stare, causing Jamison to cringe.

"That leaves means," she continued. "She's big enough to swing a bat—and they probably wouldn't have expected it. But to pick up a man Nolan's size—all dead weight—and put him in the front seat of the SUV? If it *was* her, she'd need help."

"I agree," Jenna stated. "What else?"

Jamison rolled her tongue around her lips. Lifting an inspired finger, she answered, "She refused to give a DNA sample, so maybe she has something to hide." Jamison's countenance fell and her shoulders slumped. "She just doesn't give me a killer vibe, you know?"

"They don't always," Jenna instructed. "It's good to use your gut as a compass, but you still must dot all the 'i's and cross all the 't's, because sometimes—especially with a sociopath—they're excellent liars. Her shoe size doesn't match the impression beside the road, although she could have worn larger shoes on purpose. The big thing that doesn't jive for me, is Picasso. Claire may hate any number of people, but she loves dogs. I just don't see her whacking the little Pom and then burying her four feet deep. Do you know how long digging that hole must have taken, and how much hard work? No wonder there was sweat on the driver's side seat; I just don't think it's Claire's."

Jamison narrowed her eyes at Jenna suspiciously. "If you don't think it was her, why'd you push me in her direction?"

"I wanted to hear your thought process—decent—and we must assume nothing."

"So, does she go above or below the home invasion robbers in suspect ranking?"

Jenna's lips twitched, and she rubbed her temples as if the decision mattered. It didn't. It wouldn't be either. "Put them on the same rung—still in the running, but not favored to show, place, or win. We need to take a trip down to the DMV office and talk with Nolan's supervisor and co-workers. Maybe there was an incident with an angry customer on Friday or even someone who was a repeat troublemaker."

"Sounds good," Trisha chirped, back in her usual good spirits. She scooped up a half-full bottle of water and her purse, and Jenna followed her out. "Wanna take my car?"

"No." If Jenna wasn't in charge, she got antsy. She'd let Owens drive sometimes, especially if she was busy with some immediate detail or a high-speed chase was involved, but Trisha drove too slow and her expensive car invited too much attention.

Walking into the crowded center, with rows of chairs for folks who had to take a number and lines at plexiglass windows, reminded Jenna it was a Monday. To one side of the central area were private booths for taking written driving tests—two of which were occupied by teenagers. High counters and protective barriers lined two walls, separating employees from the public. There was a camera spot, where several people stood waiting to have their pictures taken, and two security guards wearing uniforms—one at the door and the other parading about the space. It was hot, sticky, and reeked of dismal impatience.

Jenna showed her badge to the pudgy guard at the door. "We need to speak to whoever's in charge. It's about Nolan Baxter."

A vein pulsed in his neck, and he shuffled his feet, rubbing a hand over his wide chin. "That'd be Mrs. Phillips. She's the department supervisor and she briefed us on what happened. Terrible. Here, I'll take you back to her office."

More than a few heads turned when Jenna, accompanied by Jamison in heels, a form-enhancing summer dress, and her luxurious strawberry-blonde tresses bouncing down her back, strolled past. The doorman left them with an older woman sitting at a desk piled with folders and an ancient computer monitor.

"May I help you?" sounded her fatigued greeting.

Jenna presented her badge again. "Lieutenant Detective Ferrari and Detective Jamison. We're here to talk with you about Nolan Baxter."

She sighed and peered up with bags under her eyes that looked like they'd been packed for a month-long trip. "I'm just so shocked—we all are. Nice young man like that and he just got married. What happened?"

"That's what we're trying to piece together, ma'am," Jamison replied in a sympathetic quality. "We are sorry for your loss."

"Blow to the gut is more like it." Mrs. Phillips leaned back in her office chair. "Won't y'all have a seat?"

Jenna and Jamison sat in the twin visitors' chairs across from her.

"I know things can get a little heated in offices like this," Jenna opened. "Nolan's sister mentioned he'd get irate customers from time to time."

"Yeah. It's why we have two security guards instead of just one. Nolan was a second-tier assistant, not just a window clerk. He taught a driving safety course and would often perform road tests. Now, back when he worked the counter, he took some abuse, but, in his new position, not so much."

"When was the last time he was in to work?" Jamison asked. "We know he only recently returned from his honeymoon."

"He was back in on Thursday and Friday after taking a week and a half off," Mrs. Phillips said. She shuffled her hands from her chair arms to her lap and then laced her fingers together. "My daughter and I went to his wedding. Sheila was in his class in high school, so they were friendly. It didn't influence my decision to promote him," she explained defensively. "He had a steady temperament and was a great communicator, exemplary record, no conflicts with other employees. Nolan was skilled at defusing situations before they got out of hand. I can't think of any recent incidents with angry customers or arguments, heated or otherwise. I wish I could help."

"You're helping," Jamison assured her. "The more suspects we can cross off our list, the closer we get to finding the right one. What about his wife, Alexia? Did she ever come into the office? Did people see them together?"

A nostalgic smile brightened Mrs. Phillip's face for the first time. "No, not as a rule, but this is where they first met. It was right before Nolan got his promotion and he was making licenses. She had come in to swap her out-of-state license for a Virginia one, and he assisted her. He filled out her information, took her new photo—retook it when she frowned at the first one, which is never done—and printed up the card. They smiled at each other enough to brighten up even *this* place. There was a scruffy fellow who got upset because he spent so much time with her, but that was nearly two years ago. It was kind of like love at first sight, only they didn't rush into anything. Then he found out she worked at the same school where his mother taught. What are the odds?"

It was a sweet, meet-cute for a couple people seemed to like—only someone disliked the Baxters enough to murder them.

"So, no threats have been made against Nolan recently? Someone who failed their driving test or maybe an angry parent?"

"Detectives." Mrs. Phillips sighed and shook her head. "You can't think someone would murder two people over that, can you? Besides, there were no unfortunate incidents on Thursday or Friday. Oh, maybe a month back, he had to fail a boy on his driving test because he clearly wasn't ready. The kid ran a stop sign, couldn't parallel park, and nearly sideswiped a garbage truck. As I recall, the boy's father was plenty mad, but at the kid—not Nolan."

While the world is full of angry, thoughtless people ready to unload their wrath on the nearest individual they can blame, Jenna didn't see someone fed up with the DMV following Nolan Baxter to discover where he lived, and then waiting for him to return from his honeymoon to bludgeon him and his wife. It was too much trouble, too much effort, and they wouldn't want to delay their fury for that long. If an incident had occurred on Friday, one day would give the felonious nutcase time to get his nerve up. If Mrs. Phillips' testimony was correct—and Jenna saw no reason for her to lie—she wouldn't find the killer here.

***

Randi parked her pickup truck on the curb in front of the Baxters' house and slid out with a flower arrangement and a covered dish. Not taking time to prepare something homemade—as is customary—she picked up a Chicken Alfredo at the deli. She'd eaten from there before, so she knew the extra herbs, cheese, and bacon bits they added gave the pasta a boost. Her hands full, she was about to ring the bell with her elbow when Susan opened the door, an uncharacteristically lethargic golden retriever at her side.

"Dr. McLeod," she greeted, with a pleasantly surprised expression. "And you brought stuff."

Randi attempted to poke a hole through her heavy heart to smile. She knew Susan pretty well after reading her essays and listening to her observations on famous literary works for three out of the past four years. She was a typical student, by most standards, yet displayed an enthusiasm for reading many others lacked.

"Dean Stanley wanted me to remind you that you're one of ours, and the faculty and staff wish to support you at this difficult time," she began. Susan took the flowers and ushered her in.

"Thank you," Susan gushed, her eyes tearing up. "Mama, Dr. McLeod brought food and flowers," she called over her shoulder.

"I talked with your teachers, and you're exempt from final exams," Randi continued. "Your record is sound, and Dean Stanley said it's all right if you don't make it to graduation; he'll get your diploma to you and anything else you need."

Mrs. Baxter met them at the door and the sweet-natured dog slunk off into the front living room. Randi could tell the family pet registered everyone's grief, which confused and troubled him.

"Dr. McLeod, thank you so much for coming by." Kathleen dutifully took the covered plastic pan loaded with food from Randi's hands while Susan set the bouquet with other flowers that had arrived in the front room. With her hands free, Susan returned to where Randi stood in the entry with a longing expression. Randi enveloped her in a comforting embrace and the young woman sunk into her, taking every ounce of energy and emotion her teacher bestowed.

Her mother disappeared and reappeared without the dish before Susan was ready to let go. Randi wasn't sure what to say. She remembered all the people coming by to offer their condolences when her mother, and then her father, died in quick succession, yet she didn't remember a thing any of them said—only that they cared. She concluded that was enough. Words couldn't help a tragedy like this, though knowing people loved and cared about them might.

"Please tell everyone thank you," Susan responded. "Do you want to have a seat?"

"I don't want to intrude," Randi said. "I'm sure you'll have family arriving."

"Our pastor was just here a little while ago," Mrs. Baxter said. "He prayed with us and gave us a book."

"*A Grief Observed*, by C.S. Lewis," Susan said, glancing toward where the book lay on the coffee table in the adjoining sitting area.

"Anything by C.S. Lewis is wonderful and meaningful," Randi said. "When you're more settled, you should read it."

"We went to the police station earlier today to see them—Nolan and Alexia," Kathleen related. "It's all still so surreal, like something in a dream."

"They killed their little dog too." Susan's eyes flashed with hatred, and she wiped a hand across her brow, staring down at her feet.

"Yeah, I know," dropped from Randi's lips. "But Lieutenant Ferrari will find out who did it and arrest them. She's leading this investigation, and she's the best detective on the force."

"Oh, do you know Lieutenant Ferrari?" Mrs. Baxter asked.

"Yes, Mom. Remember—I told you Dr. McLeod and Lieutenant Ferrari are getting married on Saturday."

"Sorry. I must have missed that part."

"Listen, I don't want to be in the way," Randi repeated. "I just want to let you all know how sorry the faculty and I are about this horrible tragedy. Susan, don't worry about anything school-related. You are graduating with honors, and there's nothing else you need to do for that. Also, if there's anything I can do for you or you just want to talk, I'm available all week. Then I'll be gone a few days, but I'll be back, and you can always reach me by phone or e-mail. We don't always understand why things happen, and maybe we aren't supposed to. Just understand that you are surrounded by a community who loves and cares for you. You're not alone."

"That's what our pastor said," Kathleen commented. "We don't understand it, and I don't know if I'll be able to cope, but we sure appreciate knowing how many concerned friends we have, praying for us to pull through. I hope Lieutenant Ferrari can catch who did this so they can't kill anyone else, but it won't bring my children back."

Susan put an arm around her mother, gathering her against her shoulder. "I was going to come to the wedding, but—"

Randi offered her a soft smile and shook her head. "Don't worry about that. Just grieve and heal and help your mother. You are a smart, sensitive, strong woman, Susan Baxter. The two of you look after each other for now. I'll just let myself out."

Mrs. Baxter held out a hand to Randi in a weak wave. "Thank you for the flowers and food and mostly for being such a wonderful mentor to my daughter. She has loved all your classes and would often come home and repeat one of your lessons to me. We appreciate you."

Randi nodded with a bittersweet smile and closed the door behind her, hoping she left some measure of comfort to tarry with them for a while.

When Randi arrived home that evening, still wearing her gi from karate rather than taking time to change, she could only stop and stare at the unusual scene before her. Byron and Bandit played a bizarre game of "try to catch my tail" with each other, and Jenna stood in the kitchen with the stove on and the spicy aroma of food filling the air.

"You're cooking!" Randi blinked and wearily stole into the main room where the Twilight Zone happenings took place.

"Why are you looking at me like that?" Jenna retorted. "You don't do all the cooking. It's not like I never step foot in the kitchen."

"Yes, but, when you make dinner, it's always takeout." Randi dropped her bag beneath the coat rack and rounded the corner to see what Jenna was up to.

Jenna smirked at her and stirred something in a pot. "OK, so it's your spaghetti, but I'm perfectly capable of reheating leftovers. Oh!" Jenna grabbed a potholder, opened the oven, and pulled out a tray containing two healthy-sized slices of garlic bread with only the edges tinged black. "Whew! Almost forgot—because of your accusations that I never make dinner. Less than a week," she sang out with a big grin.

"You're in a good mood," Randi observed. "Do you have a viable suspect, a murderer in custody?"

"Neither," Jenna confessed. "Can't I be happy just because you're home?" She popped a quick kiss to Randi's lips and scooped pasta and meat sauce onto the plates with the bread.

"Of course you can, and I'm thrilled that you are. I was just picturing what a fabulous little wife you will make, being all domestic, taking over the cooking and cleaning while I prop my feet up with a beer and watch a ball game."

"Hey!" Jenna wagged the serving spoon at Randi. "You must never want to see me in the kitchen again with threats like that. Besides—you don't even like beer."

Randi caught her arms around Jenna and possessed her mouth in a searing kiss. "Thank you for heating up dinner. I appreciate everything you do around here, and, don't worry, I won't expect you to change a thing when we're married."

With a playful look in her dazzling blue eyes, Jenna quipped, "So that means I can keep seeing the cute little gal from the deli behind your back?"

Randi laughed, squeezed her waist, and let her go. "No."

Jenna snapped her fingers with a grimace. "Darn."

Laughing, Randi carried her plate to the table. With the prospect of spills, both Byron and Bandit abandoned their game and trotted over expectantly. "These two?"

"Are you kidding?" Jenna slid into her chair. "I had to feed them first, or I'd have gotten no peace. How was your day?"

"I went by to see the Baxters—well, Susan and Mrs. Baxter. Susan is excused from all her exams. I'm sure you made some progress on the case."

"Yeah." Jenna's good mood deflated like a popped balloon and Randi wished she hadn't mentioned it. "I suppose. I mean, I discovered a passel of people who didn't kill them, so that narrows it down, I guess. Randi, it was brought to my attention that there might be some members of the community who won't be happy about you and me getting married, and they might try to make trouble for you. I never intended—"

"Not another word, Jennifer Lynn Ferrari," Randi snapped, jabbing her fork at Jenna. "I don't live my life or make my decisions based on what *some people* might think, say, or do. Let them try to come after either of us. I feel sorry for any idiot who does."

"Sure, the law is on our side now, but that could change. If right-wing politicians take power—"

"Let them. It won't change how I feel about you. Even if they revoke our license, we'll still be married in our hearts and in the eyes of God. Some politician in Washington or Richmond isn't the boss of me, and I know they aren't the boss of you. Is this what has been bothering you? You're worried we could have our marriage taken away?"

Jenna swallowed a sip of water and pushed the food around her plate with a frown. "I'm worried someone might try to kill you."

"Sweetie." Randi reached across the table and took her hand. "People have tried to do that already, if you recall. It won't happen, and, even if it does, I don't care. They could just as easily try to kill you."

"That's different. I'm a cop—"

"And your life is always in danger, blah, blah," Randi interrupted. "Do you want to marry me?"

"With every fiber of my being," Jenna declared.

"Then it's settled. We aren't going to worry about anything because there's nothing you and I can't handle together."

10

Tuesday, May 14th

"Hey, Ferrari," Owens called as Jenna strolled into the criminal investigations office that morning. "We got a hit on a suspect in the home invasions. This guy, Holden Baird, did time for robbery and was recently released. His size matches one of the thieves on the video, so we're having him picked up and brought in for questioning. Bauman's going to run the booth, record his voice, and do a comparison. If he matches, we'll be able to get a warrant for his residence and car and grill him until he gives up his partners."

"If he matches, I want to ask him about the Baxters," Jenna declared. "And maybe, if he thinks we're after him for murder, he'll confess to a lesser crime."

"OK, I'll cut you in. But I'm going to need Bauman most of the day, and the crime scene investigators for the evidence search—just so you know," he said, pointing at her with a wink.

Officer Stewart from the front desk stuck his head in. "Sergeant Owens? Your suspect is here, and he's spitting furious."

Owens grinned. "Good! Bauman, let's go make his day even better." Bauman dutifully left his station to follow the sergeant.

"I'll keep working the murders with you," Jamison volunteered. "I'm following up on the shoe tread and the fiber from Picasso's teeth."

"Excellent." Jenna had just settled at her desk with her coffee and a blueberry muffin from the pastry box when she heard a deep, commanding voice resound from the doorway.

"Lieutenant Ferrari," Captain Myers addressed. "A couple of FBI agents are here to consult with you on the Baxter case."

Jenna spun in surprise to spy a man and woman standing beside him. "Let me introduce Special Agent Edan Pane and Special Agent Dustin Hawkes from the local Roanoke office."

She rose and crossed the room to meet them. "Ferrari," she introduced, shaking each hand. From her tall, lean athletic build to her textured, tousled pixie cut, Edan Pane struck Jenna as unapologetically butch. Sporting an alert posture, the African American agent studied Jenna right back with keen, walnut eyes beneath naturally full eyebrows set in an angular face topped with ebony hair. At five-foot-eight and a hundred and fifty pounds of condensed power, her handshake was firm and decisive. Fine lines around her eyes and neck informed Jenna she was probably in her early forties. Jenna liked her in an instant.

Agent Dustin Hawkes appeared younger and every bit a stereotypical FBI agent in his black suit and polished shoes. He stood a little shorter than her captain at around six feet and wore his acorn hair in a military cut.

"Pleased to meet you," Agent Hawkes said.

"And this is Detective Jamison," Jenna introduced as her partner joined them. She also shook hands with their guests.

"What brings you to our humble abode?" Jamison asked what Jenna had been thinking.

"They're here to exchange information with us on a serial murder case the FBI's been working for the past month, and I've assured them of the RPD's full support in this matter." Captain Myers, as always, filled the space with his presence, both physically and energetically. "Since Detective Owens and Specialist Bauman are away, I figured we could use your office for the briefing."

"Yes, sir." Jenna's interest was piqued. "That would be convenient. Does this relate to the Baxters' murders?"

"It does," Agent Pane affirmed.

"Are either of you behavioral profilers?"

"No," Hawkes replied, "but we have a profile the BAU compiled for us."

"If it's alright with you, Captain, and the agents, I'd like to invite Dr. Grayson to join us," Jenna suggested. "I was ready to ask for her input anyway."

"Fine with me," Myers stated. "Special agents, any objections to including our department profiler in the meeting?"

Agents Pane and Hawkes exchanged a glance. Hawkes shrugged, and Pane granted a minimal nod. "Very well, if you like. May Dustin use that empty station to load our presentation on your screens?" She motioned toward Bauman's desk with its multiple computers and monitors.

"Yes," Jenna replied. "That's our tech station, and he can operate everything from there. Would you care for coffee?"

"Thank you, Lieutenant." Edan Pane strode to the table in the approximate center of the room.

With a nod, Jamison moved to the coffee station and asked, "Cream or sugar?"

"Black," Pane specified.

"Cream and sugar, thank you," answered Hawkes as he loaded a thumb drive into Bauman's computer.

By the time Captain Myers returned with Dr. Grayson, they were all sitting around the table with file folders in front of them. The elegant psychiatrist glided in beside Jenna with her studious glasses in place and a light, fruity fragrance swirling around her like a breath of crisp mist.

Captain Myers made the introductions and turned the meeting over to Special Agent Pane.

"Thank you, Captain Myers, Lieutenant Ferrari, and team," she began. "We are not here to step on your investigation but to ascertain if we seek the same unsub." She glanced at her partner, and he pushed the remote-control button to the big wall screen. Displayed were a variety of images and abbreviated case notes for three murdered couples.

"We were contacted by the Syracuse Office and brought on board after they learned of your newlyweds' murders." Maintaining a professional air of respect and authority, Pane filled them in.

"The first victims, George and Kathy Waite, had been back from their honeymoon for two days when they were brutally murdered in their home on April 6th. You can read in your files that they were bludgeoned and then posed, lying in their bed. The killer cleaned the crime scene with bleach and left no fingerprints, DNA, or murder weapon behind. The Syracuse M.E. determined the murder weapon was a cylindrical metal object—probably a crowbar or tire iron. Forensics narrowed it down to a particular style of tire iron, and the SPD was actively interviewing persons of interest when a second murder occurred two weeks later in Binghamton. The M.O. was the same, only the couples had nothing in common other than being recently married."

Jenna flipped a page in her folder to view information regarding the second pair of victims and took a sip of her coffee. This could be a viable line of inquiry. Even though the weapons differed, the COD was the same.

"Haval and Aveen Barzani were from the Middle East, not born in New York like the Waites," Pane continued. "The evidence says their attacker gained entrance to the home, hit each one in the head without attracting the attention of witnesses—just like the first murder. Then he posed their bodies in lawn loungers in their back yard and cleaned up the scene with bleach. When Syracuse Police discovered the like crime, they contacted Binghamton who then called the BAU in Quantico to ask if they had a serial killer targeting newlywed couples roaming their state. Note the profile I included in your folders."

Jenna noticed Dr. Grayson—Jane—flipping to the profile at the same time she did. It was still hard for Jenna to think of her therapist by her first name, no matter how many times the woman requested she do so. It would be too much like calling Captain Myers "Jerome." Older and with more degrees to her name, it was only respectful to refer to her as Dr. Grayson.

"When a third pair of victims turned up in Harrisburg, Pennsylvania, the perpetrator had crossed state lines and the threshold for calling the killings serial. Jacob and Emily Dierdorff were in their twenties, like the other victims. They had returned home from their two-week honeymoon without time to unpack before they were struck on the heads and posed sitting together on their living room sofa. Harrisburg detectives suppose the killer could have already been in the house waiting for them to return. This time, the murderer used a cylindrical, wooden implement as the weapon—most likely a bat or rolling pin. No prints, no DNA, and no witnesses. A bureau-wide alert went out, and the Roanoke director pinned it to our bulletin board with a dozen other notifications. I don't want to tell you how many of those are for missing children," Pane added with a hint of grief.

"It seems there's no racial component," Jenna mentioned. "George Waite was half Onondaga of the Iroquois Nation, the Barzanis Middle Eastern, and the other targets were White."

"The similarities are young and recently married," Hawke added. "They don't share religion, political affiliation, or economic status. Emily Dierdorff had a million-dollar trust fund while the Barzani's barely scraped by."

Agent Pane's eyes turned cold, and her jaw stiffened. "The press wants to give him a fancy name—the 'Newlywed Killer.' We're calling him 'Unsub Seventeen' because he's our office's seventeenth murderer of the year."

Dr. Grayson glanced up from her folder. "The BAU profile says we're most likely looking for a man in the same age group who had his engagement broken, or a fiancée or new bride who suffered a sudden, violent death. Additional stressors could include the loss of a job or home. But they didn't have all the information available to us now. See how all the murders—especially if ours is one of them—have occurred along the I-81 corridor? This could indicate he travels that highway for his work. With the first murders occurring in Syracuse, that may be where he lives, but we can't neglect the possibility he and his wife or fiancée were visiting—or even honeymooning—there when she was taken away from him. If suffering a psychotic episode, or even a common fit of rage, he could think, 'If I can't be happy, neither should you.' He's organized, as your profile suggests. He might search newspaper society sections or church announcements for wedding photos, then study the suspects to see who is going on a honeymoon. That also seems to be a box to check for Unsub Seventeen.

And he's knowledgeable, wearing gloves and cleaning up after himself. Posing the bodies is also important to him, to leave the victims in positions where you would find a happy couple—in bed together, sitting on their back porch, or snuggling on the couch. It could be a fantasy he plays out of what he wished he could do with his wife if she was available to him."

Jenna agreed with everything Dr. Grayson added to the profile, but a thought occurred to her too. "What if Unsub Seventeen caused his wife or fiancée's death? Maybe not on purpose, but the guilt and remorse over killing the woman he loved—thereby ripping away his own happiness—would provide a powerful catalyst for a young man who already wrestled to retain his sanity. If his religion, or simply fear, prevents him from committing suicide, he might turn his guilt outward. If we're checking records for persons of interest, I'd add a young man who was somehow involved with his lover's death, be it a car accident or whatever else."

"Good observation, Jenna," praised Dr. Grayson.

It wasn't so much a good observation as dark places she feared her mind might go if she ever endangered Randi in a way that led to her death. No, Jenna was confident she'd never devolve into a serial killer, but suicide? That could be possible. Suffering an emotional or mental breakdown? Almost assuredly. And yet, Randi had provided her the stability and hope to give marriage and a life together a shot. "Just because a thing could go wrong doesn't mean it will go wrong," Randi reminded her often. "Try focusing your attention on everything that could go right instead." Jenna tried; sometimes she succeeded.

"We might have something to contribute if this is the same guy," Jenna stated. "Our lab has a DNA sample from our crime scene that we believe is from our killer. Dr. Gupta ran it through the database and came back empty."

Both agents perked up at Jenna's share. "Let me check it against the FBI databank," Hawkes proposed. "We'll have more records."

"What about pets?" Jamison asked, rocking Jenna from her thoughts. Suddenly the question held great merit in Jenna's mind.

"Pets?" questioned Agent Hawkes.

"Did any of the victims own a dog or cat and was it harmed at all?" Jenna clarified.

A disconcerted expression formed on Pane's face, deepening its lines. She opened her folder and flipped through the pages. "Either the answer is 'no,' or they didn't forward that information to us. We only got this case late yesterday afternoon, when Syracuse determined our local murder could be Unsub Seventeen's latest. I'll call them and ask. Is that relevant?"

"It is in our case," Jamison answered. "Whoever murdered our victims also killed their little dog and then spent hours burying it in their backyard."

"That's curious," Captain Myers commented. "Could it be a sign of escalation?"

"I don't see how going from killing a young couple returning from their honeymoon to taking out the pooch is an escalation," Dr. Grayson answered with a puzzled expression. "Typically, it's the other way around. They start off murdering pets and work their way up to humans."

"There's another difference," Jenna noted. "Our victims weren't posed in a happy, domestic setting. They were stuffed into their SUV and driven off the road, down an embankment, and into a tree. They weren't even side-by-side in the vehicle. You could call it posing the bodies, but—"

"Unless!" Excitement lit Agent Pane's expression as she voiced a thought. "If your idea about the killer having inadvertently caused his lover's death in a car crash is accurate, he could be trying to recreate the incident with these last two victims. There are numerous instances to research, men whose significant other was killed in an accident in which he was driving or at fault. If we divide up the load, we can make headway today. Also, can you give your DNA report to Dustin so he can start checking it against our national records?"

"Sure," Jenna agreed.

Captain Myers stood, stretching his long legs. "Excellent. I'll leave you all to the investigating. Please keep me in the loop."

"Will do, Captain," Jenna affirmed.

"Agent Hawke, I can walk you over to our DNA lab," Jamison offered.

He rose to join her, leaving Jenna, Dr. Grayson, and Edan at the table. "You're welcome to stay and make use of our workroom," Jenna offered.

Gathering her things, the FBI agent shook her head. "Our office isn't two miles from here. I'll run back and shoot you a list to check out. Let's keep in touch on this and see where it leads us."

Jenna walked Agent Pane to the door, hoping they had just caught a major break. *If this I-81 serial killer is our perpetrator, we'll get the full support of the FBI to identify and catch him. And if a suspect isn't in custody by Friday, they can carry on without me while Randi whisks me off on a grand adventure. So, why don't I feel more relieved?*

II

―――――◆◇◆―――――

With Captain Myers and the FBI agents gone, Jenna turned to meet Dr. Grayson, making her way toward the door. "Do you think Unsub Seventeen is your guy?" the psychiatrist asked, arching a brow.

Jenna exhaled a thoughtful breath. "It would be simpler if he is."

"What's this cloud I see, hovering around you with negative energy? Nothing to do with the wedding, I hope." Jane rested a fashionably manicured hand on Jenna's arm. Her painted nails were decorated with sparkly things, accentuated by the glimmer of the two rings on that hand.

"No, not really." Jenna frowned. "My mother probably won't come because she thinks two women getting married diminishes the Catholic sacrament of marriage or something. And, OK, sometimes I let a case get in my head, and I worry someone will be lying in wait for us when we get back from our honeymoon."

"I was worried you were off to a dark place when you brought up our perpetrator acting out of guilt for being responsible for his bride's death—if that's even the case. Any number of stimuli could cause a fragile mind to break."

"Only for a few seconds," Jenna promised. "My brain tells me we're far more likely to be struck by lightning than attacked by gay-bashing lunatics or a deranged serial killer. Then I hear Randi's voice in my head telling me to think about all the things that could go right."

"I may have a medical doctorate and a Ph.D, but the best advice I can give you is to listen to that angel in your head. Randi may not be a psychiatrist, but she's certainly the expert when it comes to you," Dr. Grayson concluded with a smile. When it faded, she probed, "Anything else I should know about?"

"I've been practicing clenching my jaw when I want to spew out a heated retort—give myself a moment to breathe and gather my words carefully. I find a regular workout schedule to siphon off excess nervous energy and being distracted by wedding planning and my fiancée have me in a good place."

"So, really, it's just disappointment over your mother's refusal to be present for the most important day in your life that's bumming you out."

A chuckle escaped Jenna's lips, and she shook her head. "It's so odd to hear phrases like 'bumming you out' coming from you. It isn't nearly clinical enough."

"Perhaps not, but it's accurate." Dr. Grayson lifted her hand and shifted between Jenna and the door. "Is that how it makes you feel—disappointed, not angry?"

"I was mad as hell at first, but disappointed, and ..." Jenna met her gaze with complete honesty. "My mother's in poor health, and we haven't made as much progress in a year as I had hoped. I worry we won't get to where I want us to be by the time she passes away. Jamison and I spent a little time with Joel and Kathleen Baxter, and I could see how much they loved their children and Alexia, how close they were, how devastated. My mother is so impossible to please, and she didn't enjoy a close relationship with her mother either, so nothing to model ideal behavior on. I guess it's OK—I mean, at least we talk to each other now. I understand some people never have an intimate relationship with their parents. Randi did, and I think it gave her an immense head start in life."

"My mother was a medical doctor, a surgeon," Jane confided. "She was brilliant, proper, and professional. She made a point of doing everything by the book, which back then meant following Dr. Spock. In her opinion, she was the best mother who ever lived, but we were never close. She was as emotionally distant as your mother, from what you've told me. I think, when that's the case, the parent suffers just as much, if not more, than the child."

Jenna considered that for a moment. "Thank you for breaking your rule about, 'we're here to talk about you, not me.'"

"Well," she blushed and grinned, appearing far more like a friend than a cold, distant professional. "We aren't in a therapy session now, are we?"

A smile brightened Jenna's eyes at the carefree moment, then she confessed, "I just want Mama to know what it feels like to love and be loved, to lower all her defenses, throw out her excuses, and just know something better than she's experienced so far in her life. It seems like she's always struggling. I'm learning to let go of the struggle, and I wish the same for her. So, despite it all, I suppose that's evidence I love the woman who was complicit in throwing me away."

Dr. Grayson's intrepid gaze bore into Jenna's. "And that is what will make you whole." She leaned in, kissed Jenna's forehead, and, without another word, whisked out of the office.

Feeling the radiance of Dr. Grayson's approval and a burden lifted from her shoulders, Jenna went back to her desk and was about to sit when Jamison returned, accompanied by Owens and Bauman.

"We got us a hot suspect!" Owens announced with gusto.

"Bravo!" Jenna cheered half-heartedly. While she wasn't sold on Unsub Seventeen, she felt he was more viable than the home invaders with the too-narrow bat. Still, she'd take a crack at the fellow. "Want me to trick him into spilling his guts?"

"In a little bit," Owens replied. "Ethan, here," he announced with pride, slapping a hand on Bauman's shoulder, "got a perfect voice pattern match to a robber on the video and *I* got a judge to sign a search warrant."

"Some of Jamison's magic pixie dust must have rubbed off on you," Bauman teased and headed for his desk. He stopped short and glowered. "Hey, someone sat at my computer—and touched things!"

"FBI," Jamison chirped from her spot across the room. "You think I have magic pixie dust?"

"FBI?" Owens' brows shot up and he sucked in his gut. "What'd the feds want?"

"The serial killer they're after could be our guy," Jenna relayed in a condensed version.

"I thought my home invaders were your killers." Owens took on an offended expression. As if not to be one-upped by the bureau, he snatched his coffee travel mug, squared his shoulders, and called, "Come on, Ethan; we don't have all day. Let's go toss Holden Baird's place for evidence and call it a win. Oh, and he's in holding, waiting for his public defender to arrive. FBI," he muttered on his way out the door.

Jamison giggled. "Sergeant Detective Owens doesn't want to be outmaneuvered by federal agents."

"I gathered as much," Jenna smirked. "Oh, that was fast," she exclaimed when the e-mail from Agent Pane pinged in her inbox. Jamison, keep researching who bought a wooden baseball bat locally in the past couple of weeks. Most folks use aluminum, so maybe one of the sporting goods store clerks will remember. Did you get anywhere with the shoe tread?"

"I coordinated with CSI Wilcox. She's headed out with Owens and Bauman, but she told me where to search. According to the SoleMates database of over 42,000 shoes, the specific chevron tread pattern on our casting matches three brands of hiking boots for men and boys and one woman's brand style. Considering a man's size nine is average, while it would be quite large for a woman's shoe, which converts to a ten-and-a-half, I'll check on the men's first."

"That's good, Jamison. If we can pin down the shoes and the bat, we'll know exactly what to look for." Taking out her phone, she texted Owens.

Include in search hiking boots size nine and a wooden baseball bat. It was worth a shot.

Hours passed, giving Jenna a headache and hunger pains. Picking up the phone to call for delivery, she asked Jamison what she wanted from the deli down the street.

"I'm hungry today," she admitted. "A turkey and provolone panini on rye, please, with a big pickle. Thank you."

Jenna made it two, and they ate at their desks. She felt no closer to unveiling the identity of Unsub Seventeen when Owens and Bauman waltzed in with evidence bags and triumphant grins. *Figures they'd solve their case first.* Then her thoughts brightened. *Unless they are the same case.*

"What've you got there?" she asked, putting her searches aside.

"This," he gloated, swinging a plastic bag with a weighty object inside, "is the pocket watch Cheri Easton gave her husband for their twenty-fifth wedding anniversary, engraved with their names and wedding date. And this," he gleamed, presenting a second bag, "is Mrs. Easton's stolen jewelry. CSIs Wilcox and Davenport are still there, dusting for prints, swabbing for DNA, and bagging up heaps and piles of computers, flatscreen TVs, laptops, tablets, and cell phones. They've likely sold some of the loot already, but it would be too suspicious to unload it all at once. We have Baird cold for the robberies. It won't go well for him with his prior record, and I think we might just get him to talk—lawyer or not."

"Well, then, let's get cracking. I want him to confess to the murders so I can call it a day." Jenna swirled out of her chair and downed the last sip of her Diet Coke from lunch. *Water, she* reminded herself. *I'm supposed to be drinking water.*

"Stewart is going to have him moved to Interview B. Kyle Konrad is here to represent him. Nice kid, but, when we call Altman in, he'll be so ready to deal his client'll never know what hit him."

Jenna glanced back at Trisha. "Jamison—" was all she got out before her partner answered.

"I'll stick with sifting through accident reports and men in their twenties who travel I-81 for their jobs who wear a size nine shoe, have no DNA on record, and might live in Syracuse."

"You're a good detective," Jenna commended and followed Owens to the interview room. Bauman made for the booth.

"Hang on," Jenna said when they reached the door. "I'm going to give Altman a heads up. He might have to schedule another time to hack things out with Konrad and your collar, and you get the credit on this arrest, even if he turns out to be my murderer. You've earned it."

Jenna sent a quick text and waited a minute for a reply.

'Might can swing by. If not now, then later.' It was good enough. Owens escorted her into the small, windowless space dominated by a table, chairs, a two-way mirror, and a bright overhead light. The uniform who stood guard tipped his hat and retreated into the hallway, pulling the door closed behind him. Already seated was a broad-shouldered, forty-year-old man marked with black ink and enraged snake eyes that glared at her and Owens. His dusky skin tone and straight, black hair informed her he could be mixed race or of Slavic, Mediterranean, or some other darker-complected ancestry. She was almost certain his foot would never fit a size nine.

Beside the scowling lump of the caught-red-handed felon sat his young, idealistic public defender, recently out of law school. Kyle Konrad was a likable fellow and in decent shape for a desk jockey, though a little wet behind the ears.

Owens swaggered over, jerked out a chair, and plopped in it, gently dropping the evidence bags on the table. Jenna took her seat less dramatically, setting a file folder in front of her.

"Now, Mr. Baird—or do you prefer I call you Holden?"

He crossed his arms and curled his lip at Owens, who merely shrugged. "Our technical specialist has verified a ninety-nine percent accurate voice match between you and the home-invasion robber who, with two accomplices, illegally entered the home of Bryan and Whitney Johnson on the night of May 8th. Didn't know they had in-home security cameras recording everything, did you?"

Jenna watched his eyes morph from cynical to frightened and his face lose some of its depth of color. He licked his lips and glanced away, but only shrugged rather than reply.

"These," Owens continued, "were recovered from your residence along with sundry electronics, including a laptop and iPad that you hadn't even wiped the lawful owners' information from yet. Tsk, tsk." He opened one bag and read the inscription from the back of the watch. "'Celebrating twenty-five years with the man I love. Cheri and James 4ever.' Isn't that sweet? But ..." he presented a puzzled expression to Baird. "You aren't old enough to be married for twenty-five years and, unless you have another identity, your name isn't James."

"I found it lying on the ground in the park one day," he claimed, motioning toward the watch.

"I suppose you found this bag of Cheri Easton's jewelry too? Even if that was true," Owens allowed, "our voice recording evidence proves you and two associates—another man and a woman—robbed the Johnsons' house after you kidnapped and bound them, threatening their lives with a lethal bat.

"I'd like to see a copy of the voice-matching results," Konrad requested. Jenna pulled it from the folder and slid it across the table.

"You can see the marker matches across the feed," Jenna said and tapped her finger on a particular line. "This is where your client read from the paper Owens handed him, repeating the exact words from the video recording."

"I wasn't present for that," Konrad noted. His lip twitched. Leaning his mouth to Baird's ear, he whispered something.

"No!" Baird glowered at him. "I can't give them the names of people I don't know and was never in that house with."

"But you were there," Jenna stated calmly. "You wore gloves and a mask, but we have your physical likeness, the way you walk, and your voice all recorded. Now, unless you can prove you were somewhere else on the evening of May the eighth and the other nights when home invasions took place, Owens is going to place you under arrest, and we will return you to your cell to wait for an arraignment. Won't Judge Michaelson be so happy to see you back in his courtroom only months after you were released from the stint you just served for felony robbery?"

"Do something!" he shouted at Konrad. "You're the lawyer. You're supposed to get me off."

"I can get you a better deal than going to trial with the evidence they're going to present against you," the young public defender explained. "But even Cinderella's godmother couldn't wave her magic wand and make these charges go away."

Baird pulled his brows together and snorted at Konrad. "You probably work for them."

"That is not true." Konrad didn't shout it, but he used a forceful tone. Twisting toward his client, he leaned one arm on the table. "I'm here to represent *you*, to get you the best deal possible, reduce your sentence. Sure, I'd love to have a jury declare you 'not guilty,' but with stolen property in your possession and a video recording of you committing the crime, that's not going to happen. You need to calm down and listen to my professional advice."

"Calm down?" he bellowed. "Are you telling me to calm down?"

Konrad backed away, and, if Baird hadn't been handcuffed to the table, he might have struck his attorney.

"That's it, "Owens declared. "Holden Baird, you are under arrest for four counts of trespassing, unlawful breaking and entering, kidnapping, possession of a deadly weapon, threatening homeowners with a deadly weapon, aggravated robbery, possession of stolen property with intent to distribute, two counts of first-degree murder and disposal of dead bodies, and one count of animal cruelty. You have the right to—"

"Wait a minute!" Baird yelled. His startled expression extended throughout his body as his hands shook. "What? Did you say murder? And kidnapping—really? Deadly weapon? Where are you getting this from? Mr. Konrad, nobody got hurt. What is he talking about?"

"Just be quiet, Holden." Konrad raised his gaze to Jenna, who withdrew crime scene photos of Nolan and Alexia Baxter and Picasso.

"What went wrong at the Baxters' house on Saturday?" Jenna asked as she laid out the gruesome scene before Baird's eyes. "Did the tiny dog scare you and your crew? Did Nolan Baxter fight back? Was Alexia Baxter an unfortunate witness who had to be silenced? All three were bludgeoned in the head with a bat in their home in a nice neighborhood just ripe for being robbed."

"No, this is wrong," he stated emphatically and dropped his head into his hands. He combed his fingers through his sooty hair and lifted a sickly expression to Jenna. "We—I was nowhere near these people's house. Check my record; you know I have one. I've never hurt anybody. Try to scare them, maybe. Threaten—OK, but you can't convict someone for saying they're going to do something they never actually do. Mr. Konrad, help me out here," he pleaded.

"May I have a moment to confer with my client in private?"

Jenna nodded, and she and Owens stepped out.

"What do you think?" Owens asked.

"I think he's going to plead to the robberies, possibly name his accomplices, and Konrad will get Altman to drop the kidnapping down to unlawfully detained against their will. I don't think we'd have gotten threatened with a deadly weapon to stick because—really—anything can be a deadly weapon, even a pencil, and that tire bat's purpose and typical use isn't to inflict harm like a gun or hunting knife. More points to Baird if all the stolen goods are returned, but he'll do more time."

"What about your murders?"

Jenna shook her head. "He's not my guy."

12

By the time Jenna returned home that night, she was wiped out. She and Jamison had marked fifty potential suspects off a list of over two hundred that Special Agent Pane had sent them and, while one home invader was in custody, charged, and working on a deal, he was off her murder board. To support her belief, Wilcox and Davenport found only size eleven shoes in Baird's closet and no baseball bat. An examination of the painter's coveralls he'd worn in the video turned up no dog hair or transfer from the Baxters' home. Right now, Unsub Seventeen was her strongest lead. At least the FBI was helping. Maybe by tomorrow they'd get a hit on the DNA or run across an ideal candidate who checks all the boxes. For tonight, it was dinner and relax time with Randi.

Jenna would have never conceived the idea to barbeque catfish, but Randi had created a recipe and technique that would put a New Orleans chef to shame. Coupled with foil-wrapped corn on the cob she threw on the grill—still inside its husk, of all things—and her homemade coleslaw, it was another delightful meal. The flavors of blacking spices and beer still rolled around her tongue when she pressed her lips to Randi's where she reclined in her arms on the couch. A comedy—cleverly written in Jenna's opinion—played on the TV. Bandit had commandeered the recliner chair, doing his best to cover the entire seat, while Byron lay on the rug by the hearth, licking his privates as if nobody else were in the room. It was glorious, and it was home.

The peaceful moment of relaxation was broken when Jenna's phone played off the theme song to *Game of Thrones* and/or *House of the Dragon*. She groaned, shifted, and reached toward the coffee table. With her longer arms, Randi plucked up the phone and handed it to her, pausing the program they were watching.

"Hey, Dad," Jenna answered, trying to bolster her voice with some enthusiasm. While never having taken an interest in the fantasy series before Randi introduced it to her, the posturing, plotting, and cruelty of various heads of houses inspired her to assign the tune to her father's calls.

"Hey, honeysuckle." There was a tension in his tone, and Jenna braced herself for bad news.

"What's wrong?" Her pulse sped, and she felt her heart thump against her chest.

"It's your mother. She's OK," he added hurriedly when Jenna sucked in a breath. "Well, she is, and she isn't. We just got back from the emergency room with a boot on her foot. It rained today and, when she went out on the front porch to walk down and check the mail, she slipped and fell down the steps. The doctor said her ankle is sprained and broken, and she can't walk on it for six weeks. They gave her crutches and said she has to keep it elevated and iced when the boot is off several times a day for the next three days or until the swellin' goes down. They gave her a hefty dose of pain meds and she's lyin' in bed asleep. I'm afraid we won't be makin' it to your weddin' for certain now."

He sounded like he was telling the truth, but it sure sounded awfully convenient. Mama just happens to slip and fall down four little steps and break her ankle? Can't take a car ride to her wedding that she was trying to get out of to begin with? All her settled emotions and loving resignation erupted in the hurt and pain of rejection, just as it had the night her dad threw her out of the house.

"What—she can't say to my face that she just doesn't want to come? She's too timid to tell me what a disappointment I am again, and how ashamed she is of my life choices?" Jenna ripped herself off the couch and out of Randi's arms of comfort to pace the floor. Byron tucked his tail and rushed out of the way, while Bandit sat up to watch her, ears perked with interest.

"No, Jenna, that's not it," Dad charged in an authoritative voice. "Don't you think we'd make up something better? Go ahead and call Vince Jr. or Angie.

They saw her at the hospital when they put the cast on. I had to get her up off the ground, and your mother's no featherweight."

"Yeah, right," Jenna muttered. This wasn't supposed to happen. Her mom was supposed to weigh her love for her daughter—or at least her sense of duty as a mother—against the medieval stance of the church and choose her. For once, her mom was supposed to stand up for her. And from what her brother and sister—and even her mom—said, Dad had been trying to talk her into coming. Dad—the mean, nasty, abusive one—was taking her side while the weak, stand-by-and-ring-her-hands-and-do-nothing mother had dug in against her. This was Renita's chance to make everything right, and she slips down steps she'd been using for the past thirty years just in time to provide her with a legitimate excuse.

Jenna could hear it now. "I had finally decided to come and be there for you, to give you my blessing when I was befallen by a terrible accident. Oh, I wish I could be there to see you marry your sweetheart. If only I wasn't old with rheumatism and joints that don't work. My knee must have just given out on me. Or maybe the step was slick from the rain. I'm so sorry, baby girl."

The more the thoughts and emotions streaked through her, the more upset she became. Any notion of stopping for a few deep breaths or counting to ten or any such nonsense flew out the window. Jenna felt the rumble begin like the birth of an earthquake and she struggled to hold back the tide of raw emotion.

"I'm tellin' you, she's got her foot in a goddamned cast. What do you want me to do—leave her here alone when she can't even get up to go pee?"

"Then she did it on purpose," Jenna fumed. "If the two of you aren't faking it, she intentionally fell, so she'd have a viable excuse to not come. She never wanted to. All she ever said was, 'We'll see.' Well, we see now, don't we?"

"Jenna." Her dad's timbre softened, and the throbbing in her ears wasn't loud enough to obliterate the tenderness she heard. Maybe he cared. Maybe after thirty-three years, he finally cared about her.

"Honey, I can't tell you what goes on inside your mother's mind. There's some things she'll talk about with me, and we discuss and argue and laugh. And there's things she keeps hidden inside like a high-security bank vault. You need to reflect a little, kid, 'cause I've seen that tendency in you too."

"Well, there's plenty I want to say right now," she allowed. Jenna hadn't realized she was shaking until Randi's arms came around her to steady her. She pulled Jenna close and held her in silence, stopping her march and slowing the surge of grief.

"I'm sure," her dad responded. "All I can say is the X-ray showed a break, and I saw a swollen ankle turning purple. Whether she consciously or subconsciously was lookin' for an excuse to get out of what she saw as a no-win situation, I can't say for certain. I know she's in pain—probably physically and emotionally. She cried and hollered, and she doesn't do much of that. I've been tryin' to get her to open up and let stuff go, but she just says she's fine and everything's good when I can see it isn't. She'll sit doing her cross-stitch while a ballgame is on and just stop sewin' and stare off into space like she's in another world somewhere. I've been doin' better, now, I swear. I only go out to the bar or poker night with my friends once a week and come right home after work to help her out or just spend time together all the other days."

"I know, Dad," Jenna admitted. "You are doing better. You helped pay for Angie's training course and now she has that job driving the ambulance for the emergency care facility at the University of Kentucky. It's a great job, and she says she feels better about herself than she ever has. And Vince told me that you've been talking about using your nest egg to go in with him on opening his own mechanic shop. Ferrari and Son," she said with a laugh.

"Well, I pull enough parts off the cars at the junkyard, I figure I could do the same to further my son's career and maybe build a legacy for myself in the process. I'm not quite ready to put out to pasture. Still, things look different from this side of fifty than they did when I was y'all's ages. I know I put you through it—Vince the most. Well," he fudged. "Except when I kicked you out. I thought it was tough love when it was just stupid and arrogant. I'm a grandfather now, and it's so easy to see parental mistakes when you aren't the one makin' 'em. I owe it to Vince. And I have to accept some responsibility for not helping Angie get off dope right when the problem started. I just looked the other way. Now, I'm counting my years and I want my years to count."

"I'm glad for that, Dad." Jenna meant it. She felt her body returning to an even keel safe in the harbor of her lover's arms. Together, they slowly rocked, an inch to the left, an inch to the right, a gentle sway like a lake's water lapping the bank.

"I love your mother," he attested. "Renita was a beauty when she was young, and she put up with all my crap when she could have—probably should've—left me. She tries to do what's right, and I've witnessed acts of kindness from her. She never raised a hand to you all—that was me. But the water of that placid pool runs deep, and I worry something dark and dangerous lurks at the bottom. I'm worried it'll eventually kill her."

Jenna sensed the same. Randi had said her ailments could all be caused by unresolved emotional trauma, guilt, unforgiveness, things she holds onto and won't let go of that consume her health and devour her joy. Maybe it was a subconscious sabotage that caused her misstep off the porch.

"I think she sees herself as a failure and has convinced herself it's too late to do anything about it. The more she focuses on her pain, the more pain she's in. But if she keeps insisting she's fine and won't talk about the root of it all ..." Jenna sighed and leaned her weight against Randi's firm body in surrender. "I told her I've been seeing Dr. Grayson, a psychiatrist and licensed therapist, and it's helped me. I mean, does she even talk to her priest?"

"She goes to confession at least once a month, but I don't know what she says to him. I doubt it's the whole story if it's even any of it. I'm sorry, Jenna. We all like Randi and I can see how good for you she is. Try not to worry about Mama. She loves you the best she knows how, and so do I."

"You're trying—I'll give you that much. I think we're better, you and me. Maybe not all the way to best buds, but better. I wish—" Jenna swallowed and choked back a tear that caught in her throat. "I was telling Dr. Grayson today that I loved Mama even though, despite it all, I wish she and I could be close. That may never happen, and I need to learn to accept it. I still want her to be well and happy. Thank you for looking after her. I love you too."

"You're a fantastic daughter, Jenna," he avowed, choking up himself, she could tell. "Better than I deserve. I want to tell you a secret. Back when I'd get after you, and you'd stand up to me, fight back? Even when you refused to back down and left that night—I might have been mad about it, but I admired you. A part of me was so proud, tellin' the stupid part of me, 'That's my daughter! That's my strong little girl.' I'm glad we're on a path to reconcilin'. Tell Randi we're sorry and I'll take her for a daughter-in-law anytime."

"Will do." Jenna hung up the call, tossed her phone onto the couch, and turned in Randi's embrace. Bringing her arms around her, Jenna pressed her face into Randi's neck and they both held on for a long moment.

"Are you all right, Jenna?" Randi continued to hold her close, breathing in sequence, soothing her with a blanket of loving vibrations. Jenna noticed the hot tears on her cheeks and wondered how they'd gotten there.

"I don't think so," she admitted. Clinging to Randi helped her get a grip on herself as well. "I don't understand what's wrong with me. I thought I had put this all behind me, was resigned to the fact Mama is never going to fully accept who I am, and just this morning I told Dr. Grayson ..." Jenna swallowed and took that deep breath she was supposed to.

"It's a process, sweetie," Randi reminded her. "It only still hurts because you care, and that's a good thing. You have a driving desire to save people in trouble, to protect them from their most potent dangers. That's an admirable trait. It's not a sign of weakness that you can't fix everything."

"No," Jenna agreed, feeling more vulnerable than she had in a long time. "Not being able to control my emotions is, though. You heard me—you saw. It all came back up and tried to swallow me. I got mad and hurt all over again and there's no reason, no excuse. I knew she didn't want to come and was looking for an out. Why did it surprise me when she found one?"

Jenna pulled back enough to peer into Randi's compassionate gaze, keeping her fingers locked around her waist. Randi moved one hand to brush a tear from her cheek. "Because a part of you still hoped she'd change her mind."

"I don't get it." Jenna scrunched her face in discontent. "Once I've compiled evidence against a criminal and presented my case, he goes to prison, or whatever, and that's it. I don't have to keep rehashing the same facts and details over and over to convict him anew every day. So why do I have to keep repeating this process inside me? Why can't I just say, 'I'm not going to worry about that or let that bother me or be hurt by old news anymore,' and let that be the end of it? I should be able to close the door on it all. So why do little girl Jenna's feelings of rejection still raise their ugly head at me and spin me around like a bottle at a frat party?"

"Little girl Jenna will always be a part of you, just like wise, old Jenna, and in-her-prime action Jenna," Randi answered. She stroked her face and brushed a gentle kiss to her lips. "Little girl Jenna wants to enjoy the childhood she missed out on, and responsible action Jenna hasn't taken the time to give it to her. Be easy on yourself. You can't make fifty years of your mother's problems disappear overnight, or even in a year—or maybe ever. But you can choose to love her where she is, flaws and all, and love yourself where you are, flaws and all. From my perspective, the flaws are teeny weeny compared to all the awesomeness."

Jenna snorted a jarring chuckle. Anger and anguish had evaporated to a neutral numbness. Randi's words and the love that inspired them pushed her an inch over the line toward feeling better.

"You are prejudiced," she accused playfully. "Those glasses of yours must have rose-colored lenses in them for you to see so much good in me."

"Me?" Randi's eyes widened and her jaw dropped in pretend shock. "There's not a prejudiced bone in my body."

"OK, biased then, partisan in my favor. You just see what you want to see."

"That's true of everyone, Jenna," Randi corrected in a more serious tone. "We all see what we look for. Nobody can control their emotions all the time and I don't even think we are supposed to. I get mad or discouraged sometimes too; I just don't let myself pitch a tent and stay there for the weekend. Sensei Yoshita Moro teaches us there is no such thing as failure, only learning opportunities. Einstein called it 'success in progress.'"

"Yeah, yeah," Jenna quipped, feeling both relief and embarrassment over her emotional rollercoaster. "And Edison failed a thousand times before inventing the light bulb. Maybe I expect too much of myself. I mean, I'm only human, right?"

Randi smiled, and Jenna could see tiny cogs turning mischievously in that big brain of hers. "I think you expect exactly the right amount from yourself. After all, to whom much is given, much is required. You just need to be patient and not expect it all right this red-hot minute. To live is to grow, expand, accumulate the points, beat the boss, and move up to the next level. I think you leveled up a notch tonight. Why don't you shower while I whip up a little dessert so we can celebrate? Or just snuggle and finish our show. Don't feel bad because you aren't perfect yet. If you were, where would you have to go for the next sixty years?"

Jenna laughed and shook her head. "You're amazing; do you know that?" She kissed Randi and gave her another squeeze.

"In a few days, I'll be more amazing, because I'll be married to the love of my life and the most extraordinary woman in the world."

With a delighted grin returning to her face and a twinkle in her eyes, Jenna replied, "I can't wait to see what you cook up this time. Be back in ten—and I might skip the bathrobe," she added with a wink, and was warmed by Randi's dazzled response.

.

13

---◆○◆---

Wednesday, May 15th

Jenna beat everyone to the office by at least half an hour. She was anxious to solve her case and focusing on it took her mind off her mother. Later last night she'd talked to Vince on the phone, and he'd corroborated the story of her broken ankle. Making a firm declaration she had put it behind her and was moving on, Jenna dug into accident reports and criminal histories, setting a promising candidate aside.

Will Gomez was twenty-seven years old and had lost his fiancée. The young woman left him standing at the altar, fleeing town, and refused to take his calls, according to social media posts. He had a history of mental health problems—mainly depression—and worked as a private courier. From what Jenna could find, he made a lot of I-81 runs. To aggravate his situation, the bank repossessed the Baldwinsville, NY (just outside of Syracuse) mobile home he lived in just a week before the first murders.

By then the rest of the gang barreled in laughing—about some humorous account, no doubt. Jenna rolled her neck and snarked, "It's five after, you slackers."

"We were in the building," Bauman quickly affirmed.

"Girard was telling us about this thing that happened," Owens began.

"Never mind," Jenna cut him off. "Jamison, did you come across any viable suspects from the serial killer angle?" Jenna wasn't in the mood for small talk. She was driven to catch this murderer so she could enjoy her honeymoon.

"I pinned one yesterday who stood out," she replied. "Ronell Fischer." In cool capris and a stylish blouse, Jamison set down a Tupperware dish that didn't come from a bakery and started preparing a fresh pot of coffee.

Owens frowned. "I thought you were getting donuts."

"This breakfast is better," she answered cheerily. "Deviled eggs, cheese slices, and little smokies. It's better to start your day with protein than sugary carbs."

"All right, Ms. Keto," he replied with a sarcastic huff, but waddled to the container anyway.

"Forget the food," Jenna commanded with urgency. "Tell me about Fischer."

"Mr. Fischer had been driving late at night with his new bride shortly after returning from their honeymoon when their vehicle struck an unknown object in the road and he lost control, ending in a crash that killed his wife." Jamison took the seat at her desk and continued her report.

"He works as a traveling sales representative for a cleaning supply company with offices in Syracuse, Hagerstown, and Wytheville—all cities along I-81. And get this—his mother left him and his dad when he was little and family services had been called in on suspicion of child neglect. No charges were filed against his father, and he remained in the home."

"Good find," Jenna praised. Returning her attention to her computer, she shot off an e-mail to Special Agent Pane, briefing her on the two most likely suspects they'd found so far.

Glancing up, she noticed Owens sampling the healthy munchies at his desk. "Are you done with your home invasion case?"

"Not yet," he confessed. "We're still trying to identify Baird's two accomplices. No reason he should have all the fun."

She chanced a glance at the Tupperware box, but, before Jenna could snag a snack, the phone on her desk rang. "Ferrari."

"We have a guest here to talk to you—in my office this time." It was Captain Myers again. Her brow furrowed. "And just you, Lieutenant." Now her mind raced with speculations.

"Yes, sir. I'll be right there." Hanging up, she directed Jamison to keep digging.

She arrived at the captain's office with a dozen questions, but, upon seeing him sitting with a man who resembled a less ancient version of the Colonel from Kentucky Fried Chicken fame, she stopped and blinked. His hair was more steel-gray than snow-white, but the mustache, goatee, and glasses remained the same. His suit was fog-gray over a black shirt rather than white on white, and he'd left off the bowtie, but the resemblance seemed uncanny.

"Close the door and take a seat," her superior instructed, and Jenna complied, more curious than ever. "Lieutenant Detective Jenna Ferrari, meet Federal Marshal Sylvester Cyrus."

"Call me Sly," the man in his sixties, instead of his eighties, requested, in an accent drenched in the Kentucky hills, fishing ponds, cigar smoke, and Wild Turkey.

"Pleased to meet you, Sly. What can I do for you today?"

"Well, it's about your victim, Alexia Baxter," he replied, "only that's not her real name—it's Jada Styles from New York City. I work with the Federal Witness Protection Program—WITSEC—and I was Jada's handler. Four years ago, when she was eighteen, Jada witnessed a top mafia lieutenant we'd been after for ages commit a murder in an alley behind an NYC nightclub. She ran, and the FBI kept her in a safe house. The brave kid agreed to testify, so, for a year, we shuffled her around while she started her elementary education degree online. COVID was happening, so that had become a common practice. A year later, Alfredo 'Alpo' Mancini went to trial. We had the murder weapon and gunk from the alley on his shoes, but, without Jada's testimony, we probably couldn't have gotten a conviction."

Sly's story represented a mind-boggling twist to her investigation, opening up an entirely new direction to pursue.

"The Marshal's Program sent her to Phoenix first, where she spent another year working on her degree before her new identity there was compromised. Hell, poor kid's mother was dying of cancer—can hardly blame her for coming home to see her. The problem was the Mancini organization monitored her parents' house and the hospital, waiting for Jada to show up. After that incident is when she got passed over to me and moved to Virginia. WITSEC created the new identity for her, including tacking on a couple of years to her age. Instead of a student, she'd be a graduate. I mean, how many college classes do you really need to teach five-year-olds their ABCs?"

Jenna recalled Kathleen Baxter mentioning the fundamental importance of kindergarten teachers in children's development.

"So, she was only twenty-two and never actually attended UV," Jenna concluded aloud.

"That's correct. Our office does this all the time, so we're good at planting documents where they can be found and have the full cooperation of institutions to do so. We set her up with a birth certificate, driver's license, diploma, and a back story about her family dying in an accident. Unfortunately, her mother did pass away."

"But she still has a father, siblings, grandparents, people I need to contact?" Jenna asked. "They have to know what happened to Alexia—or Jada."

"Well, now, hold your horses." Sly lifted his palms and waved down her proposal. "First, we need to determine what actually happened here. The Witness Protection Program has an almost spotless record of protecting folks who abide by the rules. I've been in touch with Alexia Smith, then Baxter, every week since she arrived in Roanoke. I approved her taking the job at the school—which is what she'd wanted to do, be a teacher. You know, we try to give our witnesses a new identity they can live with and be happy assuming. Otherwise, they just go rogue. You can't take an artist and turn him into a factory worker or a teacher into a trash collector. It just doesn't work. So, we worked with Jada to become Alexia and have a happy, fulfilling life away from the Mancinis. We even gave her the green light to marry Nolan after thoroughly picking through his life from birth to the present. By all indications, his whole family is clean and didn't suspect a thing. She hadn't told them, either, which is why I'm so baffled."

"You think the mafia discovered she was actually this Jada Styles and killed her for payback?" Jenna questioned. "Even though old man Mancini was already convicted and serving a probable life sentence?"

"Sure," he remarked casually. "They're big on revenge killings."

Captain Myers voiced something Jenna was thinking. "But doesn't the mob usually shoot people in the head execution style? And, if they don't want the bodies found, they won't be. Seems like the M.O. used here doesn't fit mob standards."

"You're right; that's what they typically do. However, there have been exceptions in the past. The only other time I'm personally aware of that something like this happened, a fellow federal marshal had been compromised by the organized crime family and revealed the location of a witness under duress. The hitman the boss hired made it appear someone else unassociated with the mafia committed the crime to protect their mole. We only found out because the marshal experienced such remorse that he recorded his testimony, put it in a lockbox with a short paper trail, and turned it in before committing suicide. Captain, Lieutenant, I was the only marshal—the only person—who knew where to find Jada and what name she was using, and I didn't compromise her safety. She loved Nolan and wanted this new life. She grew up in a crime-infested, rickety neighborhood; living here was like heaven to her. I don't believe she would have broken a single rule and risk losing it."

"Then how would Mancini and crew know Alexia Baxter was Jada Styles?" Jenna asked.

"I don't know, and I'm not sure they did. Do you have a suspect?" Sly leaned back in his chair, studying Jenna with an interested expression.

"A few," she answered without conviction. "Sort of."

"Why don't you fill Marshal Cyrus in on everything you have in the case so far," Captain Myers suggested.

With a nod, Jenna did so, including all the evidence, witness statements, potential suspects, and theories.

"Well, now, that's very interesting," he concluded as he rubbed the splotch of hair on his chin. "I have a little hope that the sweet couple didn't die because of my negligence. However, there is a lead I'd like to check out. Observing law enforcement courtesy, I'll invite you to come along."

"A lead?" Jenna asked, expectations rising.

"Alpo Mancini has a nephew, Frankie, who lives a couple of hours' drive from here up in Buffalo Gap. He claims to have broken all ties with his uncle and the Mancini organization, and the FBI has been keeping a loose watch on him, but it wouldn't be hard for him to run down here and whack a couple if Alpo made him do it. Seeing how he doesn't want to be associated with the mob, he might have tried to make it look like a car crash to throw off an investigation. I want to talk to him, find out where he was on Saturday, and look him in the eye. Wanna come?"

"I sure do!"

"In that case, let's take my car." Sly pushed up from his seat and flashed Jenna a charming grin.

"You two be careful," Captain Myers warned. "No playing cowboy."

"You can count on me for perfect care, Captain," Jenna replied honestly. "I've got a wedding to attend in a few days."

Jenna buckled into Sly's late-model charcoal Jeep and listened to his stories all the way up I-81 to where they turned off at Staunton. The hill country was green and spotted with tobacco farms.

"How do you know he'll be home?" Jenna asked as he turned onto another country road.

"My FBI contact gave him a call, said we had a few questions for him, and made sure he'd be available. Frankie knows we keep tabs on him and, so far, he's cooperated to keep the feds out of his hair. Now, mind you, Frankie has never admitted his family runs an organized crime outfit. He swears his uncle and father are businessmen, but he knows. He just doesn't want a hitman coming after him. So, the bureau gives him some space and keeps a low profile but watches him all the same."

He turned the Jeep up a gravel drive that ran through rows of grapevines clinging to their trellises, their leaves waving merrily in the breeze on a cloudy day. Jenna recalled Randi saying they could use a nice rain, that it was too early for the summer drought to set in. Jenna figured Frankie would agree. She suspected he took his share of the family fortune to buy this place and get out of the life over a woman and wondered if she'd find that to be the case.

The house appeared spacious and in good repair, but not grandiose. No armed men stood guard or vicious dogs barked. Instead, their vehicle was greeted by a black and white border collie and six bounding puppies.

A brawny man with shaggy, dark brown hair and three days' worth of scruff shuffled along behind the dogs. Sweat beaded on his forehead and dampened the curls hanging about his neck. Standing a little taller than Marshal Cyrus—though not as tall as Randi by Jenna's estimation—he moved with an uneven gait, peeling off work gloves as he neared Sly's Jeep.

When the pups rushed forward, all tongues and wagging tails, yipping playfully, their mother leaped between them and the strangers with a bark of reprimand. They were friendly dogs, but the mother wisely didn't want her progeny stumbling into danger.

Jenna bent from her waist, held out the back of her hand toward the Shepherd to sniff, and smiled, projecting a friendly vibe.

"She doesn't take to just everyone," the man said. "I'm Frankie Mancini, and I suppose you're the federal marshals."

"Marshal Cyrus," the older man stated and shook Frankie's hand. "And this is Lieutenant Detective Ferrari from Roanoke."

His brow lifted as he gripped Jenna's hand. His fingers remained clean from being inside the glove, but his broad palm was rough from farm work. "Pleased to meet you," he said amiably. "Roanoke?"

Jenna nodded. "And who's the lady of the house?" She patted the dog's head as puppies bounced around her feet.

Frankie laughed and caught his thumbs in the belt loops of his jeans, beaming with pride at his dog. "Don't let Jessica hear you say that. This is Daisy and her four-week-old brood. I raise them, you know—AKA registered—and folks pay a pretty penny. This is no puppy mill, as you can see. Daisy is part of the family. Fellow across the ridge has the pups' sire."

He whistled, and Daisy quick-padded over to Frankie, tongue lolling, as she gazed up at him with an expression of affectionate devotion. A puppy grabbed Jenna's pants leg in its baby teeth and tugged. "Grrrr."

"Rascal, no!" he reprimanded. Then, in an excited tone, called, "Come over to me! This is where the action is." Jenna gave the puppy a gentle nudge and he scampered to join the others. It was easy to tell Daisy and her litter were happy and well cared for.

"Agent Miller said to expect you. What can I do for you guys?"

His voice carried far more New York than Virginia in it and his Italian heritage was obvious in his skin, hair, and eyes, his Roman nose, hairy body, and heavy beard. She didn't spy a weapon on him, and he didn't exude the superior, entitled attitude of a mobster.

"We're just needing to know where you were this past Saturday," Sly said in an easy drawl. "And the names and numbers of people who saw you."

With a weary sigh, Frankie plucked a bandana from his hip pocket and wiped the back of his neck with it. "Come on over here in the shade and have a seat." He led the way to his veranda, where a quaint swing gently swayed and two rocking chairs beckoned, sheltered under a broad porch covering. Daisy and the yipping, tumbling pups followed them. The mother dog went straight to an old blanket and lay down, the puppies all jostling for positions to nurse.

Frankie took the swing, leaving Jenna and Sly each a rocking chair. It was a pretty place, and, from this vantage, the entire vineyard spread before them like a Tuscan painting.

"Saturday I was home alone tending to my vines. My wife, Jessica, took our three kids to Play-a-Day-in-May-Away in Staunton. They were gone for about seven hours while I was home alone. So, if I need an alibi for something, I guess I'm out of luck."

Jenna ran calculations in her head. *It took an hour and a half to get here, so three hours round trip gives him exactly four hours to kill the Baxters, bury the dog, and stage the scene. It's feasible.*

"What do you think I've done this time?" he asked, as if being hassled by law enforcement was a cross he must bear for being related to a mob boss.

"Say, when's the last time you talked to your uncle Alpo?" Sly asked, changing the subject.

"Check the prison logs," Frankie said. "I haven't called, written, or been to see him since he got arrested on that murder charge. Look, I moved here to get away from that life. I love my wife and kids and I don't want them anywhere near danger. Nor do I want to get locked up or killed and leave them to fend for themselves."

"Where is your family now?" Jenna asked, taking a glance around the property.

"Jessica volunteers at the food bank on Wednesdays and my girls are in school," he replied.

"Since you're being so cooperative and all, Mr. Mancini, would you mind letting Lieutenant Ferrari here swab your cheek for DNA?"

The motion of Frankie's swing stopped, and he glanced at his folded hands for a moment. When he looked up, his expression had hardened. "Who are you trying to place at a crime scene? My brother, Kid, my cousin, Shorty? Surely not little Luca—he's only sixteen."

"We aren't here about your relatives, Mr. Mancini," Jenna stated. "We're looking into a crime that occurred in Roanoke County. DNA was left at the scene, and we just want to rule you out as a suspect."

"Roanoke?" The offense in his manner bloomed into bafflement. "Why are you up here interrogating me about something that happened in Roanoke? I thought maybe a bank had been robbed in Staunton and you were here to blame me since you had no leads. Roanoke?"

"You would have had plenty of time to drive there, commit the crime, and be home working in your vineyard while your family was at the festival," Jenna extrapolated.

Frankie shook his head, a hopeless expression filling his face, and rolled his eyes. "I didn't drive all the way to Roanoke to extort money or oversee a prostitution ring or open a new illegal gaming club or any of the crazy things you cops and federal agents are always trying to accuse me of. It's like, 'Oh, who could have committed this crime? I'll bet it's Godfather Mancini's nephew. Who else could it be?' Doesn't it ever get old?"

"I'm surprised your DNA isn't already in a national database," Sly commented.

Leveling his gaze on the old marshal, he replied, "I've never committed a crime."

"Never?" Jenna questioned. "You grew up in a mafia family and never once broke the law? Heck, I even did some shoplifting as a kid—got arrested for it too."

He looked her straight in the eyes. "I left the family *because* I grew up in that environment and I didn't want it for Jessica and my children. I saw the way my mother suffered, and my aunt, cousins. The men all cheat on their wives, bully business owners, and I'm not saying what they do is criminal, but it isn't right. I don't want a penthouse in the sky. This is what I love," he confessed, extending an arm around him. "My grape-covered hills, my wife and kids, my dogs, and a peaceful, quiet life. Why is that so hard for everyone to understand?"

"So, you won't volunteer your DNA?" Jenna probed.

Frankie grimaced and glanced away. "It was a condition for leaving the family," he said. "There were certain requirements to ensure I didn't become a liability, you see? And my wife and daughters, to guarantee their safety. It's not just the FBI that watches me, Lieutenant Ferrari. You're Italian, right? You know how it is."

Her family in the impoverished hills of Kentucky had been a world away from the millions and the lifestyle of the Mancinis. Still, she understood the concept that loyalty to family was everything. She shifted her gaze to his work boots. "What size are those?"

"Huh?" He glanced down, confused again. "A nine. Why?"

"Do you own a baseball bat?" She queried without answering him.

"My oldest girl plays Little League," he said. "We have a few bats in the garage. Your questions seem so random."

"May I examine the bats?"

"Sure." He rose and led the way. A parade of border collies trotted after them. Behind the bicycles and lawn mower, propped in a corner, were two tennis rackets, three fishing poles, and two baseball bats—one aluminum and one wood. Jenna slipped on her rubber gloves and lifted out the wooden one. She examined the label, the wear, the grip, and the cap. While there was no visible sign of blood, the fibers of the wood would have soaked in minuscule drops, even if it had been sanitized after the fact. It would need to go to the lab.

"Mr. Mancini, I'll be honest with you," Jenna stated. "You don't strike me as the perpetrator we're looking for, but, if you want to be cleared and left alone by the Roanoke PD, I'm going to need to take this bat back to our lab. If it doesn't match the one used in our crime, I promise to return it to you so quickly that your little girl won't even know it was gone. Would that be OK with you?"

"My daughter's bat?" He scratched his scruffy face and Jenna speculated it must itch. "I guarantee nobody used it in a crime. It's been right here the whole time unless we're playing in the yard, at her practices, or a game. There was nothing in the family rules about baseball bats, so, sure—take it. Run your tests and then clear me from your list of suspects."

"Thank you, Mr. Mancini, for your cooperation."

"Thanks, Frankie," Sly said with a courteous nod. "I'm glad to see you're doing well and staying out of trouble."

Jenna laid the bat on the back seat and climbed into the front.

"What do you think?" Sly asked as he cranked the Jeep. "Is he your man?"

Jenna let out a frustrated sigh. "He loves his dog."

14

⸻◆⸻

"What does that have to do with anything?" Sly asked as they rumbled over the gravel drive. "I love my dog too—Horatio, an English bulldog. He looks like Winston Churchill and marches around the house like a sentinel. But I still could have murdered countless people. He has no alibi, wears the right size shoe, refused to submit his DNA, and handed over the possible murder weapon—probably thinks it's clean. And there's a heap of ways a mobster could get messages in and out of prison with nobody making a record of it. His story has more holes in it than a fishing net. I'm not convinced."

"I didn't mention the crime was a murder to see if he'd slip up, which he didn't."

"He's neither stupid nor an amateur," the marshal stipulated as he stared at the road in concentration. "But I'm glad you didn't. In case he wasn't involved, I don't want him to find out your victim was the girl who put his old man away."

"Agreed."

"I'll bet the lab finds traces of blood soaked into the wood of that bat," Sly grumbled.

Jenna sighed and shook her head. "Twenty says you're wrong."

"You're on!" Sly readjusted his grip on the wheel. "You know where he got the money to buy that nice vineyard, don't you?"

"I'm sure it was his share of the family fortune," Jenna admitted. "But just because his uncle and other relatives have committed murder doesn't mean he did."

"I reckon that's fair. Now, what's this about loving his dog got to do with it?"

"Everything. Whoever killed Nolan and Alexia Baxter—Jada Styles—also murdered their Pomeranian," she explained. "Now, I'm not certain if burying it deep in their back yard was a sign of remorse—in which case, I could be mistaken about Frankie—or an attempt to hide the body. But it was an unnecessary cruelty. The little fluff ball couldn't have weighed more than ten pounds and posed no threat to the attacker whatsoever. Suppose Mancini found out from prison who and where Jada was and secretly got a message out to Frankie. I don't see it, because why not send a professional hitman? Why enlist the black sheep of the family who choose a life apart from the Cosa Nostra? But suppose he does. Maybe Frankie would take out the witness who testified because he felt he had no choice, but why also kill her husband, and why the harmless, tiny dog? I don't get a cruel vibe from him. Anyway, we'll see what the lab says about the bat."

***

Randi ambled around her spacious classroom, keeping a close watch over her Freshman English Literature Two class as they scribbled pencil marks into answer bubbles on their score sheets. She tolerated many things; cheating was not one of them. Besides requiring the students to skip every other seat, she had taken the added precaution of printing out two versions of the test. Since she had never given an all-multiple-choice exam with the computer-scored grid sheet, there would have been no point trying to get help from last year's class or attempting to steal her key. To be fair to the would-be cheaters, Randi informed them of this before passing out the tests. Experience told her one or two would still try to peer at their neighbor's answers.

The students were instructed to turn their papers in and quietly leave the room as they finished and to enjoy their summer vacation. Now only one young man remained—Trip. She noted he spent more time chewing his fingernails that were already up to the quick than bubbling in responses. He scrubbed his eraser back and forth, tearing a hole in the scantron sheet. He raised helpless, nearly tear-filled eyes to her. Randi calmly walked over and placed a fresh one on his desk.

"You have fifteen minutes remaining. I suggest you carefully transfer the answers from the ripped bubble sheet to this one, then make your final selections."

"Yes, ma'am," Trip uttered in despair. "My dad's gonna kill me."

"I truly doubt that," Randi replied, offering him a smile. "Finish up now, and we can talk after the bell."

Returning to her podium, Randi slipped the stack of test question booklets into her briefcase and sorted the scantrons into their A and B stacks. Trip continued to fuss over his exam until the bell sounded and then trudged to the front, dropping his test and bubble sheet onto her desk with a groan.

"Dr. McLeod, I wanted to talk to you about the essay assignment from last week," he said, shifting his weight from one tattered sneaker to the other. His black and teal hair stuck up in a short Mohawk and a stud pierced his eyebrow. He tugged at the sagging back of faded, black cargo pants, clearly stalling.

Randi remained placid and raised her brows. "You mean the one you never turned in?"

"Yeah ... that one," he stammered and scratched his head. "I ran into a snag, but I really can't have a zero. I don't think I can pass with a zero. So, I was hopin' you'd let me turn it in late, you know? Even a fifty is better. I might pass if I get a fifty on it."

"You know I'm turning in all my grades on Friday night—no exceptions."

"Yeah, I know. You've got that wedding thing."

Randi wasn't certain if the dark circles under his eyes were from staying up partying or cramming for finals, but Trip was struggling; he had been all semester.

"The wedding thing," she confirmed. "Don't waste my time with a piece of crap or something you copied off the internet, Trip. You know points are deducted for late papers, but tomorrow is Thursday. If you bring me something worthwhile by four o'clock tomorrow afternoon—which is when I leave for the day—then I'll give it a fair shake and replace that zero with something higher.

By the way, unless you aced this exam," which Randi found doubtful, "you're right about not passing with a zero on a major assignment."

Trip hung his head, the rise of his colorful hair flopping into his face. "Yes, ma'am."

"I know college is supposed to be fun," Randi sympathized with the nineteen-year-old, "and young people are so excited to have some liberty to stay up as long as they want, to hang out, and try crazy stuff. But your parents paid for you to be here, and they expect you to spend some of your time on academics. What's your major?"

He shrugged. "My guidance counselor said I don't have to decide yet, that the first two years are mostly required, general classes. He said to see what I'm interested in."

"And what are you interested in?"

"Art and music, only my dad says I can't get a job that pays any money for those."

"You can for certain if your degree qualifies you to teach one of those subjects," Randi said in an encouraging tone. "To be honest, school districts seem to swing with the economy on how many art and music teachers they keep on staff, but it is a steady, respectable profession that allows you to pursue your talent in a more applied manner in your spare time. What I mean to say is that you could teach elementary or secondary art or music classes and still draw, paint, or compose and perform in your spare time. Perhaps the best perk to teaching is all the time off we get."

Trip wiped a hand under his nose and laughed. "Me, teach? I can't even keep my grades up. I'll probably have to drop out and go to a vocational school."

"I suspect your lack of results speaks to your lack of effort. I see you sleeping in class, which means you've been staying up too late at night. Go on, now. Write your essay, proofread it, and get it turned in tomorrow. With any luck, your dad won't kill you and you'll come back in the fall ready to apply yourself."

Her student chuckled and met her gaze. "I'll try applying myself. Thanks, Dr. McLeod. You didn't have to accept a late essay."

"I know," she quipped and jerked her head toward the exit. Randi noticed Trip had a bit more spring in his step on the way out.

She gathered the scantrons and keys and headed to the workroom to run them through the machine, double-checking her A and B sheets carefully to ensure they were scored correctly. More than a few made A's, and the majority fell into the B and C columns. A relative few failed. Seeing the names, Randi wasn't surprised. They belonged to students who rarely showed up and made minimal effort when they did. The bubble sheet Trip had agonized over just made the passing mark by one point. He wouldn't return home for the summer with flying colors, but if he wrote an original essay that made any sense at all, he wouldn't have to repeat English Lit.

Randi went to her office to eat the sandwich and fruit she'd brought from home and to call Renita. Her mind had played over what to say practically all night while Jenna slept like a rock. That was good—she needed to. But Randi wanted her mom to know they weren't ticked off at her and that they wished her a quick recovery. Such a message would stay truer to its intent if it came from her instead of Jenna.

It wasn't that Jenna lacked communication skills. Randi knew when operating in a professional capacity, Jenna could strike just the right chord. However, her mother was another story. Her words—or lack of them—elicited such a strong emotional response from Jenna, and it was easy for Randi to understand why. She pushed in the number, hoping Renita had a phone by her bed or chair or wherever she was resting with her foot up.

After three rings, a weak voice answered. "Hello."

"Hi Renita, it's Randi. Did I catch you at a bad time?"

"No, just lyin' in bed readin' with my foot on a pillow. I was about to doze off when you called. Vinnie went out to pick up somethin' for lunch. I feel so stupid and useless, and now he has to miss work to take care of me—at least for the first week. Then I'm shooin' him back before he decides I'm more trouble than I'm worth." She allowed a self-deprecating chuckle that Randi found void of humor.

"Ah, no such thing," Randi responded. "It's good for him to take care of you for a change. And I'm sure Vince Junior and Angie will come by and help when they can. Did they give you good pain meds?" Randi used a tone that invited a laugh, and she wasn't disappointed.

"Yeah, but only enough to last through today. The doctor said they could be addictin' and that's the last thing we want, sure enough!"

"Angie says she loves her new job."

"She does, and Vinnie and me are so proud of her." Renita's voice perked up as the conversation turned away from her accident in favor of praise for her youngest. "I haven't seen her in it, but I can just picture it—the big, white ambulance with the red stripes and the light flashin' and siren blarin', my baby girl racin' to the rescue." Pride permeated her words, and Randi could imagine the smile lighting her face.

"Listen, Jenna is up to her neck in a double-homicide case, but we both wanted to call to say how sorry we are you hurt yourself yesterday. Not too long ago I did a silly, thoughtless thing and fractured my wrist—had to wear a brace and limit my activities for weeks. I berated myself over and over for not paying close enough attention, and not following safety protocols, all because my mind was focused on something else, so I know it does no good."

"But it *was* a stupid mistake. I didn't have a firm enough grip on the rail, and, yes, my mind was on other things besides watchin' my step," Renita rebuffed. "Still, I didn't do it on purpose, as I'm sure Jenna thinks. I would never put myself in such an embarrassin', helpless, painful position by design. I have enough ailments to fake one without havin' to go and fall down the steps."

"No one thinks you consciously planned to hurt yourself," Randi responded gently. "I think you were just worried, trying to decide what to do about Saturday, and didn't notice a slick spot." *Or, subconsciously, your brain provided you with a way out.* "We're sorry you can't come and would have been if you had decided it went too much against your convictions, but neither Jenna nor I wanted to see you break your ankle. We love you and would have understood if you couldn't come; you just needed to say so."

"But Jenna would see it as another rejection of her when it ain't." Tension strained through a voice that otherwise sounded like a pout.

"From your perspective, it's her decision you can't approve of, not Jenna herself."

"That's right. Only whenever I try to talk to her about it, everythin' comes out wrong. I don't know how to be friends with my grown children. You should have been around for the fiasco when Vince Jr. got Dawn pregnant out of wedlock. I was fit to be tied and so ashamed."

"His actions shouldn't make you ashamed, and neither should Jenna's. You love Eli. Can you imagine not having him in your lives?"

"Of course, I love Eli," Renita avowed. "He's a precious little boy, and it wasn't his fault. But I'm their mother. And when Angie was on drugs?" She sighed. "I have to think I'm to blame. I wasn't a good enough mother and did everythin' wrong. I think God must be punishin' me and that's why I have the arthritis and the pre-diabetes and all the other ailments, and probably why I broke my ankle. Somehow, I've got to get back on God's good side, and I can't do that by condonin' a same-sex marriage."

Randi's heart went out to Renita. She didn't believe any of the nonsense about God punishing her with disease and accidents; however, it was completely believable that her self-image, stress, anxiety, guilt, and shame played havoc with her health.

"Ah, Renita," she empathized. "Surely you don't believe that. It makes no sense. Jesus went everywhere healing the sick, which is inconsistent with the suggestion God punishes people with illnesses. We all make mistakes, but look at your kids now. Vince is a talented mechanic about to go into business with his dad, Angie is saving lives driving an ambulance, and Jenna is a respected detective and one of the youngest to make lieutenant in Roanoke history. You have a lot to be proud of where your children are concerned. But this is the time in your life when you get to focus on yourself. The kids are grown, and your husband is starting a new business with Ferrari and Son. I'm sure there's a women's group at your church you could join. Plus, there are worthwhile charities and even money-earning jobs you can do from home or for just a few hours a day. You don't need to sit at the house alone, dwelling on what you could have, should have, or would have done differently."

"I reckon you're right about that," she admitted. "I need to contribute somethin' to this world. It's just been a month of Sundays since I felt like doin' anythin'. And I know I'm supposed to trust the Lord and not worry constantly, but how do you not worry? I know you believe what you and Jenna are doin' isn't wrong. It just grates against everythin' I've always been taught to believe."

"It isn't easy to change one's mind about anything, much less a long-held belief," Randi allowed. "You're Jenna's mom, and she loves you. Sometimes it's hard for her to separate your staunch disapproval of a part of who she is with how you feel about all of her. She wants to have a good relationship with you, and I think she's almost as frustrated about it all as you are."

"But what if I can't resolve it?" Renita pled in anguish. "I feel like I'm damned if I do and damned if I don't."

Randi bit her tongue. She had so much sage advice she wanted to give. *Stop looking backward. Let it go. Do what gives you peace, what makes you happy. Quit subjugating yourself to the dictates of the Catholic Church. Put your love for your daughter first. Learn to love yourself, for crying out loud.* But she didn't feel it was her place to instruct Jenna's mother on how to solve her issues.

"Things sometimes feel that way for me too," she said instead. "And I might make a mistake—as I've done plenty. But when I think about the love, compassion, and character of God, I think I'd rather err on the side of grace. If I do wrong, I want it to be because I loved too much, not too little. We love you, Renita, even if we don't always like the choices you make, either. And maybe that's enough. We pray for your speedy recovery, so you'll be up and around and getting into mischief in no time. Tell you what—we'll send you some pictures from the wedding."

Randi thought she heard a quiet sob and a sniff. "I love you both too. Tell Jenna I'm sorry and I'm not rejectin' her."

"I will."

15

———◆○◆———

"How's it going?" Jenna asked when she returned to the criminal investigations office after bidding Marshal Cyrus farewell. He planned to check on some other mafia contacts in the area while waiting for the lab report on the bat.

Owens glanced up mid-munch as he ate lunch at his desk. Bauman, whose mouth wasn't full, answered, "We're going through all of Baird's known associates, other folks he served time with, friends going back to high school. So far, we've isolated four guys and two gals who look promising as his accomplices."

"What he said," Owens affirmed as he swallowed his bite. "Where have you been?"

With a slow spin of her chair, Jamison regarded Jenna with an expression that silently questioned why she had been left out, making Jenna wince. "On a secret mission with a federal marshal. He didn't say I couldn't tell you all, although he wants to keep this angle quiet. Since his information is highly relevant to our investigation, you need to know. Confidential, OK?"

Her three team members nodded somberly as the insult faded from Jamison's face. Jenna told them about Alexia's original identity, the situation of being placed in WITSEC, and their visit to Frankie Mancini's place.

"First it was the home invaders, then the FBI's serial killer, and now a mafia boss?" Owens voiced in incredulity. He shook his head, making a baffled expression. "What'll drop into your lap tomorrow? You've got so many angles on this case."

"That's for sure," Jamison agreed. "But I think we've eliminated your robber and his accomplices."

"I could do some runs on the Mancini family," Bauman volunteered. "Probably nothing the FBI doesn't already know."

"Stay on Unsub Seventeen search for now," Jenna requested. "While it is entirely believable Mancini would send a hitman for Alexia without blinking an eye, he had to know she was Jada Styles first. And if he did, it wasn't Frankie. The lab's running the baseball bat we collected from his garage, but I'd bet the prize racehorse I don't have it'll come back clean."

"You said no alibi," Owens recalled, "and, if he's that eager to keep his family clear of mob business, he'd be willing to do anything."

"True," Jenna admitted. "But this murder and the attempted coverup appear too amateur for a kingpin's nephew. First, someone gains access to their home. No doors or windows were busted, and no scrape marks were detected on the locks to indicate they'd been picked. OK, so maybe that's a sign of a professional, but it could also point to someone they would open the door for, like a delivery person, maintenance worker, or an acquaintance. Unsub Seventeen might use just such a disguise to trick his way into people's homes—or, if he's a traveling salesman, use his products as a ruse. Then the killer doesn't use a gun. Something like seventy-five percent of all murders in the U.S. are committed with guns, yet our intruder uses a bat, and they kill the dog."

"And bury her," Jamison added.

"That could be a sign of remorse," Bauman pointed out. "Maybe the dog got in the way or interfered with the perpetrator's plans and had to be eliminated, but he felt bad about it afterward since the dog had never been the intended target."

"A reasonable theory," Jenna commended. "Maybe it was a crime of passion, an escalated argument, and the bat was handy. It could have been a weapon of opportunity. We know the Baxters engaged in athletic activities, so maybe one or both of them was taking up baseball. But why put their bodies in their SUV, clean up the crime scene with bleach, and put everything back so it would appear no fight had occurred—a poor job of it, I must add—and then drive their car off the road? If he or they *really* wanted it to look like an accident, why not put Nolan in the driver's seat, Alexia in the passenger seat, and leave both safety belts unlatched? The way it was staged, even a child could guess someone else was driving."

"Yeah, definite amateur hour," Owens concluded.

"Or the killer panicked," Jamison suggested. "Maybe once he realized what he had done, he just wanted to get rid of the evidence in a hurry and didn't think it through."

"You know what?" Jenna asked in frustration and met each of her team members' eyes. They held hers questioningly, eagerly awaiting her insight. "It doesn't sound like a mob hit or a methodical serial killer. We have to keep them on the list, but I want to reinterview friends and neighbors. Jamison?"

Her butt was out of her chair faster than a rattlesnake strike. "I'm with you, boss."

"Good. Owens, Bauman, interview your accomplice suspects and close your case so you can help us tomorrow. I'll enjoy my honeymoon much better with this killer in custody."

Jenna and Jamison caught up with Brenda Zellner at Carilion Roanoke Memorial Hospital, where she worked as a tech in the radiology department. Her supervisor sent them to a private consultation room to talk.

"Have you made any progress?" The young woman's brunette strands hung in a long tail over her scrubs, and she twirled her fingers in nervous circles.

Jenna took a seat, followed by Jamison. "Here, we have a few more questions." Jamison patted the chair beside her, and Brenda obediently sat, eyes wide and lips parted.

"Were Alexia or Nolan taking up baseball to your knowledge? Do you recall seeing a bat at their place?" Jenna asked.

"Is that what killed them?" she answered, her breath coming quick as she reacted to the news. "Oh, God!"

Jenna realized the panic rising in her witness and, on cue, Jamison reached a hand to cover Brenda's arm.

"You're all right, Brenda. Just take a breath. I know this is all horrifyingly fresh in your mind. We are working to identify the murder weapon, and anything you can tell us will help."

"Yes, of course," Brenda answered, visibly attempting to rein in her emotions. "I don't remember Alexia or Nolan mentioning an interest in baseball. They liked kayaking, hiking, and bicycle riding, and had just started going to one of those ninja gyms—you know, like the television show."

No team sports, Jenna noted. *Things they could do together whenever they wanted without being locked into a schedule. Randi's mentioned the new ninja gym. I bet she'd be great at it with her long arms and legs.*

"What about a dispute with a neighbor or someone who did part-time work for them?" Jamison asked, bringing Jenna's thoughts back to the moment.

Brenda pinched up her face and stared at the wall in thought. "Nothing major. I mean, a few words here and there, but—"

"Anything could be important," Jenna assured her.

"One day when Tommy and I were over, Mr. Halbach—that's the old guy next door—pounded on the door to complain about Picasso. She was just barking at a squirrel; it wasn't a big deal. Alexia brought her in, she quieted down, and that was it. It wasn't even late at night, but I suppose someone his age might have been going to bed at eight o'clock. I remember checking the time so I'd know how much longer before Tommy and I would have to go home. Honestly, they got along well with everyone in the neighborhood—unlike Ricky Finstermeier. He's the real scourge of the hill."

"Tell us about Mr. Finstermeier," Jenna prodded.

"Oh, he keeps junk cars—says he's fixing them up—and lets weeds get knee high before he'll mow his grass," Brenda reported with enthusiasm. "He's a hoarder, too, and has this humongous, vicious dog in his yard. Sometimes he puts it on a chain in his garage, and it chased a kid on his bike once. The mailman won't even go to the house when the dog is out front. Whenever someone tries to visit or be nice to him, he yells and grumbles and curses at them. Most folks just avoid him. I don't recall Nolan or Alexia ever attempting to interact with him, though. His house is on another street a block away from theirs."

"Thanks," Jamison said. "We'll check him out. Can you think of anything they may have mentioned about a disagreement or a competitor, an angry parent, or anything they were concerned about?"

Brenda wilted, turning a withered gaze to Jamison. "They just got married. They were flying too high to be worried about anything."

When her eyes glistened, Jenna stood. "Thank you, Ms. Zellner. We'll let you get back to work. You're helping your friends, and I want you to know that."

The young woman nodded and dabbed at her cheek.

"We will let you know when we have something substantial," Jamison promised.

"Do a run on Ricky Finstermeier," Jenna instructed as she and Jamison got back in her car. "We'll talk to the grumpy old neighbor again and then pay him a visit. Hopefully, Marshal Cyrus or Agent Pane will turn up a hot lead. In the meantime, we do the legwork, reinterview people, and wait on science."

From Halbach's front porch, Jenna glanced at the Baxters' residence, invigorating her with renewed determination to solve their murder. The yellow tape had come down around the house that would never build the happy memories of years together, children growing up, and a couple growing old together. Who knew? Maybe they would have ended up divorced in eight or ten years, but they deserved a chance to try. They deserved a chance to live.

An average-sized man with salt and pepper hair answered the door. "May I help you?" he asked with a pleasant expression.

Jenna held up her badge. "I'm Lieutenant Detective Ferrari and this is Detective Jamison. We're here to see Ralph Halbach." She peeked past him into the house.

"That's my dad," he said. His shoulders slumped and his smile drooped. "I'm Carlin. This must be about what happened to the neighbors. Car accident, was it?"

"No," she answered with a somber expression. "They were murdered. May we come in? Your father was home at the time, and he might remember something now that he didn't when we spoke to him Saturday evening."

Shock and dismay overtook Carlin's features, and he pulled the door wide. "Murdered!" He swallowed as he ushered them inside. "Dad!" he called, then turned back to Jenna with a hard scowl. "This is supposed to be a safe neighborhood. That's why I helped Dad choose this house. I read in the paper about the home invasions. Is that who you think did this? Have they escalated to murder now?"

Before Jenna could respond, Carlin raced a few strides to meet his elderly father. "Dad, did you hear? Now you must promise me you'll start locking your doors, and not just at night."

"What's all this about?" Ralph grumbled and wiggled a bony finger in his hairy ear.

Carlin grabbed hold of his arm. "The cops are here, and they said the Baxters were murdered—right there in their home. Let's go sit down. They want to ask you some questions, so try to be civil and remember what you heard and saw."

The lines deepened in Ralph's face and he hmphed, pulling away from his overprotective son. He waddled toward the living room furniture. "Come on, then. Murdered, you say?"

"Yes, sir," Jamison replied as she and Jenna followed them in and took seats.

A glance around informed Jenna this was a man's house, void of a feminine touch. A painting of a deer in a forest clearing shared the wall with old portraits and various military remembrances. An ashtray half-filled with butts and ash rested on a rectangular end table beside the big stuffed chair Ralph took. The smell clinging to drapes, carpet, and furniture reminded Jenna of her parents' house.

"An arrest has been made in the home invasion cases," Jenna said, "although the investigation is ongoing. They may not have been responsible for the Baxters' death. Mr. Halbach, you stated earlier that you didn't see or hear anything out of the ordinary Saturday afternoon, but what about earlier—say, around eleven or twelve o'clock?"

He frowned and smacked his lips. "If I recall, I ate lunch, then turned on the ball game, sat out here with a beer, and must have dozed off. When I stepped out onto the porch to collect the paper, their garage door was open, and the SUV was gone. That weren't unusual. Young couple always went somewhere or did somethin' on Saturdays."

"This part is important," Jamison said, leaning forward with her elbows on her knees, presenting Ralph with an irresistibly imploring expression. "Did you hear their dog barking when you went out for your paper, or any time Saturday?"

Both Carlin and Ralph trained their attention on Jenna's partner. The old man cocked his head. "Come to think of it, I don't think so. It sure woke me up that mornin'—I remember that. Bark, bark, yap, yap, but not after I'd had lunch. I didn't hear it again. Say—what happened to Yappy anyway? Did y'all ever find it?"

"Yeah," Jenna answered sorrowfully. "We found her."

"I'm going to get you a big dog like Finstermeier's," Carlin stated with resolution. "That little orange powder puff was no protection for your neighbors, and Nolan was a fit young man."

"I don't need no damn mutt for protection!" Ralph growled at his son with a scathing glare. "I'm perfectly capable of defendin' myself. I fought in Nam, and I have guns. No ne'er-do-well would dare cross my threshold."

"Mr. Halbach." Jenna turned his attention away from quarrelling with his son. "How did Nolan and Alexia get along with the other neighbors? Did you ever see one of them arguing with someone or a visitor at their house, not from around here?"

"Well, now that you mention it ..." Ralph thoughtfully rubbed the stubble on his chin. "I doubt there's anythin' to it, but the Black fella across the way—Kirby, I think—paid a bit too much attention to Alexia, if you get my meanin'. He and Nolan raised their voices outside last week, but it weren't none of my business."

"Thank you, Mr. Halbach, Carlin. Hey, your business is in security, isn't it Carlin?" Jenna asked as she stood.

"Yeah," he answered and rose to walk her and Jamison to the door. "It's my day off, and I came over to check on Dad. This entire ordeal has been upsetting to him."

"You told him to lock his doors," Jamison said. "Does he leave them unlocked often?"

"I'd wager everyone up here does. Used to be a time when you never had to worry about locks. Folks were decent and didn't try to rob you blind. If you need anything else, detectives, don't hesitate to call. I want this criminal caught and locked away. Dad doesn't seem worried, but maybe *I'll* sleep better at night."

"You know," Jenna commented to Jamison as they strolled across the street to speak to Mr. Kirby. "If the Baxters didn't lock their door, anyone could have just waltzed in and hit them over the head with no fuss at all. Honest people are too trusting." She considered ways to improve security at her and Randi's house—large, intimidating dog notwithstanding.

16

"No, Nolan and I weren't arguing," Mr. Kirby swore when Jenna and Jamison confronted him at his front door. The fellow appeared to be in his late forties or early fifties, with close-cropped hair. Sporting a wiry build and an average height, he seemed to lie comfortably between athletic and lethargic. Taking a glance at his feet, Jenna supposed his sneakers could be a size nine.

"Sure, I complimented him on his pretty wife, but he wasn't mad about it," he explained.

"Mr. Halbach said he heard you two yelling at each other," Jamison declared.

"Oh, that." Mr. Kirby laughed and shook his head. "One of the neighbors was mowing his lawn, and we had to shout to hear each other over the noise. Look, detectives, I'm a happily married man. Now, there's no denying Alexia was an attractive young woman, but I would never—and neither would she. She was very well respected and well liked."

His countenance fell, and he let out an anguished sigh. "It breaks my heart what happened to that nice couple. I sure 'nough had nothing to do with it—wasn't even home Saturday. I took my wife to the flea market, and she and Winnie hunted for bargains while I sat with her husband Dwayne eating ice cream and shootin' the breeze. Maybe if I'd been here, I would've noticed something."

If no stronger leads presented themselves, Jenna could always check his story. If he truly had three witnesses to his whereabouts, it would prove a tight alibi.

Mr. Kirby leaned on the doorjamb and hung his head. "Do you want to come inside?"

"No, thanks," Jenna replied. "That won't be necessary. Thank you for your time."

The visit to disreputable, disliked Richard Finstermeier proved no more productive. It was easy for Jenna to understand why neighbors would complain about him, and his guard dog could have turned Byron into a snack. He never invited them in and kept the screen door closed throughout the brief interview. A balding man about Carlin's age, he might have worn a size nine shoe. Jamison got him to admit to being agoraphobic. The only time he left his house was to go into his yard to tinker with the two nonfunctioning automobiles on concrete blocks, and he put his dog on a long chain to protect him whenever he did. He had all his groceries delivered.

The man complained about everything—the neighborhood children were mongrels, the adults were useless vermin, and his delivery employees were inexcusable. He claimed he didn't even know who Nolan and Alexia Baxter were. Jamison suggested, if he had killed them, he wouldn't have buried poor Picasso but would have brought her home as a chew toy for what could only have been the largest bull mastiff in recorded history.

When they returned to the office that afternoon, Owens greeted Jenna with a lab report. "This came back on your bat. Not even the slightest hint of blood, skin, hair, bone, or brain matter. Wilcox declared it the cleanest bat she'd ever processed. So, not the Mancinis?"

"Not Frankie Mancini," Jenna clarified and looked through the folder. "And your guys?"

"We nailed the female accomplice," Bauman announced.

"Yeah," Owens confirmed with a proud blush. "ADA Altman is on his way over to go back in and flip her with a sweet deal to reveal the other guy's name and testify against the two of them. She claims she was coerced and swears up and down they were casing a subdivision across town on Saturday and had nothing to do with the murders. Hopefully, we'll have it closed by suppertime."

"Good." Jenna gave him a thumbs up and settled in at her desk. A couple more hours and home to her honey. *Only three more days.* The tingle of anticipation and satisfaction expanded through her like yeast-laden dough, warm and thick. She could swear she could even smell it. Her phone rang, shattering the moment.

"Ferrari."

"Lieutenant Ferrari, this is Special Agent Pane checking in with you," she said. "Please thank Detective Jamison for sending over the names the two of you sifted out of the masses. Together with the suspects we narrowed down to, we're watching five men—well, four. We haven't pinpointed the current location of the fifth, but we have his address, and a car is monitoring his house. Both you and Dr. Grayson helped enhance our profile. As soon as our unsub makes a wrong move, we'll have him, and I'll give you a call. I know you'll want to be present for the interrogation to discover if he killed your couple."

"Thank you; I would like to be there," Jenna agreed. "And to be clear, Detective Jamison picked one out of the murky pool while I chased another lead."

"Classy to credit your partner," Pane praised.

"No, just being honest. So, where are the suspects now?"

"One's in Bristol, and the others are in Syracuse, Pittsburgh, Harrisonburg, and unknown. But I've got our tech guy scouring traffic cam footage for his vehicle. We'll put eyes on him too. He's one of the suspects you sent over. They are both excellent candidates. The FBI could use someone with your experience and sharp eye for details. Give me a call if you ever think about moving up."

"Moving up?" Jenna laughed. "That would be the captain's corner office. Roanoke's been good to me, Agent Pane; still, I'll keep your suggestion in mind."

"Excellent—you do that. Have a good evening," she bade, and Jenna returned the good wishes.

She clicked off the call and made one of her own to Marshal Cyrus. "Frankie Mancini's bat is as squeaky clean as the proverbial whistle. Now, I don't know who sits around scrubbing and polishing all these whistles, but I'm holding a report that says the bat we collected from his residence was not used to kill the Baxters or anybody else."

"Well, that's a shame. I s'pose that means I owe you a twenty-dollar bill." Jenna detected the disappointment in his tone. "I've just spent all afternoon looking up the whereabouts of every known criminal associate of the Mancinis, and none were remotely near Virginia on Saturday. So, either they've branched out and hired someone who's not on our radar yet, or good ole Alpo has no clue that Alexia and Jada were the same person."

"What's the likelihood they'd hire a stranger to do a sloppy job of taking out a witness?"

"Not very high," he admitted, "although I reckon anything is possible. On the one hand, I'm peeved because I have to drive that bat back to Frankie's, eat crow, and fork over an Andrew Jackson. On the other hand, I'm not feeling quite so guilty and unnerved about this. It's looking like the U.S. marshals didn't slip up, and this murder had nothing to do with Alexia being in witness protection. I'm sorry she's dead—just feel less responsibility for it."

"I haven't completely tossed the theory the mob carried the murders out, but it's way down on my list," Jenna said. "It wasn't well thought through or executed, and the attempted coverup was a joke. I grant you permission to sleep easier tonight. Hey, does this mean someone can notify Jada Styles' family now? They need to know what happened."

A long sigh blew over the phone. "I reckon that's my responsibility. I'll take care of it. Say, you wouldn't like to drive back up to Buffalo Gap with me tomorrow, would ya?" Sly's smooth, Southern drawl spread through his invitation like honey over toast.

Jenna laughed. "Sorry, Sly. I have to stay here and catch my killer but say hi to Frankie for me."

"Yeah, I'll do that," he said with a tinge of regret. "I'll be by to pick up the bat first thing, in case you change your mind."

Jenna pictured "the colonel" winking and grinning at her temptingly. "See you in the morning, then."

Hanging up the phone, Jenna continued to pry into everybody Alexia had known in Roanoke and everyone Nolan had known for his entire life. Owens and Bauman met with Altman and their home invader to talk deals while Jamison poured through social media accounts. Bauman had taken a few minutes to hack both of their phones, which had been recovered from the Baxters' house. There were no threatening messages or red flags at all.

When the clock hit five, Jenna turned off her computer and pushed out of her chair. "Go home, Trish," she directed, "or wherever you go after work. I'm calling it for today."

Jamison swirled around with a glowing smile, showing off pearly whites in contrast to her rose-petal lipstick. "Only three days!" she sang with glee. "And only two days until the rehearsal. Oh, Ferrari, I'm so excited!"

Jamison shimmied up to her with enough energy to make Jenna feel like a lethargic snail. She allowed a smile at her friend and coworker. "Me too." Though her voice lacked the enthusiasm that radiated off Trisha, she meant it deep in her core. A day she never thought would happen for her was about to become a reality. *I'm not alone and I won't be alone. Randi loves me and she wants to marry me—me!* "And nothing is going to go wrong," she declared.

"Of course it won't," Jamison assured her in a confident tone. "*I'll* be there!"

***

Randi and Byron returned from their run along the shoulder of her country road, down a trail, and back in plenty of time before dinner. While she was winded and sweaty, Byron could have done it all again with ease. Randi was glad to have all her exams scored and grades recorded except for tomorrow's two classes—and Trip's final grade. She suspected he'd have something on her desk in time. Being sticky, she headed straight for the shower to be presentable and smell fresh when Jenna got home.

She had taken out chicken to thaw that morning and planned to whip up a stir fry with veggies and Kung Pao sauce to go over a small portion of brown rice. As a timesaver, she used the instant variety, and, honestly, chopping all the ingredients took the longest. Still, it was a tasty, healthy meal whipped up in less than half an hour.

Jenna surprised her by arriving at a decent hour. "Something smells divine," Jenna cooed as she rounded the corner. Then, taking a peek at the pan, added, "And the food isn't half-bad either."

Randi met her for a greeting kiss, delighted to feel Jenna's hands encircle her waist. "You adorable pest," Randi teased.

Jenna sniffed Randi's neck, then lifted an elbow to smell her armpits. "I've got time for a quick shower, don't I? That way we can relax after dinner."

"Sure, but hurry. I don't want to overcook the vegetables and make them mushy," Randi answered.

"Quick as a wink," Jenna vowed. Planting another quick kiss on her lips, Jenna spun and dashed away.

Randi liked showering with Jenna—lathering her up with soap, gliding her hands over her smooth skin and shapely form, checking all the nooks and crannies. It was also invigorating to have her back scrubbed and enjoy Jenna's soapy hands on her body, taunting and teasing as well as washing. Shower time could turn into sex time on a dime. Good thing the master bath was equipped with a roomy, separate shower rather than the confines of a tub shower with a flimsy plastic curtain.

Baths were enjoyable too, with the bath salts or oils, soaking in steaming water, with music and candles. The only problem was the tub wasn't large enough for them both at the same time. Randi reserved bath time for when Jenna had to work late or was out on a stakeout. Thinking about it made her a little dizzy.

By the time Jenna's ten minutes were up, Randi had fed the pets and had dinner and tea on the table. "Did you finish your exams and semester grades?" Jenna asked as she slid into her chair across the small dinette from Randi, wet droplets still moistening her black hair. She was a vision to behold, from her button nose to her firm body and lusciously squeezable breasts and buttocks.

Dynamite comes in small packages, she mused to herself. "I did—all but a couple who have late work," she answered aloud. "But I was firm that tomorrow is the last day for everything."

"Good. This is delicious, by the way. You didn't pick this up at the Wok N Roll Kitchen, did you?"

Randi laughed. "No, silly. You know I made it. I was glad you got home at a decent hour. Did you catch your killer yet?"

"No." Jenna's expression twisted toward frustration. "There are a lot of potential suspects, but none that stand out. I guess the serial killer angle is the best, but I don't know. Too many things don't add up."

"The Baxters are such a nice family," Randi lamented. "I know you're doing everything you can to discover who did it. And not all cases get solved in a week. I mean, don't most take a good, long while? If you don't have him in custody before we leave, you have a strong team, and they'll carry on without you."

"You're right. Only I'm not sure how much longer we'll have Bauman." Jenna stabbed a forkful. "You know how it is when you find someone special." A light returned to her eyes as she flashed them at Randi.

"I do," Randi returned with a wink. After a bite and a deep breath, she said, "I called to check on your mother today."

"And?" Jenna's fork froze in mid-motion, and she met Randi's gaze, appearing breathless. Randi hurried on.

"She said thank you, that the doctor only gave her a few of the strong pain meds and she was about to be out, and that she didn't do it on purpose. She doesn't want you to think that."

"Well, maybe not consciously on purpose," Jenna mumbled and took a breath.

"Jenna, your mother loves you," Randi conveyed with powerful ardor. "She said she doesn't know how to be friends with her grown children."

"Figures. She didn't know how to be friends with her young children either." Jenna took another bite. "I'm not mad anymore—just resigned. I've got to stop getting my hopes up. She just smashes them every time. How do I do it, Randi? And what's the limit? When do I give up?"

Randi stretched her hand across the table and took Jenna's, rubbing a finger over her knuckles and pressing her thumb into her palm. "The only thing you need to give up is expectations. You will keep reaching out and forgiving and showing her love without needing a favorable response. That's what unconditional love is. What I think will help is to really put yourself in her shoes, in her headspace. Look at the world and you and me from her perspective. She's lived her whole life being indoctrinated into Catholic beliefs and traditions and can't do a one-eighty in a year, if ever. She's conflicted and burdened with guilt and who knows what else. So, she can't come to our wedding. We're still getting married."

"You bet your sweet patootie we are!" An aroused gleam lit Jenna's eyes, increasing the brilliance of their blue. "In three days, I get to stand in front of the city and say my vows to you, put a ring on your finger, and you put yours on mine. I don't think I'd have the courage or the confidence to do this with anyone but you."

"You?" Randi couldn't help but laugh. "Lack courage or confidence? Those are two of your strongest virtues, Jenna Ferrari."

"Maybe concerning most things, but not marriage. The thought of turning out like my dad loomed over every relationship I attempted. The fear of suffering rejection made me push away anyone who got close. But it's like you see everything that I'm thinking or feeling and have a way of soothing the savage beast I still fear is inside. Maybe it's in a cage right now, but ... I know you can physically put me in my place if you have to, and I can't express how much of a comfort that is. You stuck with me, and you love me despite all my baggage. I love you, Randi, with everything I am or will ever be. And I am so proud to marry you."

A surge of emotion flowed through Randi at Jenna's words. She squeezed her hand and smiled. "I love thee to the depth and breadth and height my soul can reach when feeling out of sight for the ends of being and ideal grace."

Jenna tilted her head. "That sounds familiar. One of yours?"

Randi chuckled and shook her head. "If only! Elizabeth Barrett Browning. But I do, you know—love you with all my soul can reach, with every breath, every beat of my heart, every firing synapse of my neurons, every dream that fills my sleep, and every thought in my waking day. Remember that when we get on the plane to embark on our surprise honeymoon."

"Ah ha—a clue!" Jenna cheered in triumph. "While I could resort to using my vast collection of resources—namely one Ethan Bauman—I won't spoil your fun. I know I'll love whatever you've concocted in that creative brain of yours. And if it's as good as this stir fry, I will not be disappointed."

Randi grinned with satisfaction.

17

---•◦•---

Thursday, May 16th

Jenna was tired of waiting on science. After filling her favorite, silly coffee mug that read, "I like big busts and I cannot lie," opposite a smiling cartoon cop and his squad car, she marched to the lab. "Good morning, Dr. Gupta." She parked herself in front of the counter, took a sip, and set her mug out of the way. "Surely, you have that genealogy report by now."

"You would be surprised how long it takes to perform a thorough ancestry search," the scientist replied in a lovely, exotic-sounding accent. At once, despite the discouraging report, a feeling of appreciation for Asita Gupta, Jose Marcus, Destiny Wilcox, Rudolph Valentine, and all the brilliant specialists who worked with the department struck Jenna. It was this wedding. It was causing her to be uncharacteristically emotional, and there would be no hugging. Maybe at the church, but categorically, not in the office.

Jenna's anticipation melted. "So, no news," she moaned.

"I didn't say that." With a smirky grin and a twinkle in her brown eyes, Dr. Gupta retrieved a folder and rounded the counter, spreading out the contents before Jenna and herself.

"I knew it!" Jenna enthused, pumped with fresh energy. "You could have been a magician if you weren't a scientist."

"I had extra motivation to move swiftly. I have a wedding to attend on Saturday."

"Oh, do you now?" Jenna pressed her lips together to keep from bubbling. *Bubbling? You're on the job, Jenna. Be professional!*

"Yes. Well, here's what we have on your unclaimed sample of DNA. The first sheet is the basic analysis. We are looking for a male with O-positive blood type—which is the most common one. He has blue eyes and blond hair—although, in many men with the gene for blond hair, it darkens with age and can appear brown, but never black or red. Red hair is a whole other story, and I mustn't go off on a tangent. Depending on his age, it could be gray. The gene for male pattern baldness is present, but there's no determining at what age it might present. Some men with this gene never lose their hair, while others have a receding hairline in their twenties."

While Jenna found this all fascinating, features that may or may not be present weren't of much help to her. "So far, we have a man, O positive, blue eyes, and light-colored hair. Can we get any closer?"

"Let me finish." Dr. Gupta eyed her like a disapproving teacher when Jenna would act out in class. She tapped a finger to a line on the page. "Your suspect has a genetic disorder that will narrow him down significantly from the others; however, it's probable he doesn't know he has it. It's called Fragile X syndrome."

"Fragile X?" Jenna furrowed her brows. "I never heard of it before."

"Well, it's an inherited condition that causes intellectual disability and a range of physical, behavioral, and emotional symptoms. These may include learning difficulties, movement or communication problems, anxiety, or produce no symptoms at all, and still be passed on to their children. In severe cases, it can cause autism, though I doubt your killer is autistic."

"No," Jenna agreed. "That wouldn't make much sense." She thought about the odd, disagreeable Mr. Finstermeier. He indeed displayed anxiety, behavioral, and emotional indicators.

Turning a page, Dr. Gupta continued by pointing to a graph. "Geographic markers place where his ancestors originated. You can see here—51% German, 27% English, 9% French, 6% Danish, 3% Polish, 2.5% Spanish, 1% Italian, and .5% other. It's safe to say your suspect is of northern European descent, non-Scandinavian or Celtic. Of course, German includes Austrian and a whole swath of Hungarian, Danish, Belgian, and Dutch peoples. And who's to say how far back that line goes because Saxons were Germans who invaded—or moved to—England hundreds of years ago. Therefore, his family could have come over from the British Isles as far back as the Mayflower. Then again, they could have immigrated from Germany after World War II."

"Does it tell us how old or how tall he is? Shoe size?" Jenna asked hopefully.

Dr. Gupta shook her head. "No. But based on the standard genetics of that region of the world, we can safely assume he is probably not as tall as he would be with a large Swedish or Norwegian contribution nor as short as if he was predominately Slavic or Mediterranean, as Poles, Spaniards, Portuguese, Greek, and Southern Italians tend to be shorter than other Europeans. However, I can't rule out extreme height or shortness, only that he doesn't carry a dwarfism gene."

Yeah, Jenna thought with long-held regret. *I had to inherit those Southern Italian short genes.*

"Average height or a little on the shorter side would fit with the size nine shoe. We're forming a picture—a broad picture, but a picture all the same. At least we can determine who he isn't," Jenna stated. "Anything else?"

"If you're asking if I've come up with cousins or other relatives to match him to, the answer is that will take a lot longer. While many interested citizens put their DNA test results into ancestry databases in hopes of discovering relatives they were unaware of, many others choose to keep their reports private. Your suspect would have to have relatives who post their genetic samples on the bulletin boards. With the help of a colleague at the University of Virginia, we are searching for familiar markers in common. You do realize all humans share 99% of their DNA, right? We're only testing the one percent of unique genes, and even those contain an ocean of data."

"I realize it isn't as easy as picking plums off a tree. Thanks, Dr. Gupta. I'll work with this, and it helps."

"I have additional data to add to our investigation," Jenna announced upon returning to the office. She waved the file folder, attracting her team's interest. "The DNA genealogy report from the driver's seat of the Baxter's car. We know we're looking for a size nine hiking boot, but this paints a more detailed picture."

Owens shoved the last bite of his cruller into his mouth while Bauman pivoted away from his screens and pushed up his glasses. Jenna shot a glance at Jamison, who just looked gorgeous and smart at the same time.

"We can eliminate anyone who doesn't meet the following criteria: White, male, blue eyes, light-colored hair, of Germanic non-Nordic and non-Celtic descent, with O positive blood type, and a rare genetic disorder called Fragile X syndrome. He carries the gene for male-pattern baldness, which may or may not have presented yet, depending on his age."

"What's Fragile X?" Owens asked, crinkling his nose.

Jenna repeated Dr. Gupta's explanation while Bauman nodded. "That rules out all members of the Mancini family and most members of their organization," he deduced. "Also, the neighbors Mr. and Mrs. Kirby, as they're African American, and Brenda Zellner, who reported the crash, although she was never a strong suspect. On the other hand, that describes about half of the white supremacists in the area if we want to reexamine that angle."

"While Finstermeier fits, he's a long shot," Jamison mentioned, "unlike Ronell Fischer." She pulled up his photo and switched it onto the big screen. "He has light brown hair, blue eyes, and a German surname. While we don't have his shoe size, his driver's license puts him at five-foot-ten and a hundred and sixty-five pounds, so nine is reasonable as a shoe size. In the photo, you can see a high hairline, and it looks a little thin on top to me. Plus, his psychological profile was down to the penny."

Jenna nodded absently as she studied the picture and info on the screen. He certainly seemed to check all the boxes. "The FBI is watching all five of the most likely suspects we pushed to the top of the list. Special Agent Pane said they're still looking for Fischer but I'm sure they'll have eyes on him soon too. Meanwhile, we can't sit around twiddling our thumbs and congratulating ourselves on an unproven theory. Bauman, get me a list of every member of any Whites-only clubs—the Proud Boys, KKK, Patriots First, and all the rest."

"You've got it," he replied and spun back to his keyboard.

Owens cupped a hand to his mouth and whispered to Jenna, "It's Patriot Front."

"Whatever," she muttered. "None of them are worth remembering, stupid assholes. If the Baxters made a habit of leaving their doors unlocked, anyone could have wandered in. Some kid jacked up on drugs, a mental patient who went off his meds, a petty thief. We've got to scour the city until we find a dude to match this DNA, and we have to do it in two days."

Everyone got busy compiling lists of residents who fit the profile. Jenna knew they would range in the thousands, but it had to be done. Most detective work wasn't car chases and shootouts; it was exactly this—looking for a tennis ball in a sea of tennis balls.

When Jenna stared into her empty coffee mug a while later, her office phone rang. "Ferrari."

"Hey, heads up," agent Edan Pane said excitedly. "Two agents from Wytheville just picked up Ronell Fischer outside of a sporting goods store, carrying a brand-new baseball bat, a pair of athletic gloves, and a package of rags. They said he was wearing size nine hiking boots, and they're bringing him to us."

"Hot damn!" Jenna exclaimed. "I'm going to be presumptive here and say I get in on the interview."

"I said you would, especially how you and your team picked this guy out of the pack and showed him to us. They should be here in about an hour."

"I'm on my way," Jenna declared as she spun out of her chair. "Do you want me to bring anything?"

"We've already got your DNA report."

"I've got more. I'll bring it. See you soon, and thanks, Agent Pane."

"Despite the perfunctory plots of cop shows on TV, we don't just swoop in and take over local investigations," she said with a laugh. "I'd be happy if all three states and the federal courts convict him of these murders. I look forward to seeing you again."

"Hey, boss, what's the good news?" Jamison asked.

"I'm meeting Agent Pane to interrogate Fischer. The feds just picked him up. I'd invite you, but I think it's going to be crowded already, and, if we stack up too many cops, we might only get the word 'lawyer' out of him."

"No, I understand," Jamison answered, her tone remaining cheerful. "I have to pick up my dress from the dry cleaners anyway. Can I take an early lunch?"

Jenna flashed her a grin. "Sweetie, you dug Fischer out of the pile. As far as I'm concerned, you can do whatever you want." Then, shooting a commanding stare at Owens and Bauman, she directed, "But in case it isn't him, stay on the hate group angle. I'll be back."

With that, Jenna whipped out of the office with a spring in her step and closing her case on her mind.

18

———◆◇◆———

J enna arrived at the Roanoke FBI office before the agents bringing in Ronell Fischer, and Special Agent Pane met her at the front desk. Shaking hands, Jenna said, "Thank you so much for calling. Remember when I told you we have more?" She passed the report folder to Edan.

"Thanks," she said and almost smiled. Pivoting on her heel, she led Jenna down the hall to a stark interview room wired, no doubt, for sound and video like the RPD's. "Now, what am I looking at?"

"It's a genealogy study on the DNA sample my guys collected from our victim's SUV. Someone drove it off the road and this is that someone. It's consistent with Fischer. What about the evidence you collected from his vehicle, and how'd you manage that?"

"He ran, resisted arrest, and took a swing at an agent with the bat," she answered smugly. "We had probable cause."

"Excellent," Jenna praised. "We don't like it when judges throw out evidence on technicalities."

"The FBI isn't overly fond of that, either."

Sharp, younger Agent Hawkes swept in, wearing his black suit and tie, to join them. "Jones is running the booth," he reported. "Jensen says they're about twenty minutes away."

"In that case, let's head over to the lounge for a Coke, and I'll fill you in on how I want to run this," Pane suggested.

She shared the evidence collected from Fischer's van and her strategy, gaining Jenna's confidence that this would work. Bees buzzed in her stomach instead of butterflies as Jenna's anticipation grew. *Close this case today, the paperwork tomorrow, and then the wedding. We didn't forget anything, did we? That's what the rehearsal is for, to make sure. I hope Randi'll like the vows I wrote. I don't think anything can beat what she said to me last night.*

Half an hour later, Agents Pane and Hawkes sat with Jenna across from a twenty-five-year-old man with a high hairline of sandy-loam strands sticking up like a fist full of straw. He wore a blue and navy button-up shirt, checked in a tight, fine pattern, and khaki pants over brown suede hiking boots. A shiner marred the flesh around one blue eye. He sat expressionless, as though he had been hewn from granite. To ensure no more misbehavior on his part, a two-foot chain connected Fischer's handcuffs to the loop on the steel table, which was securely bolted to the floor.

"For the record, today is Thursday, May 16th, ten-twenty a.m.," Edan stated. "Special Agents Pane and Hawkes of the Roanoke FBI office and Lieutenant Detective Ferrari of the Roanoke Police Department are present in this interview with Ronell Fischer of Hazleton, Pennsylvania. Mr. Fischer, have you been read your rights?"

The morose young man passed a veiled stare from Edan to Dustin to Jenna, without saying a word. He posed as if having his portrait painted—spine erect, shoulders squared, chin slightly raised. Only his steely expression spoiled the illusion.

"You have the right to remain silent," Dustin recited. "Anything you say can be used against you. You have the right to have an attorney present for questioning. If you cannot afford an attorney, one will be provided for you. Do you understand your rights?"

Fischer shifted his glare to Dustin and flared his nostrils.

"Mr. Fischer, I see you are observing your right to remain silent," Edan said. "But please tell me, are you on any medications or other substances?" He snorted with a sarcastic eye roll. "Are you having any trouble understanding where you are or what's going on in this proceeding?"

Fixing his gaze on Agent Pane, he lifted both middle fingers at her.

"I'll take that as a yes," she stated neutrally. "Let the record show Mr. Fischer responded with an obscene gesture. Please be advised that this interview is being recorded."

"Mr. Fischer, may I offer you a drink?" Dustin asked. "Water, coffee, a soft drink?"

Ronell narrowed his eyes at Agent Hawkes. "Do you think I'm stupid? You're trying to trick me into getting my DNA. I watch TV."

"Suit yourself," Dustin responded apologetically.

"Have you ever been interviewed by law enforcement before?" Edan asked while Jenna studied Fischer's every response. He seemed completely void of emotion except for paranoia. Paranoia wasn't an emotion, yet he seemed suspicious without being thrown into the fear column.

The intensity of the man's deadpan stare transformed his youthful visage, making him look ten years older. "Yes, and no. You know this. After the accident, the police talked to me for hours on end."

"Tell us about that," Jenna prompted. "I know it must have been impossible. There you were—a victim of a crash that killed your bride. They should have been providing you comfort and support, calling in the chaplain, not harassing you in your grief."

Fischer cocked his head at Jenna as if examining her under a microscope. "You talk like you understand. You're just trying to play me."

"No, really," Jenna responded, imitating Jamison's natural empathy. "I'm about to be married, and I can't imagine anything more heartrending. Tell us about it."

Fischer had to lean slightly forward to brush his fingers through his hair due to his restraints. It was then Jenna noticed he was still wearing his wedding ring. For the loss of his young bride, Jenna could honestly feel compassion for him, but the thought of his innocent victims froze her heart.

A shoulder muscle loosened, and he released a sigh. "They called it a no-fault accident," he said in a human voice. "I'm sure you studied every detail of my life, the abuse, abandonment, foster system, the bullying ... But I got a job for a cleaning products company and excelled. I got put in charge of distributing sample products to businesses all up and down Interstate 81. It was a good fit for me because I didn't have to get along with co-workers, just give short presentations. I spent most of my time alone."

Fischer shifted in his seat, assuming a more comfortable position, and a light flickered behind his eyes, bringing them to life for a brief second. "I met Hannah at a networking mixer my boss ordered me to attend. I expected to be bored and have a horrible time, and I would have if Hannah hadn't spilled her drink on me. It might be cliché, but it started us talking and led to a date. I'd had a few dreadful dates, but Hannah really got me. She was the nicest person I'd ever met, and she shared her music, poetry, and dreams with me. She said she was normally shy, but she felt a kindred spirit with me. We were each other's first real relationship. Two years later, I asked her to marry me, and she said yes. I was never so happy and thought my bad luck was behind me."

"There's no doubt you had a rough start," Edan sympathized, "and to lose the love of your life must have been devastating."

He flicked a mechanical glance at her before returning it to Jenna. "We were married for fifteen days. I was driving home from a party at Hannah's friend's house, and it was very dark—no moon, or maybe it was behind clouds. This big semi-truck's lights were blaring in my face, blinding me. He must have had his brights on and didn't dim them. Plus, there were all these lights all over the cab." His tone hardened, anger and anxiety cutting through, and he flexed his hands into fists.

Emotion is good, Jenna thought. *Now we might get somewhere.*

"There was something in the road, but I couldn't see it for those damn lights! I felt the car hit it, a front tire blew, I lost control of the wheel, and the next thing I knew ..."

Fischer stopped to compose himself. No one spoke while they waited for him. When he continued, he resumed his detached manner.

"I woke up in the hospital. It was hours before they told me Hannah had died. A police officer talked to me, asking about details of the accident. I told him what I told you—it was the truck driver's fault. There should be laws against all those blinding lights. When I got out of the hospital, the cops had me come in and they asked questions for hours, then declared it a no-fault accident."

"Did the police ever try to blame you?" Jenna asked.

He took in a breath and released it before answering. "They never accused me, but I could tell they thought it was my fault. Why else would they keep asking questions, like they expected me to slip up and give a contradictory response?" A hard, excruciating glower enveloped his ordinary-looking face.

"Did you ever blame yourself?" Silence hung in the room after Edan's question.

"By all accounts, it was a tragic accident," Jenna said after a minute. "You shouldn't blame yourself, but I can understand why someone would. 'I was driving. If I had done something different, if we had left sooner, or later, if I had stopped or not stopped somewhere, I wouldn't be passing that truck at the same time a foreign object obstructed my lane.'"

"It was the truck driver's fault, and he didn't even stop. The car behind us called 911, and its driver moved the debris from the road. He's a hero; that truck driver is a killer. He killed my wife."

"I don't think the truck driver intended to kill anyone," Dustin said, gaining him a glare from Fischer.

"It wasn't my fault," he declared sternly.

"What about Hannah's family?" Jenna asked with sensitivity. "Did they blame you?"

"At first, yes. They were distraught and angry, but, after the police called it an unavoidable accident, they apologized and reached out to me. We all took it hard."

"I'm sure you did," Edan affirmed. "And the accident occurred about a month ago?" He gave a somber nod. "What about your employer?"

"He understood. He gave me as much time off as I needed. After two weeks, I had to get out of the apartment and back on the road. I was going crazy. Everything reminded me of Hannah. So, I was back making my rounds when these FBI goons showed up out of nowhere and punched me in the face." He motioned toward his shiner.

"Agent Jensen said you ran, resisted arrest, and assaulted him with a baseball bat," Dustin said.

Fischer's glare shot darts at the agent. "I didn't know they were law enforcement. Big goons with guns—of course I ran. People steal our samples when they can. Our cleaning products are the best on the market, guaranteed," he rebutted in a huff.

"I'm sure they are," Jenna agreed. "I'll bet they can even get blood out of carpets."

"Damn right," he replied. "And wine, tomato sauce, coffee, chocolate—even dirty, black, motor oil. They leave carpets and hard floors looking brand new. So yeah, people try to steal them. And they think I have money on me. So, I ran, and I fought back. When the dust settled and they could show me their badges, I cooperated—just like I'm doing with you."

Jenna flicked a glance at Edan, and she continued with the next question.

"Mr. Fischer, do you know George and Kathy Waite of Syracuse, New York?" The experienced agent placed a wedding photo of the couple facing Fischer on his side of the table. "Maybe you did business with them when you were in Syracuse."

Jenna detected the vein in his temple pulse and a slight twitch disturb his cheek. Aside from the subtle response, he remained impassive. "I don't recall their names or faces."

Placing another wedding picture before him, Edan asked, "What about Haval and Aveen Barzani? They're from Binghamton, New York. Do you recall them?"

Fischer ground his teeth and wiped a hand across his mouth. "Nope. Don't know them."

"But you do have a stop on your route in Binghamton," Edan half-stated, half-asked.

"There's fifty-thousand people in Binghamton. You expect me to know them all?"

"What about this couple?" She pushed across another wedding portrait. "Jacob and Emily Dierdorff, Harrisburg, Pennsylvania."

"Look, agent," he said in a bored tone. "I don't know any of these people. What do they have to do with me?"

"Because our agents found all these in a lockbox in your van," Dustin declared with authority. He slapped newspaper clippings of their wedding announcements on the table in front of him.

Fischer's face reddened and his cool eyes blazed hot, yet he merely shrugged. "I started collecting wedding photos from the paper months before we got married. Hannah and I wanted to see what other couples were wearing. I guess I continued to clip them out of habit. And what were you doing opening my lockbox anyway? You just blew your case," he smirked.

Dustin passed him the warrant. "You shouldn't have attacked our agents. It gave us probable cause to search your van, and a judge signed the warrant."

With a sneer and a hint of erupting anger, Fischer replied, "You can take this warrant and shove it up your ass!" He thrust it back at Agent Hawkes with a look of contempt.

"Then how do you explain these?" Edan set the foot-long metal box on the table and withdrew items. "A pair of women's panties, a man's wedding ring, a pair of earrings, a locket with tiny pictures of Emily and Jacob Dierdorff inside, a watch with George Waite's name etched on the back? Just what were you planning to do with that baseball bat, Mr. Fischer?"

"Start a new sport," he snarled. "That's all circumstantial."

Jenna shrugged. "Maybe. But we also have DNA from your latest victims' crime scene. Now, how could that have gotten there if you saw none of these couples?"

His solid wall of control blasted apart in an explosion of fury. "You're lying! You didn't find my DNA anywhere."

"Because you thought you were so careful," Edan supposed, "wearing gloves, possibly a surgical mask and cap, so no hair or sneeze droplets could be left behind to tie you to the murder victims. Only, you couldn't protect against sweat. It seeps through clothing, drips off your body, and is most inconvenient. We've got you. Now, why not walk us through it?"

He glowered and tried to cross his arms over his chest, except the restraints prohibited him. "You can't know that's my DNA. It isn't in the system. It's not on file anywhere. You're just making things up to trick me."

"But this warrant," Dustin held it up again, "permits us to take your cheek swab now."

On cue, a lab tech walked in with a sterile swab and a glass vial.

A look of genuine shock spread over his expression, like cracks in a windshield that had been hit by a rock. "How did you even know to look for me? There's nothing tying me to any of these dead couples. There was no goddamn reason for FBI agents to be looking for me!"

"It's called police work," Jenna stated. "The FBI and Roanoke Police divided up thousands of potential suspects based on a psychological profile and other particulars, and a member of my team picked you based on how your story lines up with the murders. She's got a good eye and excellent instincts."

He merely stared at Jenna in disbelief for an instant.

"Now, Mr. Fischer, we can avoid the humiliation of a trial and maybe even work a deal for diminished capacity because of your recent trauma, but, to do that, we need you to tell us what happened. Why did you kill total strangers for seemingly no reason?"

Tick by tick, he pivoted his face to Edan. He propped his elbows on the table and steepled his fingers, regaining his passionless demeanor. "I was textbook perfect. There is no explanation for how you rent-a-cops discovered it was me. I'll do as you request on one condition." His penetrating gaze bore into Edan's as he flicked a finger toward Jenna. "That the detective who pulled my name out of thousands and said, 'he's the one,' is here asking the questions. I'll talk to her, and her alone."

19

Special Agents Hawkes and Jensen escorted Ronell Fischer to a holding cell and offered him lunch, which he refused, while Jenna called Jamison and filled her in.

"I'll be right there," she assured her. Then Jenna joined Edan for a quick bite at a Greek place down the street.

When Jamison arrived, Jenna and Edan briefed her and replayed a bit of their earlier interview.

"He specified he'd talk to you and you alone," Edan told her. "People like this are very unpredictable, but he'll be chained, so you should be safe. Just don't get close to him, do you understand? We'll be right next door in the observation booth and an armed agent will be standing by on the other side of the door."

"I'm not worried," Jamison responded in a professional tone. "Jenna and I have interviewed murderers before."

"But have you ever been in a room with one alone?" Agent Pane raised a brow at her.

"I have full confidence in my detective," Jenna encouraged. "Trisha is smart and instinctual. She has a way of coaxing things out of suspects and witnesses alike. Let's be clear—I'd rather be with her. But she can get the job done, and you can take that to the bank."

"Thanks, Ferrari." Jamison met her gaze with assurance. "I'll try to make you proud."

Jenna wanted to break into a sappy smile, hug her partner, and proclaim how she always made her proud. Considering the setting, she merely nodded and turned her over to Agent Hawkes. Then she and Edan stepped into the booth where a tech already had sound and video running.

Ronell Fischer didn't look like a serial killer. Then again, what did a serial killer look like? Jenna reconsidered. He didn't look like a hardened criminal who had spent years in a penitentiary, boasting no tattoos or scars from a fight. Neither was there anything particularly sinister in his presence. Maybe that was because he had only started killing a few weeks ago. He had already revealed much. Hopefully, he would spill his guts to Jamison, and that would be that.

Trish had taken a few minutes to freshen up, brush her coppery strands to a brilliant shine, give her cosmetics an expert touch, and arrange the lay of her knee-length gray skirt and friendly floral blouse just so. She unfastened the top button for good measure and strode in on sturdy heels.

Jenna's anticipation level skyrocketed when she witnessed Fischer's jaw go slack and his eyes light at the sight of her detective. He abandoned his robotic posture and leaned his elbows on the table, studying her in wonder. "Are you Detective Jamison?"

"I am," she replied. Jamison unclipped her shield from her belt and opened its black leather backing so he could see her photo and read her name.

"It looks real," he confirmed.

"Perhaps you think I'm too young to be a detective or too attractive to be intelligent," Jamison stated with official elocution. "But earlier this week, as Lieutenant Ferrari and I scrolled through endless pages of licensed drivers who fit our profile, something about you stood out. I looked closer, dug out the details, and added your name to our list of most likely suspects. It takes diligence and focus, but not an extraordinary amount of talent or experience. I'm familiar with your file, and I understand what a traumatizing blow it was to lose the woman who had finally made your life complete."

Fischer leaned back, his aspect returning to cold cynicism. "You only know what someone wrote in a report. Don't think for a minute that you know or understand me, what I've been through, what torture does to a child's development, how it twists up fact and fantasy, right and wrong. There have been times I didn't even know who I was. Then I found Hannah. With her help, I could be normal. For the first time in my life, I felt loved. When I look at you, Detective Jamison, I see a happy childhood, a comfortable, stable home, and an excellent education. I see money and privilege and every advantage a person could hope for. Don't pretend to know where I come from or what makes me tick."

Jamison folded her hands on the table and gazed at him openly. "Then tell me. Help me understand how killing these couples would improve your life. It certainly wasn't going to bring Hannah back."

"No," he muttered as a hint of sorrow crept into his hard eyes. "I don't know." He propped his elbows on the table and leaned his head into his hands, dragging slender fingers through his straw hair. With a deep sigh, he glanced at Jamison and then away, rearranging his feet. He rubbed his chin pensively, then swung his jaw from side to side.

"The best part of me died with her in that crash. Of course I blamed myself. I blamed the truck driver, the idiot who dropped something in the road, the doctors who couldn't save Hannah, her friends who invited us over that night, the weather, the moon, the stars, God—I blamed everybody. I tried to pull myself out of it, but there was nothing to live for."

Jenna spotted Jamison's characteristic expression of empathy and kindness as she listened to him ramble. Fischer dropped his fists with cuffed wrists to the table, taking on a faraway look. He regarded Jamison curiously and continued to speak.

"I heard a voice—not an audible one but inside, you know? It kept saying, 'Why do all these other young couples get to be happy when your love and joy were taken away?' I felt as if my very soul had been ripped from my body and all that was left was a thick, oily, black substance, a gloom without end, a misery with no relief." Absently, Fischer rolled his thumb and forefinger around each other.

"At first, I pushed back. Then, after a while, I started to believe it. What makes them more worthy than me? Why do they get to live happy lives when I never had—only for a shining moment," he added with a gesture of his first two fingers pressed to his thumb to emphasize the point.

"I started back to work to get my mind off it, but all the long hours of driving gave me just as much time to think. Everywhere I went, I'd stop and buy a Sunday paper with all the wedding announcements. I cut out pictures of the couples our age who looked the most joyful and beamed at each other with unblemished love and devotion. It's not that I wanted to kill them—I just hurt so bad, and there was no reprieve. I remember feeling like I was falling down a deep, deep, bottomless well, tumbling into darkness. I began to think about things Hannah and I might be doing if she were with me. And I saw these happy couples getting to do them. It wasn't fair."

"No, Ronell, it wasn't fair," Jamison sympathized. "But it wasn't George and Kathy Waite's fault. It wasn't fair that they be murdered. Why them?"

"Because," he answered with a puzzled expression, suggesting Jamison—and the entire world—should understand. "They taunted me. You saw their wedding photo. It's like they were laughing at me, rubbing it in my face. I had to hit them in the head. That's how the doctor said Hannah died—traumatic brain injury from a massive head wound. Once they were lying there dead, I thought, 'That won't do.' So, I took them to their bedroom and undressed them, then arranged them in bed, cuddled together, like a loving couple should be. That seemed better ... peaceful," he decided.

"That's when it hit me—I helped these newlywed couples freeze the moment in time when they were most blissful and brimming with promise. By killing them right then, when they were riding the high of an inexplicable joy, I was doing them a favor. I wasn't the bad guy here, but the hero, preserving the moment for all eternity. Because of me, they'll never argue and fight; they'll never cheat or get a divorce; they'll never get old and crotchety." His countenance darkened. "They'll never abuse or abandon their children."

A sick feeling surged through Jenna as if she had ingested a bowl full of slimy slugs. If he was telling the truth—and he probably was—this was a very warped individual. That's what happens when you let darkness consume you, when you do nothing to halt your descent down the rabbit hole. She knew those dank places, icy cold and blanketed in coal dust. She had glimpsed them, dipped her toe in, and made a conscious choice of her will to pull it out. Yet even though such temptation lurked in the recesses of her psyche, Jenna felt confident that, even if the worst happened, she wouldn't plummet to their depths. Randi's faith and optimism had their talons dug deep enough into her soul as to keep her from falling. *Even if death steals her from me, I'll never become him.* The thought brought Jenna solid comfort.

Jamison maintained perfect professionalism, avoiding any recoil or expression of disgust. She merely nodded and continued with the next question. "How did you gain access to their home?"

"I watched them for a few days," he responded with a shrug, "checked their social media. They were perfect—so much like Hannah and I were. It was hard to wait and plan, but I was disciplined. I had seen George go in and out of the house through their garage door several times and knew it was unlocked. When I noticed nobody else in the surrounding houses outside and no cars driving by, I took my tire iron, waltzed right into the open garage, and through the door. It was so easy. I hadn't thought it would be so easy," he mused, cocking his head, "but it was."

In a display of patience and stamina Jenna had seldom witnessed, Jamison walked him through each of the next two murders. Once he reverted to expounding about the cruelties he suffered as a child, which Jenna had to admit surpassed her experiences—if the tale was true. Occasionally, Fischer would get off on a tangent or interject psychotic fantasies, but the intrepid detective steered him back on track each time. A bubble of warm pride in Trish welled within Jenna's chest. She had picked her for her team, taught and molded her, and encouraged her to take her detective exam. Still, if Jamison hadn't had the goods, she wouldn't be in that room today.

Three hours later, they finally got to the part about Alexia and Nolan. Jenna sat up and listened closely.

"Let's talk about the most recent two victims, the ones from last Saturday in Roanoke." Jamison laid a photograph on the table facing him. Jenna didn't recall seeing a newspaper clipping of the Baxters in Fischer's lockbox, but he might not have had a chance to put it in there. Or he could have left it at home in his residence.

"Nolan and Alexia Baxter."

Fischer fingered the glossy print, picked it up, and studied it with a peculiar expression. "Yes, this would be a good choice. Note how their heads lean into each other, how close their shoulders press together. You can see in the glow on their faces how in love they are. But they weren't the next on my list. I hadn't picked up a Roanoke paper, so I didn't see them."

The breath froze in Jenna's lungs, her heart racing, beating in her ears like a bass drum. She gripped the edge of the equipment table in front of her and leaned closer to the monitor with her jaw clenched.

"Are you certain?" Jamison asked again. "You used a wooden baseball bat, struck them in the head, and posed them in their car. You drove it off the road into a tree, mimicking the accident that killed your wife. We just couldn't ever figure out why you killed their little Pomeranian. Ronell, are you afraid of dogs? Did it try to bite you?"

Fischer set the picture down, the sound of his handcuffs clinking as he ran his fingers through his hair, making it stand out from his skull like a scarecrow's.

"But I didn't. It would've been perfect. Maybe recreating the accident could be my grand finale. Maybe it'll calm this driving urge to kill another couple. The feds caught me buying supplies. I was going to Troutville to stalk the Andersons. If they were truly in love ... but I didn't think about recreating the crash."

"Are you telling me you killed the three other couples but not the Baxters?" Jamison asked, her voice strained and rising in pitch.

"Saturday, I was giving a presentation at an office building in Hagerstown. You can check. There were at least twenty representatives of companies with offices in the building present." Fischer touched his chin and stared into space. "Re-create the accident. Why didn't I think of it? That's what I'll do."

"Mr. Fischer." Jamison addressed him in the soothing tone one uses to deliver unpleasant news. She collected the photograph, withdrawing it to her side of the table. He peered back at her questioningly.

"You won't be killing any more couples or staging an accident. The federal agents will take care of you now. They'll get you a lawyer and talk about how to proceed, but you aren't going to leave here a free man to continue this."

His expression fell into a disappointed pout.

"I know how difficult and unfair life has been for you, but it doesn't give you the right to kill innocent people. The Waites, the Barzanis, and the Dierdorffs had nothing to do with your wife's death. They didn't deserve what you did to them, and you must pay the consequences for your actions. Maybe with enough counseling and psychiatric care, you can at least regain some semblance of humanity. You'll spend the rest of your life institutionalized, but at least you'll have a life. You took that away from your victims."

He shot her an icy glare and flared his nostrils.

"Yes, I know you were a victim too. But smashing their happiness, cutting short their lives was wrong, and couldn't ever rebuild your own joy. Just because you were hurting didn't give you the right to inflict pain and premeditated murder on others. Do you understand what you did was wrong?"

That point was important from a legal standpoint. Jenna would praise Jamison for this interview.

Fischer's resistance wavered. His shoulders slumped and his brow furrowed as he tossed his head from side to side. "I knew it wasn't right," he huffed out. "I just didn't care." Lowering his face into his hands, Ronell Fischer wept.

20

Friday, May 17ᵗʰ

J enna's disappointment had been palpable when she realized that Ronell
Fischer hadn't killed Nolan and Alexia. His alibi checked out, and he
had no reason to lie about that murder after confessing to the others.
She expressed her pride in Jamison, who was completely drained after her
performance in the interview. Jenna sent her home and, after checking back
in with Owens and Bauman, went home herself. Randi indulged her with
pizza for the second time in a week and snuggled with her on the couch to
watch back-to-back episodes of *Rizzoli and Isles*. It was completely unre-
alistic, but Jenna and Randi both loved the main characters' relationship
and banter. Not an episode passed without one of them hollering, "See!
The writers toy with us. These two should *so* be a couple!"

It was the relaxing night Jenna needed after being bumped back to
square one in her case. She *would* discover who killed the couple and their
dog; it just might be after returning from her honeymoon.

"I've got an easy day," Randi told her at breakfast. "Update late grades,
oversee discussion for the students who bother to come, and upload final
grades online. Then two whole weeks before summer classes start, and I
only have two. I'm going to get so in shape this summer!"

"You're already an Amazon," Jenna commented between bites of bacon and eggs. "I'll bet you want to go to that ninja gym."

Randi's mouth fell open. "How did you know?"

"I'm a detective," Jenna smirked.

"Don't you want to come with me?"

Jenna glanced down at her body. "I've watched that show, you know. My boobs are too big. I'll stick to punching bags and mat sparring."

Randi's brown eyes sparkled at her. "I think your boobs are just right. May I add wrestling and grappling to our floor exercises?"

Jenna cracked a smile. "I thought that's what we always end up doing anyway."

Randi winked before switching gears. "I know you want to catch this killer, but, remember, the rehearsal is at six o'clock. Then we have the rehearsal dinner afterward, so—"

"I know," Jenna affirmed. "I'll be on time."

"We need all your wedding party cops too," Randi reminded her. "Angie said she and Vince will be in this afternoon. I told them they were welcome to stay here, but she insisted she and Vince were staying at a hotel. I tried to tell her they wouldn't be in the way."

"Yeah. It's OK. Everything will be wonderful. I promise not to ruin the occasion."

"You can't ruin it, Jenna," Randi encouraged. "You're the reason for the occasion in the first place. Whatever happens will be precisely what is supposed to happen."

Jenna rose from the table and leaned over to kiss Randi's lips. "I will not be late, and hopefully not bleeding or wearing a black eye."

Shooting her a horrified expression, Randi gasped. "Jenna! Don't even joke about it."

Jenna laughed. "I love you, and I'm ready to spend the rest of my life with you. See you at six."

After filling her coffee mug, Jenna waved for her team to join her around the table in the middle of the room. "Owens, Bauman, you should have seen our young woman running that interview like a seasoned FBI director. She was outstanding."

Trisha blushed. "I just asked the questions Jenna and Agent Pane gave me."

"No," Jenna rebutted. "You handled that murderer with finesse and professionalism. Unfortunately, he wasn't our guy. So, where did y'all get with the hate groups?"

Owens leaned back in his chair and linked his fingers over his protruding gut. "The hard thing is finding folks whose DNA isn't in our database. So many members of these groups are also petty criminals and drug dealers. We made a list of thirteen men who have a violent history but no felonies and the light-colored hair, blue eyes, et cetera."

"Then we scrutinized their activities on Saturday," Bauman picked up. "Two were on-shift at their jobs, one posted a video of a pool party he and his wife attended, one was still in lockup from a drunk and disorderly Friday night. That left us with nine who we can bring in for interviews today if you want us to."

"How many names did you go through to get these thirteen?" Jenna asked.

"Sixty or seventy," Owens supposed. "I hate to say it, but that's probably fewer than half of the pool."

Jenna sipped her coffee with deliberation. "You know, there's someone else we could take a look at. Jamison, remember when we talked to Ralph and Carlin Halbach at their house the other day?" She nodded. "I thought nothing of it then, but, when I told them the Baxters had been murdered, Carlin said, 'Murdered right there in their home next door,' or something to that effect."

"Yeah, I remember," Jamison said. "He was acting worried for his father's safety."

"Only I never said they were killed in the house. Sure, it's a safe assumption, but they were found in their car, and theoretically could have been killed anywhere. Then there's the fact he works as a security guard. He would have a bat or nightstick. I know the lab said, based on the size of the wounds, a baseball bat was the weapon, but we haven't seen Carlin's bully stick. Maybe it's thicker than standard."

"Both he and Ralph are matches to the genealogy report," Jamison mentioned. "Ralph has lost a heap more hair than Carlin, but as Dr. Gupta told you, the gene might be present without presenting."

"What I'm not getting," Bauman interjected, "is motive. Why would an elderly veteran—respectable by all accounts—or his fifty-year-old son want to kill this young, newlywed couple?"

"I stood toe to toe with Ralph," Jenna declared, "and, even though he was fit for an old guy, I don't think he could have put Nolan in the front seat of the SUV—Alexia, maybe, but not Nolan. Sure, his shoes could be a size nine, but, if he jumped out of a moving vehicle, he'd have probably fallen and broken a hip."

"True," Jamison mused. "Still, I don't see how Carlin could have whacked the neighbors without his dad knowing about it. Do you think they were in it together?"

Owens shook his head. "I think you two are grabbing at straws. Some old geezer and his security guard son killing their next-door neighbors for no reason?"

"Well, now," Bauman considered. "Just because we don't know what the reason was doesn't mean there wasn't one. Maybe a simple altercation that got out of hand."

"Yeah, but neither father nor son had even the slightest injury," Jenna noted.

Jamison displayed a worried, sorrowful, pitiful expression. "When we talked to folks, everyone said Picasso was adorable, cute, sweet, and so forth, except Mr. Halbach used the term, 'yappy,' and seemed irritated with her barking."

"You don't kill someone because their dog barks," Owens exclaimed.

Jenna's spirit sank, and she bemoaned, "There was that kid who killed another kid because he used the neighborhood court to play basketball. And the hulky white supremacist who killed a Black kid for skimming three hundred dollars from his mom's bank account. The bozo who tried to kill a random psychic for something a practitioner in Louisiana did, and let's not forget the meth lab operators who blew themselves up because they were idiots. Owens, you forget—people don't need a legitimate reason for the cruel and stupid things they do."

"Do you really think they could have done it?" Bauman asked.

"I know I want to bring them in for another interview, on my turf this time," Jenna stated. "But I need more information. Bauman, do your magic and find out where Carlin was on Saturday. We had no reason to ask him before, but that will be one of my first questions. I want to catch him in a lie."

"You've got it!" Bauman leaped up from the table and hurried to his computer to start his search.

"Owens, do a deeper run on Ralph and Carlin—finances, complaints. See what happened to Ralph's wife. Pay special attention to a recent stressor that might have given one or both of them a short fuse or emotional distress." With a nod, he pushed his bulk from his chair.

"If it's there, I'll find it."

"Jamison." Jenna met her gaze. "I want both of their residences searched, but I'm not sure we can get a judge to sign off on a warrant. We need something more than a vague genealogy DNA report, but we need a warrant to get their DNA."

"Unless they leave it in a public area," Jamison suggested. "Maybe we offer them a drink and then collect their cup or bottle."

"Which means they need to think they're coming in to help, and I have to keep them busy long enough for you to get a sample to Dr. Gupta. Even then, we won't have the results until tomorrow."

A sly smile crossed Jamison's lips. "They don't know that."

Jenna returned a conspiratorial smile. She strolled to her desk, looked up their numbers, and used the office phone to make the call. "Mr. Halbach," Jenna greeted, reaching Ralph. "This is Lieutenant Ferrari from RPD. My partner and I talked to you in your home on Wednesday concerning the murders next door."

"Yeah, I remember you," he responded as if he had a glaring toothache. "Whadaya want now?"

"Mr. Halbach, we need you to come in and look at some suspects' photos to see if you recognize any of them. Maybe he was dressed as a delivery person, or you assumed he was a friend of the Baxters. We need you, and it will *really* help us out, especially if you recall one of them. It would be great if Carlin could come too," Jenna added. "We can send a car to pick you up and take you home, so you won't even have to bother driving down that hill."

"Well, now, I s'pose—if you need me," Ralph answered as if he was doing the Roanoke Police and Jenna personally a huge favor. "But Carlin's at work over in Salem at the warehouse."

"That's all right," she said brightly. "I'll call his supervisor and, if he can't come, we'll still have you. You're the more important witness anyway. Does an hour give you enough time to get ready?"

"I'm old, not crippled," he barked. "I can be ready in an hour."

Next, Jenna called and talked to Carlin's employer, who granted permission for her to borrow him for official police business. It was a courtesy she wanted to employ in case this theory was a bust too. Technically, officers could compel him to leave work and come into the station, but no reason to get the man in trouble if it turned out to be a dead end.

Stepping out of the office, she rounded the corner to the front desk. "Hey, Officer Stewart," she called. "I need two patrol cars to bring in suspects. Who's available?"

"The kid and I could do it," Officer Stone volunteered. She strode up in her sharply-pressed uniform and her blonde hair tucked under her cap. Murphy followed close behind.

"What's up, Lieutenant?" he asked with an eager expression on his freckled face.

She filled them in how she wanted Ralph Halbach handled as a witness. They were to be pleasant, appreciative, and all that. Then she nabbed Girard and Campbell to drive over to Salem and collect Carlin Halbach.

Pushing back into criminal investigations, Jenna announced to her team, "We've got one hour to get everything we can on these guys so we can catch them in a lie. If we can't get warrants, it's all for nothing."

"I don't know," Owens disagreed with a shrug. "A confession would be just as good."

21

Bauman hastily handed Jenna a printout. "This is what I traced of Carlin Halbach's movements. I got a video camera shot of him fueling up at a gas station a mile from Mill Mountain Estates at twelve-thirty-six. An intersection cam a block away showed him running the light as it switched from yellow to red at four-eighteen headed away from his dad's neighborhood toward town. No ticket was issued, but the shot was recorded."

"Excellent!" Jenna stuck her thumb up. "Now, wire the lounge for video and sound. I thought that would make a comfortable setting, especially with the tempting vending machines in plain view. Owens?"

"Ralph Halbach was decorated for his service in the U.S. Army during the Vietnam War. After completing his enlistment, he married Marion Berry in 1972 in Richmond, where they lived for six years. Carlin was born in '73 and the couple had two more children before they moved to Roanoke for Ralph's promotion with the post office. Their last child was born here in 1979. Marion was a stay-at-home mom who sold Mary Kay products as a part-time job. I hear women can make good money doing that, especially back then," Owens commented. "My wife's mother sold Mary Kay for thirty years or more—got one of those pink Cadillacs and everything."

Jenna pierced him with an impatient stare. "I'm just saying," Owens responded. "Now catch this; Marion Halbach suffered from Lyme disease about ten years ago, leaving her with a weakened heart. She died of a massive heart attack on May 11th of last year."

"Lyme disease can cause hyperacusis," Jamison inserted. Jenna swung her head around to stare at Jamison in astonishment. Her partner lifted a shoulder. "My favorite cousin is a nurse and, being in the country, where ticks hang out, she's treated patients who had it. While seldom fatal, Lyme disease can leave the person with long-lasting, debilitating effects. One of those could be hyperacusis, making loud noises or those with a certain pitch extremely painful."

"Things like a small dog's barking. Only, if she died last May, that was before Alexia moved in. I assumed it was her dog."

"It was," Jamison confirmed. "But there could have been other dogs in the neighborhood that Marion reacted to. Maybe Picasso reminded Ralph of them and his wife's illness."

"It's no coincidence the Baxters were killed on the anniversary of Halbach's wife's death," Owens declared in flat assurance. "You could be right."

"Owens, I need you on standby," Jenna ordained. "Bauman will run the recording, and Jamison and I will talk to them. Trisha, do you have the suspect photos?"

Jamison held up two books, each containing a hundred suspected criminals' photos. Officer Stewart pushed open the door. "Stone and Murphy are here with Mr. Halbach," he reported. "Girard says they're about five minutes away with the other Halbach."

"Thanks. Please have them bring Carlin to the lounge when they arrive," Jenna instructed. "Jamison and I will take Ralph back there now."

With a grateful nod to Officers Stone and Murphy, Jenna and Jamison greeted Mr. Halbach in the lobby. She could tell he was wearing his dentures—not from any display of teeth but because his lips didn't cave in around the gums, making his face appear sunken as it had before. She paid closer attention to the bald top of his head and the strength of his grip when she shook his hand.

"Thank you so much for coming in this morning to help us identify a viable suspect in Mr. and Mrs. Baxter's murders," Jenna gushed.

He scowled at her as if he had better things to do, then grumbled, "Whatever I can do to help out. Then maybe you'll stop bothering me."

"We surely don't mean to bother you," Jamison hastened to apologize. She slipped her soft hands around his upper arm in a friendly manner, guiding him toward the lounge. "We appreciate your willingness to aid in our investigation. This has been a perplexing case thus far, as we can't find any logical reason for somebody to have killed poor Alexia and Nolan. They were so young and in love with their whole lives ahead of them. And the poor, tiny dog." Jamison laid the sympathy on thick, and Jenna had to bite her tongue. If her partner could guilt this old man into a confession, she considered asking the captain to give her a commendation.

"I reckon there ain't always a reason," he answered in a practical tone. "These no-good hoodlums strung out on drugs—they do crazy things. Don't even remember half the time."

"That's true," Jenna agreed as she held the door open for them. "Which is why we need you to look through these suspect photos. There are too many to simply haul them all in here to interrogate. But if we had a witness who even thought maybe he'd seen one of them hanging around the neighborhood, or the Baxters' house, we'd have a suspect to pursue."

"Here, Mr. Halbach." Jamison motioned to the clean, comfortable couch. "Won't you have a seat?"

With a nod, he complied, and Jenna laid one of the photo books on the coffee table in front of him. Then, with genuine Southern hospitality, Jamison asked, "May I get you a drink? We have coffee from the house pot, not the best," she added in a whisper. "Or I can get you a Coke, juice, or water." She threw a glance over her shoulder at the vending machines.

"I suppose a Coke would be nice," he muttered and opened the book with a shaky hand.

With a brilliant smile, Jamison bounded over to the machine. "What kind do you want?"

"The original Coke-a-Cola is all I drink of that stuff," he grumbled. "It's been around longer than me. Got a nice bite, you know?"

Jenna settled in beside him on the couch without crowding him. "Take your time, Mr. Halbach," she coached. "Study each face carefully. It's all right if you don't recognize anyone. You can't get it wrong."

Jamison brought over a plastic, twenty-ounce bottle of Coke and handed it to him. Ralph absently cracked the lid and took a sip while Jenna pointed to various mug shots. A tiny thrill tingled through her when he took the bait.

He was on the fourth page with a third of his bottle drunk when Officer Girard escorted Carlin into the room.

Jamison popped up from the armchair to greet him. "Mr. Halbach, thank you so much for coming." She met him with an appreciative smile and showed him to a plush chair on Jenna's other side. "May I get you a drink?"

"She got me a Coke," his dad commented in a less irritable tone than Jenna had ever heard him use. He held it up, then took another swig.

Carlin, in contrast, appeared so angry Jenna worried he might explode. "Why did your people drag me out of work to come in here?" Carlin did not sit in the prize chair. Instead, he folded his arms over his chest with a cross expression.

"Didn't Officers Girard and Campbell tell you?" Jenna asked, blinking black lashes over rounded eyes at him.

"They said something about looking at pictures," he grumbled. "I don't know who came and went from Dad's neighbors' house."

"But you were over there from time to time, right?" Jenna prompted. "Maybe once a week? I know you checked on your dad like a dutiful son, especially after your mother passed."

Carlin relaxed his stance while keeping a suspicious gaze on Jenna. "What do you know about that?"

"Not much." Jamison put a cold Coke in his hand, and Carlin sat in the chair.

"Carlin'll do, I s'pose." Ralph glanced at his son and winked. "Yeah, he's over right regular, and sometimes he even stoops to bring his family."

"Dad," Carlin sighed in embarrassed disapproval. Jenna placed the second suspect photo album in front of him.

"Please, Mr. Halbach," Jamison beseeched. "Someone might stand out to you."

With a grimace and a nod, he twisted the top off his bottle and took a drink. "I don't think it will help, but I can look." Jamison beamed at him and sashayed back to her seat on Ralph's other side.

"It must have been difficult losing a wife you'd been married to for over fifty years," Jenna mentioned sympathetically. "I'm getting married tomorrow and I know how devastated I'd be after even a fraction of that time."

Carlin answered for his dad. "It's been quite an adjustment."

Ralph frowned and flipped a page. "Nothin's the same." His words fell with the dismal voice of one who had forsaken the prospect of ever experiencing happiness again. It almost made Jenna feel sorry for him—and would have, had he not been involved somehow in killing the Baxters.

"Would you like to tell us about it?" Jamison asked.

Ralph snarled, "No." However, after exhaling a ragged breath, he did. "I loved Marion. She was a wonderful mother to our children and a model wife. Besides that, we were best friends. Marion was the sunshine, kind of like you," he admitted, glancing at Trisha. "We traveled a bit after the kids moved out and after I retired. Then she contracted Lyme disease, and we had to take it easy. She never complained, not about a thing. Marion was up fixin' breakfast one morning while I was putterin' around the house. We had been banterin' about somethin' or another, when I heard the spatula click on the tile floor and a dish break, then a thud. I knew she had fallen, so I ran in there. Only she hadn't just fallen. I called for the ambulance, but they said she was already dead when they got there. They tried, you know, but she was gone in the blink of an eye. Didn't even get to say goodbye. Her heart. I guess it was too big, 'cause it just exploded—took her on the spot."

"I'm so sorry for your loss," Jenna soothed. "How long ago was this?"

"About a year ago," Carlin answered, as Ralph was almost in tears. "Dad's coping as best he can."

Ralph shoved the book of pictures aside. "Where's the john around here?"

Jenna pressed a button on her phone, and Owens popped his head in the door. "Right this way, Mr. Halbach. I'll show you."

He staggered to his feet and Jamison rose with him, picked up his nearly empty bottle, and handed it to Owens. "We'll get you a fresh one when you come back," she assured him.

"Did you go over to your dad's house on Saturday?" Jenna inquired once Ralph was out of the room.

Carlin took a sip of his Coke and shook his head. "My wife had things for me to do at home. My oldest daughter is expecting a baby in a few months and those women have me hopping." He let out a little chuckle and set his half-drunk bottle on the table. "I'm not seeing anyone I recognize. Maybe this one." He pointed to the most average-looking face in the album.

"Yeah," Jenna responded. "That's good. He's on our shortlist. Do you recall when you saw him? We need someone to put him in the neighborhood on Saturday, but you didn't go over to your dad's then; is that right?"

"That's right. Wednesday when y'all stopped by was the first time I'd been to Roanoke in a week. We live in Salem, you know."

Got you now! Jenna cheered with inward glee. "Hey, I've always been interested in security work. You know the police department doesn't pay nearly enough to get by, and a couple of the guys were talking about getting part-time civilian jobs. Do y'all have badges, radios, and carry nightsticks like on the TV shows?" Jenna hoped this wouldn't come across as making her look too dumb to be believed. But she was *only* a woman, after all.

"My guys have badges, uniforms, radios, the whole nine yards," he answered casually. "Only we carry stunners instead of blackjacks."

Hum, Jenna thought. *Then probably was a baseball bat. If he has a lick of sense, it's long gone, burnt up in a barrel or run through a woodchipper.*

"It's a little too warm in here," Jenna commented with discontent. "I'm going to get a drink. Would you like another? I mean, it's the least I can do for dragging you in here to thumb through suspect photos."

Carlin picked up his Coke and took a long draught. "Ah! Hits the spot. Sure, why not?"

Two clambered out of the machine—one diet and one regular.

"Here, I'll take that for you." Jamison glided over to Carlin with a pleasant smile and collected his bottle. "There's a recycle bin in the front lobby. We like to do our part to help the environment." She flashed him a winning smile and, watching his expression, it left little doubt in Jenna's imagination of what was passing through Carlin's mind.

"Thank you," he politely replied, and Jamison departed with the bottle.

Jenna turned the page, directing his attention away from Jamison's buns of perfection. "How about any of these?" She took a sip of her drink, actually glad for it. It was a little warm in the room—or maybe it was merely her glow of victory.

Jamison returned with Ralph, whom she must have met in the hallway. Jenna glanced up. "Your son recognized one," she reported cheerfully.

"I said maybe," Carlin corrected. "I might have seen him."

"I want to go home now," Ralph grumbled. "I don't remember seeing any of these people. I mind my own business. Did you talk to Kirby?"

"Yes, Mr. Halbach," Jamison answered, ushering him toward his seat on the couch. "He explained they were only shouting to be heard over the lawn mower, that there wasn't an argument at all."

"Well, I heard yellin'." With a sour glower, Ralph lowered himself back onto the couch.

After about ten more minutes of fruitless photo-perusing, Owens marched in and assumed an intimidating stance. "Lieutenant, Dr. Gupta is running the comparison right now. She should have the results in about an hour. Do you want me to go ahead and read Carlin his rights?"

"What!" Carlin exploded out of his chair, fists clenched. "Read me my rights for what?"

"Then I can take the search warrant over to Judge Hopkins to sign," Jamison confirmed.

"Just one damn minute!" Carlin thundered. "Rights? Warrant? What are you talking about?"

"The murders of Alexia and Nolan Baxter." Jenna rose to stand beside Carlin, unmoved by his anger. As Owens recited the Miranda Rights, Ralph sighed and leaned deep into the cushions, casting his gaze at the ceiling and letting his mouth drop open.

"Do you understand these rights?" Owens asked. "Would you like me to call for an attorney?"

"Damn right, I do!" Carlin thundered. "You brought us down here on false pretenses. You have no evidence, no proof. And what results will be ready in an hour? I demand an explanation."

"The DNA results from your soda bottles compared to the sample we swabbed from the driver's seat of Nolan Baxter's car," Jamison explained, now in the voice of a seasoned cop.

"Hey, you need a warrant before you collect our DNA," Carlin protested. "My lawyer will have this whole stupid mess thrown out."

Jenna shook her head. "Not if you hand us the bottles with your DNA on them. And you lied about staying home on Saturday. We've got you on multiple traffic cameras and putting gas in your car less than a mile from your father's house at twelve-thirty-six. Then we have you running a red light on the way out of town after four o'clock. You spent quite a lot of time on Mill Mountain."

"Circumstantial." Carlin jutted out his chin and clenched his jaw. "I didn't kill anyone. I've never killed anyone in my life. I'm not saying another word until that attorney gets here. Did you call one, or do I have to do that?"

Jenna opened her phone and punched in a number. "Who's on call for public defender?"

"Carol Banning."

"How soon can she be here?"

"Urgent, huh? OK, she's in here entertaining the whole office, so fifteen minutes?"

"Excellent," Jenna replied. "Mr. Halbach, you're in luck. Carol Banning is top-notch, and our prosecutor will have his work cut out for him. The thing is, if you didn't know the Baxters well, how are you going to explain how your sweat got all over the driver's seat of their car?"

"You said it yourself," Ralph stated, drawing all attention to him. He looked weary and old as he slouched into the sofa cushions. "Because he's a good son."

—◄●◆●►—

22

"Dad, not another word," Carlin commanded. "Wait for our lawyer to get here."

"Why? You didn't do anything except try to help me out of a mess. Let me tell the officers what happened."

"No, Dad; you're old. Detectives," Carlin implored, extending open palms toward Jenna and Jamison. "He doesn't know what he's saying."

"I damn well do!" Ralph shouted. He pointed a finger at his son from where he sat, and snarled, "Don't make me out to be some feeble-minded geezer. I don't want to live in that house without your mother another minute. Prison'll be like the Army. Besides, the jury might take pity on me. Lieutenant Ferrari, I'll tell you what happened, but you have to promise my boy doesn't go to jail."

"Mr. Halbach," Jenna replied sincerely, "I can't promise anything until I know what happened, other than I'll be fair. Maybe you should wait for—"

The door slammed open and an elegant, older woman in a power suit and heels promenaded in as if she was the CEO of a Fortune 500 company. "Ferrari!" She thrust up her chin in a huff. "How dare you interview my clients without me being here to represent them? I mean, really! This is outrageous!"

She sure got here fast! Jenna felt like shrinking in apology but understood it was best to stand her ground when dealing with the shark, Carol Banning. Her honey hair was wrapped in an elegant chignon and her sharp blue eyes bore holes into Jenna. Before she could reply, the woman's demeanor spun on a dime, and she presented a charming smile to Carlin.

"I'm Ms. Carol Banning, the finest defense attorney in the state. I'm even considering running for office. Pleased to make your acquaintance." Jenna supposed with her money and connections, she could not only run but win.

Dumbfounded, Carlin introduced himself and his father.

"Now, who is charged with what?" the corporate lawyer turned public defender demanded.

"Two counts of homicide and one count of cruelty to animals for Halbach senior and accessory after the fact and disposal of bodies for Carlin," Jenna informed her. "Possibly conspiracy; we haven't gotten that far."

Jenna could picture Jamison looking like Carol in thirty years—still slender with a stunning figure, gorgeous, fiery, and in charge. However, her friend would always be sweeter than the legal eagle who had just burst in on Ralph's confession.

"Really, Lieutenant Ferrari—the lounge?" Banning slapped a hand on her hip and rolled her eyes. "I need a few minutes alone with my clients and we will meet you in your interview room—like professionals."

"Ten minutes, please," Jenna stipulated and exited with Jamison and Owens.

"They had to draw her," Owens grumbled as they moved down the hallway to Interview A.

"She'll keep us on our toes, make sure it's by the book," Jenna explained. "That way, when—or if—this goes to trial, there won't be any screwups."

"I guess," he groaned and held the door for Jenna and Jamison.

A short while later, Ms. Banning, with her clients in tow, clicked in and took the middle chair across from them. Jenna couldn't ever remember having six people squeezed into the space.

"Alright," Carol began with a more civil intonation. "Ralph Halbach has informed me he wishes to make a statement. They told me how you acquired their DNA, and, while admissible, it was an underhanded trick." She scowled at Jenna like a nun at Catholic school. "Ralph says he grants permission for you to search his residence; however, I insist on there being a warrant drawn up to cover all the bases. I'll also be speaking with ADA Altman about a deal due to my clients' cooperation and his age," pointing to the older of the gentlemen, "and extenuating circumstances."

Jenna opened her mouth to object, but Banning held up a hand. "I'm not suggesting he get off scot-free. But, if we go to court, that is precisely what could happen. You better believe I can gain sympathy for him with a jury. Just bear in mind, Ralph will give you a confession based on Carlin being charged with only unlawful disposal of human remains and be sentenced to community service."

"I can't promise what a judge or ADA Altman will agree to," Jenna informed her, "but depending on Ralph Halbach's testimony, I will consider dropping the accessory charges against Carlin. You understand that Alexia and Nolan Baxter deserve justice, no matter the extenuating circumstances. Ralph bludgeoned them to death—a young couple with their whole lives ahead of them—for no comprehensible reason."

"My sympathies for the young couple, but this was all a tragic mistake. All right, Ralph," Carol said to her client. "Tell them what happened."

Ralph looked remorseful, something Jenna realized could influence a jury. Add his age, his military service, and all the character witnesses Banning would put on the stand, Jenna hoped for a plea bargain rather than a trial.

"Saturday was May 11th, the first anniversary of my wife's death," he began. "I woke up knowin' that and wasn't myself. It was a hard day," he sighed. Raising his chin, and in a more robust voice, Ralph testified, "Now I'd talked to them young folks about keepin' their dog quiet several times before. They'd apologize and try to convince me how cute and harmless the thing was, and I wouldn't hear the ear-splitting barking for a few days. Then it would start again."

Jamison asked, "Did you do something to insulate your house better? Install double-pane windows or keep them closed?"

He stared at her in astonishment. "I wasn't gonna keep my windows closed. Why should I be penalized and lose the fresh air when it was their mutt disturbing the whole neighborhood. It was their responsibility to keep that dog quiet—get it trained or put a muzzle on it."

He took a calming breath and shifted his attention to Jenna. "Anyway, I know it weren't Pinocchio, or whatever the hell its name was, but, after Marion had her Lyme disease, the sound of barking dogs would inflict so much pain—like having a migraine. So last fall, when Alexia moved in with the pooch and it barked so, I just kept thinking how much that would hurt my Marion. I don't know ... maybe for a few minutes on Saturday I forgot she was gone, thought I still had my sweet wife. And so, I marched over there with an old baseball bat I keep around for possums and raccoons and other varmints to shut it up. I just wanted to make the dog stop barking."

Ralph wiggled in his chair and glanced down at his hands folded on the table. "Nolan opened the door and welcomed me inside, like he always did, even though I had the bat. I started yellin' at them to keep that dog quiet, that it hurt my Marion's ears. Then there it was—an orange hairball baring its teeth at me with a vicious snarl. It started yappin' and I started swingin'. Alexia tried to grab the dog, and I guess I hit her on accident, but it was still hopping up and down barking its head off, so I swung again. Only this time, Nolan was kneeling on the floor lookin' after his wife and I reckon I hit him too. Finally, I shut the dog up with a solid blow to its head, but, when I checked on Nolan and Alexia, they weren't breathing. They didn't have a pulse."

Jenna mulled over his testimony. It could have happened that way, or he could have struck them all in the head on purpose. The fact was, the world would never know Ralph Halbach's state of mind or whether it truly was an accident. There was no way to prove what transpired inside the Baxters' house. Considering all the guns the old man claimed to own, she guessed it was unlikely he committed premeditated murder. Using a gun would have been much easier and guaranteed success.

"That's when I had the flashback of this time they'd sent us in to clear out a village of Viet Cong infiltrators. Our unit was ordered to sanitize the village." Ralph glanced at Owens. "You know what that means, don't you?"

Owens swept a broad hand over his long crewcut and nodded.

"The blood, the smell of it, the screaming, and then the quiet—it all rushed back. I remember kneeling over the bodies, checking their pulses to make sure they were dead ... men, women, children, old folks. Some of our guys acted like they enjoyed it—spraying everything with machinegun fire, tossing grenades, and laughing when a hut would explode, spraying the flamethrowers every-where. I don't remember if I laughed too or cheered. The Vietnamese were so small, so different from us. My sergeant used to tell us every day how they were savages, barely human, and the only thing that mattered was us stayin' alive."

Jenna hadn't been born when all this happened, but she remembered her grandfather saying how messed up things had been in the sixties, that it was a violent time. Riots and lynchings at home, war atrocities abroad, protests and long-haired hippies, and the rise of the drug culture. Grandpa had blamed rock and roll music; Jenna understood it was only the darker side of human nature.

"There was no premeditation," Ralph avowed. "I brought the bat to threaten the dog, not the neighbors. I might have killed it; I wanted to, but I never intended to hurt Nolan and Alexia."

"Why didn't you call 911?" Jamison asked. "Why not call for an ambulance?"

"Why?" He blinked at her. "Have they found some new way to raise the dead that I haven't heard about yet? It was too late for that. I was just so stunned and shocked that I called Carlin. He said sit still, and he'd be right over. I was in a haze when I took the shovel and started digging a hole in the backyard. A part of me was sure ole Pinochle would wake up and start barking again. So, I dug, and Carlin came. He was so distressed, weren't you, son?"

Carlin peered up from where he had buried his face in his hands. "Yeah. It was surreal. Still is," he whispered, lowering his face to stare a hole in the floor.

"Now, it was my idea to make it look like an accident," Ralph proclaimed, drawing everyone's attention away from Carlin. Jenna wasn't so sure about that, but she couldn't prove otherwise.

"I didn't think about the home invaders at the time," Carlin admitted. "I was too anxious and upset to think at all. Somehow, I was convinced —if we just left everything like it was—the cops would know it was my dad."

"I told him to drive them off that dangerous curve," Ralph declared with vigor—too much, in Jenna's opinion. "At least somethin' good could come of it all if the city puts a damn barricade there like they should've years ago. So, he did that part, but the rest was all me."

"The cleaning up?" Jenna inquired.

They both looked to their attorney, who granted a subtle nod. "It was a joint effort," Carlin stated. "We were scared. I should have known better, but, in all my years working security details, nobody ever got killed. And Dad was having a PTSD episode, thinking he was back in the war. Do you know why he dug that hole so deep?"

Jenna blinked at Carlin with a solemn look of agony.

"Tell them," Carlin prompted. Ralph shook his head and looked away.

"One time, when Dad was drunk, he told my brother and me a few stories from Vietnam. Once they were ordered to attack this enemy camp at night and use machetes and bayonets because they wanted it done quiet. His platoon went in there and started stabbing and hacking and soon discovered it wasn't a camp of soldiers at all, but refugees. Dad and his pals stopped and ran to their sergeant, who said, 'An order is an order, soldier. Do you want to face a court martial? Get in there and do what you were told.' Afterward, Dad found a little baby, body mutilated by blades, and something inside him broke. He wouldn't leave until he had buried it. So, when he went out to bury the little dog, he dug this deep, deep hole like he did for the Vietnamese baby.

"Detectives, I know what he did was wrong, and maybe it was wrong for me not to call and report it, but just keep that in mind when you're making out your charges and presenting your case to the judge."

Jenna did not want stories like this being told on the witness stand at a trial. Ralph Halbach may have served his country and maybe his wife held him together for all these years, but he was still a danger to society. If a psychological episode like this could happen to him once, it could happen again. Yes, he was old; he still needed to spend the rest of his life locked up somewhere—for his safety and the public's. She took out her phone and placed a call.

"Hey, Altman. Ferrari. You remember the Baxter case we've been working?"

"Sure," he answered. "I'm due in court in half an hour. What can I do for you?"

"When you get done at the courthouse, please call Carol Banning to set up a meeting where the two of you can hammer out an acceptable deal. If you can't agree on something reasonable, we'll take it to trial. My evidence is solid, but there are considerations to be taken into account."

"Is she there with you?" Altman asked.

"Yeah, she's here." Jenna smirked at her frenemy.

"Tell her to expect my call between two and three."

"Thanks." Jenna hung up and relayed the message. "We have plenty of paperwork to keep us busy until then."

"I'd like to see the evidence against my clients," Carol directed as she rose. She took Ralph's hand, and he stood beside her, looking ashamed. "Lieutenant Ferrari's team will treat you fairly, although you may have to spend some time in a holding cell after in-processing." She pivoted on a heel to Carlin, who had also left his chair. "You be on your best behavior. We'll meet with the assistant district attorney and, if we don't like what he offers, we'll take it to trial."

Carlin's shoulders fell, and he whispered in Banning's ear just loud enough for Jenna to hear. "I don't want to put him on trial, even if it means a sympathetic jury and a lighter sentence. He's eighty-one years old and I'm afraid a trial would kill him. Let's just take the deal."

Silently, Jenna agreed with Carlin.

23

---❖---

Saturday, May 18th

Randi inspected herself in the mirror in a nursery room near the sanctuary entrance, with Ellen on one side and Jo on the other. Her sister gently fluffed Randi's light brown curl, which cascaded over her shoulder, while she struggled to contain tears of joy.

"Are you sure you don't want to pin on a headpiece?" Ellen asked.

Jo made a face and shook her head. The attendants were all asked to choose what they wanted to wear—within reason. Ellen looked regal in her spring peach, floor-length gown and Jo cleaned up handsomely in her powder-blue tuxedo.

Randi twisted around to inspect the tails of her white tux in the mirror. She wore a teal blouse with a white bowtie and cummerbund and had helped Jenna pick out her black tails and plum shirt. Jenna had resisted the cummerbund, expecting it to make her look fat, but, in the tailored rental cut to fit a woman, it turned out to appear slimming.

"No, thank you," Randi stated with finality. "I told you—no veils or flowers or bows. I'm carrying a bouquet, and that's only so I can throw it at Jo."

"Me?" Her friend stepped back with a horrified expression. Randi laughed.

To save time, she, Jenna, and the wedding party had taken photos in the decorated sanctuary beforehand. The photographer snapped shots of all the groupings and individuals, and a score of Jenna and Randi in various poses, such as putting on each other's rings and lighting a candle together. A few photos would have to be taken during the ceremony and at the reception, but neither of them wanted their guests to wait for picture taking between the service and cake.

Now they waited for their cue. Randi could hear the organ music wafting in from the sanctuary—Bach's *Jesu, Joy of Man's Desiring*. They omitted the wedding tradition for the seating of the bride and groom's mothers and other close relatives. Neither of them had a mother or grandmother in attendance and their siblings were all in the wedding party. But that was OK. Randi felt her parents' love and support deep in her heart. And Jenna's parents were ... better than they used to be.

"Do you have your vows?" Ellen asked.

Randi patted her pocket, detecting the folded piece of paper. It was only there for security. She was sure she wouldn't need to look at it, but it was comforting to know it was there in case. "Right here."

"You look so beautiful and so happy," Jo gushed and hugged her.

"Thank you. I'm over-the-moon giddy like I could just close my eyes and start floating to the ceiling," Randi gushed.

"I'm happy for you," Ellen confessed and dabbed the corner of her eye.

"It's time." Tammie Ellis, the buxom wedding coordinator—who was gussied up in such high fashion one might have thought *she* was the bride—poked her head in the door. "Attendants first. Get in your order from last night."

Jo turned a sentimental gaze over her shoulder as she and Ellen followed Mrs. Ellis. "The next time I talk to you, you'll be a married woman." Her words and expression almost had Randi choked up, but she would get through this without blubbering.

Thoughts and memories rushed through Randi's awareness as she exited the waiting room with anxious joy stirring in her stomach. Each recalled image and sensation mingled like ingredients in the most exquisite recipe she had ever devised, so flavorful Randi could smell the love.

Nothing would change. Everything would change. The day Randi thought she'd never experience rushed upon her in an instant, despite months of preparation.

She glanced over to see her and Jenna's family and friends line up to march down the aisle. Owens was the most dashing Randi had ever seen him, with the glamorous Trisha Jamison on his arm. She had kept her promise, and, though sleek and appropriate, her gown didn't upstage everyone else. They stepped out to the peaceful *Canon in D* by Pachelbel.

Randi craned her neck to peek through from the foyer, surprised to see how many guests had come. It was as packed as a Sunday morning. Flowers sprung from pots and vases at the front, and all the colorful, affirming standards flowed from their banner stands in an arc. She spied some people in police dress blues and recognized a scattering of faculty from the college.

Ethan Bauman appeared more elegant than nerdish in his formal wear. Randi considered how appropriate it was for him to be escorting her very gay bestie, Jo Rodriguez.

Her heart swelling with pride, Randi watched as Jenna's commanding Captain Myers, who could easily pass for a pro basketball player with his shaved, bald head and muscular height, stepped out arm in arm with her very domestic sister. They were an odd couple, yet oddly similar. The captain was a guiding force in Jenna's life and career, as Randi's big sister had been for her.

With only one couple remaining, Randi had a clear view of Jenna from across the lobby. Forsaking the medieval practice of someone "giving away" the bride, they decided to walk each other down the aisle to the altar. With Pastor Luna's help, they had planned a gender-neutral ceremony without references to brides or grooms or the dominant and submissive role assumptions that accompanied the old guard.

Angie looked the best Randi had ever seen her, with her golden strands shining and a healthy glow to her face. *She* had a hairpiece with flowers and bows that brought an amused smile to Randi's lips. Vince boasted a dapper look with a close shave, fresh haircut, and black tuxedo. Jenna's siblings each kissed one of her cheeks before Angie took Vince's arm for him to walk her into the sanctuary.

From ten yards away, Randi washed a passionate gaze over Jenna. Man, she was hot! *And she's mine.* Reveling in the present moment, Randi committed every sight, sound, smell, and feel to memory. This was the first day of the rest of her life.

***

Jenna's heart skipped a beat as she drank in the long, lean form of the sweetest, smartest, funniest woman she'd ever met. *And she's mine.*

They hadn't flipped a coin. When Randi had asked who should carry the flowers, Jenna emphatically decreed she was not hauling a fistful of posies past all her cops. "I don't mind doing silly, sappy things when we're in private, but, if you want to do the toss the bouquet thing, you're going to carry it." Jenna had to admit it was a gorgeous display of white, lavender, and red roses separated by snowy orchids, all in a bed of frothy green and fragrant jasmine. For an instant, Jenna wished they were keeping it.

She matched every step Randi took toward her until they met in front of the open sanctuary doors. It struck Jenna that she couldn't recall ever feeling this close to God. Pastor Luna once said that being in love was akin to heaven on earth. Assessing the feeling that enveloped her, Jenna believed it must be true. The instant she took Randi's hand, every nerve and fear that had ever assailed Jenna vanished like magic, replaced by the hope and faith of fifty years as Randi's partner, come what may.

The trumpeter and organ began the *Trumpet Voluntary* by some guy—Randi knew. It was regal, and she felt like a prince marching beside her princess, or other prince, or—damn it—the most important person in her life. She never noticed her feet touch the floor as they glided past friends, colleagues, and strangers on their way to the dais.

Jenna passed a joyful gaze over the faces of their wedding party, standing guard, flanking Pastor Luna, who uncharacteristically wore her liturgical robes. A huge sphere of radiating joy emanated from Jenna's core that she knew everyone must see in the irrepressible grin that consumed her typically somber face.

Oh, to hell with what anyone thinks. This is my moment and I'm going to glow!

The couple stopped at the altar, and Randi passed the flowers to her sister. The last note of trumpet and organ reverberated through the chamber, fading to silence before Pastor Luna began.

"Friends and fellow children of God, we are gathered here today to join Jenna Ferrari and Randi McLeod for this joyful occasion, as we witness their covenant of love and devotion. Let us pray."

Jenna bowed her head, staring at the polish on her shoes—her hands clasped in front of her—and wondered if she would ever feel at home in Randi's church. It was a foregone fact that she would never step foot in hers again.

"Blessed are you, oh Lord, our God, maker of heaven and earth, life-force and sustainer, father and mother of all, comforter, healer, deliverer, and friend, for you have created joy and gladness, pleasure and delight, peace and fellowship. You are the source of every good thing, and we thank you for your bountiful love and compassion. We ask that you pour out your abundance on Randi and Jenna in their new life together. Let their love for each other be a seal upon their hearts and a crown upon their heads. Bless them in their work and their companionship, awake and asleep, in joy and sorrow, in life and death. Grant them your peace and protection, oh God, and tend their love that it may only grow stronger, deeper, and more steadfast with time."

The piano began to play, and a man from Randi's choir sang *All of Me*, by John Legend. He had a pleasant voice, stayed on pitch, and imbued the lyrics with tender emotion. It wasn't an easy song to sing, and every time it got to the line about "perfect imperfections," Jenna always thought it applied to her. When he sang, "You're my end and my beginning, even when I lose, I'm winning," it was Jenna's profession to Randi. She almost found herself singing along as she silently mouthed the words, feeling the pledge of giving herself all to Randi, mind, body, and soul.

When the music ended, Pastor Luna took a large Bible, raised it, and opened it to a page marked by a purple ribbon. "Our scripture reading for today comes from Paul's first letter to the Corinthians, chapter thirteen." As she listened to the familiar passage on love, Jenna's mind wandered to her family and her mother, who had turned her back on Jenna so many times while still claiming she loved her. "Love keeps no record of wrongs," Luna read, and the words pierced Jenna's heart. She didn't speculate how many times she would have to take an eraser to the chalkboard, but she would do it because that's the person she aspired to become.

"And now these three remain," Luna read. Jenna remembered this part and mentally formed the words as the pastor said, "Faith, hope, and love, but the greatest of these is love."

Because it's so hard for people to practice, Jenna thought.

Pastor Luna set the Bible on the communion table behind her. They had discussed whether to partake of a first communion together as a married couple, but Jenna had felt awkward. So much of her childhood had been centered on behaving in a manner that made her worthy of consuming the body and blood of Christ, as the Catholic Church taught it, that it was difficult for her to associate the mystical sacrament with what Randi's church considered a symbol of God's presence in the parishioner's life. Seeing her inner turmoil, Randi simply told Luna they would skip it.

It amazed her how Randi always knew what Jenna needed, even when she didn't or couldn't express herself to get the feeling across. And she invariably put Jenna's desires above her own. Occasionally, Jenna would put her foot down and insist Randi get what she wanted and needed. The silly woman would say things like, "I want what you want. My greatest desire is to make you happy," and other insanely unselfish things. In truth, Jenna's greatest desire was to make Randi happy—to see that infectious smile ripple across her lips and that gleam shine in her eyes and know she had put it there. That was pure bliss!

The pastor expounded for a few minutes on what it meant for two souls to join as one, and then she read a poem about vows and aspirations and undying devotion. As she talked about two lives joining as one, Jenna and Randi each picked up candles from the table and together lit the center candle, as they had for the photo session. Then they replaced their lit candles in their holders.

"The two become one," Luna explained, "without losing their individuality while gaining a harmony of purpose."

She talked about the symbolism of the rings with no beginning and no end and moved into another prayer. "Dear God, shower Jenna and Randi with your blessings such that their cups run over, and they never want for any good thing. Grant them peace and strength, and, when times get rough, remind them not to blame but to cling to each other. Be their rudder in the storm, their shade in the desert, and their blazing fire on the coldest nights. Teach them to love from the inside out. Amen."

She took Jenna's hand and joined it to Randi's. "These are the hands of your partner, young and strong and full of love, holding your hands as you promise to love each other today, tomorrow, and always. They are the hands that will pick you up when you fall, clap for you in your triumph, comfort you in your sorrow, and work with you to build your life together. Cherish these hands. Now, Jenna and Randi will exchange vows they have prepared."

Jenna had asked to go first. She knew Randi would have something eloquent and poetic to say and she didn't want to have to follow that act. Randi had said, "Do whatever you want, sweetie; it'll be wonderful."

"Miranda McLeod—Randi," she began, rubbing her fingers over Randi's hand. All at once, Jenna prickled with nerves that crawled over and through her like tingling sprites from an ancient Irish woodland. She hadn't had to speak until now. It was delightful listening to everything and feeling the cheery vibes in the sanctuary. But now all eyes and ears were on her, and it was a large crowd.

Jenna swallowed, gazed into Randi's eyes, and the world faded away. "You are my partner, my lover, and my very best friend. You are the lighthouse that brought this ship, tossed and battered, safely to shore, and I love you with all I am. I'm forever grateful that you accepted me as I was and then built me into a better version of myself. I promise to love and cherish you, to be forever faithful, to protect you and stand by you, in sickness and health, in plenty and lack, no matter what the future holds, because, as long as you're in it, it'll be marvelous. You are the love of my life and make me happier than I ever imagined and more loved than I ever thought possible. I am truly blessed to be your life partner."

Randi's expression of ultimate joy and delight reflected how Jenna felt inside, magnifying her feelings and intensifying the moment. Randi squeezed her hand and mouthed, *Thank you.*

With a nod from Luna, Randi spoke in a robust, animated, captivating voice, as if she wished the back row to hear every word. "Jenna Ferrari, heart of my heart, other half of my soul, you know I have to quote Shakespeare." A few laughs and giggles sounded around the hall, including coming from Jenna.

"'Let me not to the marriage of true minds admit impediments. Love is not love which alters when it alteration finds or bends with the remover to remove. O no! It is an ever-fixed mark that looks on tempests and is never shaken; it is the star to every wandering bark, whose worth's unknown, although its height be taken. Love's not Time's fool, though rosy lips and cheeks within his bending sickle's compass come; love alters not with his brief hours and weeks but bears him out even to the edge of doom. If this be error and upon me proved, I never writ, nor no man ever loved.'

"This pledge I make to you, dear, strong, sweet Jenna, that I am yours and you are mine from this day forth. I will love and protect you, hold you and support you, and reserve all my passion and imaginings for you alone. I will be by your side through good times and bad, as your partner and friend. And when you feel you must carry the weight of the world on your shoulders, I'll be standing shoulder-to-shoulder with you, sharing the load, because you loved me—you chose me—and that's enough.

"So today, I see these vows not as promises but as privileges: I get to laugh with you and cry with you; care for you and share with you. I get to run with you and walk with you; build with you and live with you. I am so blessed to spend the rest of my life with you, to be the winner who gets to be there for you and support you. I don't *have* to honor and cherish you—I'm thrilled and forever grateful that I'm the one who *gets* to."

Randi beamed at Jenna with genuine, unabashed, unreserved love, affection, and devotion. Jenna feared she'd melt into a puddle right there in front of her captain and hundreds of guests. She sensed the tears of joy pressing to escape her eyes. Just when she thought life couldn't get any better, it did. Jenna couldn't even form words in her mind; pure emotion consumed her, vibrations, like Randi's orchestra music, that had no lyrics and yet expressed far more than words ever could. She was vaguely aware of the pastor's voice.

"Do you have the rings?"

Jenna used her free hand to fish in her pocket and pulled out the solid wedding band to accompany Randi's engagement ring, while her partner did the same. She had told Randi not to get her an engagement ring too. Not one to prioritize jewelry, they had decided instead to splurge on matching gold wedding bands that were of high quality and had personalized engravings. Jenna never felt prouder than the moment she slipped that ring onto Randi's perfect, long, slender finger and repeated the words Luna prompted her to say.

"With this ring, I thee wed."

She tingled from head to toe when Randi placed the ring on her finger and repeated the phrase, "With this ring, I thee wed."

Pastor Luna raised her hands and in lilting, joyful tones proclaimed a benediction over them, invoking God, Jesus, the Holy Spirit, the angels, and all the hosts of heaven to drown them in blessings. Jenna didn't catch all the words, but their meaning was abundantly vibrant.

"And now, by the power vested in me and with the consecration of our Divine Creator, I pronounce you a lawfully wedded couple."

Jenna and Randi leaned into each other for the consummating kiss while Luna proclaimed, "Friends, I present to you Randi and Jenna, partners for life."

The music started and people cheered, clapping and whooping, making Jenna feel as giddy as a little kid at the fair, riding a pony for the first time. It was the most magical moment of her life. With beaming grins that could have eclipsed the sun, Jenna strode down the aisle past the implausible number of people who'd come, hand in hand with her *wife*.

Camera flashes spotted the room while people applauded, and joy abounded like a vast ocean that Jenna bobbed in, carried along by its swells. They headed straight to the nursery/dressing room for a proper kiss before joining their friends in the fellowship hall. It too had been decorated, and music played in there as well. Mrs. Ellis directed them to stand near the entrance while a reception line formed. Smiling faces wet with celebratory tears congratulated them, and everyone shook their hands.

Jenna was surprised to see people from the community whom she had helped in the past. Rhiannon Hayes, Donna Ramsey—who was still hanging on despite the doctors' grim prognosis— Chris Gates, aka Randi's student and drag queen Azalea Trayle, and even the overly sexy, rolling in millions, blonde bombshell Audra Lockwood, whose husband's New Year's Eve murder she had solved back when she and Randi were first dating.

People remember, she thought in astonishment as she shook their hands and thanked them for coming.

When the next man stepped before her, Jenna froze and quivered in disbelief from head to toe, too stunned to say a word.

"Hi, honeysuckle. I know you said to stay home and take care of Mama, but I couldn't miss this moment. Your Aunt Bess is staying with her so I could come. I sat in the back so you wouldn't see me and faint dead away from the shock during your weddin'."

Jenna surged into his arms and hugged her dad in a fierce, firm embrace. All the tears she'd held onto flooded out, dampening the skin of Vinnie's neck and his white shirt collar. "I can't believe you came!"

"Now, Jenna." His arms enveloped her with a kindness she couldn't remember from the powerful man she had once feared, hated, and loved with equal fervor. He kissed her cheek and held her. "I missed enough milestones in your life to do it again. I know you're an independent woman and sure wouldn't want me walkin' ya down the aisle, so I made Vince Jr. and Angie keep it a secret."

Opening her eyes to glance over his shoulder, Jenna spied the two traitorous siblings flashing brilliant grins and laughing eyes at her. Oh, but they had it coming!

"Dad." She swallowed a lump the size of Texas from her throat, shuddering to guess what surprise would hit her next. "It means the world to me that you came." *That you acknowledge our marriage and can give us your approval, silent or not. You came!*

"I know we won't have long to visit, 'cause y'all are leavin' on your honeymoon, and I can't hold up the line," he said, releasing his grip on her. "Hurry up so you two can cut the cake!"

Reluctantly, Jenna lowered her arms from around his neck and mopped at a stream of unbidden tears. She nodded. "We'll grab a minute before we head to the airport. I want a picture of us together and with Angie and Vince."

"Why do you think I wore the suit?" he joshed, and, with a cheerful laugh, moved on to hug Randi.

***

Everything had been picture-perfect, and Randi had been just as flabbergasted and appreciative of Vinnie showing up as Jenna had. She and Jenna laughed as they shoved cake into each other's mouths, washing it down with punch. It was such a boon to have so many friends and acquaintances sharing this singular event with them.

Randi was still floating on a cloud of bliss when she and Jenna changed into more comfortable—yet still presentable—clothes to leave on their honeymoon. The remaining guests gathered outside with tiny net bags of birdseed to throw at them for good luck. Jo warned her they were decorating her truck with signs and cans. Although annoying, it was still fun and just another way their friends said, "I love you," to them.

"It's time to spill it, my precious, secret-keeping pest!" Jenna demanded as she returned the tux slacks to their hanger. "You told me to pack a swimsuit and a bunch of shorts, so I suspect we're heading south. But how far south is the question?"

The "I've had enough of your foolishness" look that Jenna sported was priceless. It was so sexy the way she cocked a hip and quirked her mouth, drawing down her brows like she meant business when her total vibe screamed, "I just want to jump your bones, woman!"

Randi stepped closer and buttoned Jenna's shirt up the middle for her—sparing a moment to enjoy the view, of course. "You know how you missed out on a lot as a kid?"

"Uh-huh." Jenna's expression became dubious. Randi brushed her lips to smooth it away.

"We are going to Disney World," she pronounced with smug satisfaction. "I booked us four-day passes to all the kingdoms with accommodations right inside the park for convenience. You're going to see the Pirates of the Caribbean, ride Space Mountain, and get your picture taken with Goofy or some glamorous Disney Princess. We are going to have fun—just carefree fun! And, well, of course, the Star Wars attraction. We will *not* miss that!"

Jenna bubbled with laughter. "Heaven forbid!"

"Then I booked us a rental car to drive over to Daytona Beach for two more nights so we can relax by the water—and there might be a racing event you'd enjoy. You could make Vince jealous with pictures," she added with a coy wink. "Last, we drive up to St. Augustine—because I've never been, and I'm sure you haven't—to see historic stuff about the oldest city in the U.S. One night there and we fly home out of Jacksonville."

Randi's grin didn't hide the nerves that hopped around her tummy on pogo sticks. She rolled her fingers around with an anxious expression, desperate to please the woman she loved more than life itself.

Setting the hung tux aside, Jenna cupped her cheeks and kissed her with the breadth and depth of the Pacific. As Jenna's arms came around her and drew her in, Randi was sure she heard a purr of contentment emanating from her chest. "Absolute perfection. You know me so well. I always wanted to get to be a kid—even if it means climbing on a Star Wars ride and blasting through pretend space to save the galaxy. With you at my side, we can't fail."

Relief and joy, hope and assurance, all coiled themselves around Randi as tangibly as Jenna's embrace. *My wife!* she marveled and kissed her again.

Keep up with Edale Lane and never miss a new release when you sign up for her newsletter.

https://bit.ly/3qkGn95

MORE BOOKS BY EDALE LANE

The Lessons in Murder Series
Meeting over Murder
https://www.amazon.com/dp/B0B7R69R7B
Skimming around Murder
https://www.amazon.com/dp/B0B9R6FJWL
New Year in Murder
https://www.amazon.com/dp/B0BDQSPT6L
Heart of Murder
https://www.amazon.com/dp/B0BQQS57FY
Reprise in Murder
https://www.amazon.com/dp/B0C2YDKLSB
Homecoming in Murder
https://www.amazon.com/dp/B0C7M2VKSH
Queen of Murder
https://www.amazon.com/dp/B0CKRYLNSW
Cold in Murder
https://www.amazon.com/dp/B0CSXMBJLJ
Foreseen in Murder
https://www.amazon.com/dp/B0D3G5JMLP

Daring Duplicity: The Wellington Mysteries, Vol.1
https://www.amazon.com/dp/B09QDTF9YN

Perilous Passages: The Wellington Mysteries, Vol. 2
https://www.amazon.com/dp/B0B16FWN63
Daunting Dilemmas: The Wellington Mysteries, Vol. 3
https://www.amazon.com/dp/B0BMDQ8TLC

Atlantis, Land of Dreams
https://www.amazon.com/dp/B0D7TB52CG

Heart of Sherwood
https://www.amazon.com/dp/B07W4M3R5L

Viking Quest
https://www.amazon.com/dp/B097NTZVPC

Sigrid and Elyn: A Tale from Norvegr
https://www.amazon.com/dp/B0B5W48342
Legacy of the Valiant: A Tale from Norvegr
https://www.amazon.com/dp/B0BZK7Y655
War and Solace: A Tale from Norvegr
https://www.amazon.com/dp/B0CGP4WVYP

Walks with Spirits
https://www.amazon.com/dp/B09VBGQF27/

The Night Flyer Series
Merchants of Milan, book one
https://www.amazon.com/dp/B083H6WNKD
Secrets of Milan, book two
https://www.amazon.com/dp/B088HFM7Q5
Chaos in Milan, book three
https://www.amazon.com/dp/B08Q7H6DFX
Missing in Milan, book four

https://www.amazon.com/dp/B09CNXF1CX

Shadows over Milan, book five

https://www.amazon.com/dp/B09KF53VTZ

Visit My Website:

https://authoredalelane.com

Follow me on Goodreads (Don't forget to leave a quick review!)

https://www.goodreads.com/author/show/15264354.Edale_Lane

Follow me on BookBub:

https://www.bookbub.com/profile/edale-lane

Newsletter sign-up link:

https://bit.ly/3qkGn95

ABOUT THE AUTHOR

E dale Lane is an Amazon Best-selling author and winner of Rainbow, Lesfic Bard, and Imaginarium Awards. Her sapphic historical fiction and mystery stories feature women leading the action and entice readers with likable characters, engaging storytelling, and vivid world-creation.

Lane (whose legal name is Melodie Romeo) holds a bachelor's degree in music education, a master's in history, and taught school for 24 years before embarking on an adventure driving an 18-wheeler over-the-road. She is a mother of two, Grammy of three, and a doggy mom. A native of Vicksburg, MS, Lane now lives her dream of being a full-time author in beautiful Chilliwack, BC, with her long-time life partner.

Enjoy free e-books and other promotional offerings while staying up to date with what Edale Lane is writing next when you sign up for her newsletter.

https://bit.ly/3qkGn95

Printed in Dunstable, United Kingdom